ROBERT B. PARKER

D0092507

NIGHT PASSAGE

ROBERT B. PARKER'S SPENSER THRILLERS—
"ONE OF THE GREAT SERIES IN THE HISTORY OF THE AMERICAN DETECTIVE STORY!"
—*The New York Times*

EAN

9 780515 123494

50699>

"A GENUINE PAGE-TURNER."
—*The Hartford Courant*

Jesse Stone has left the LAPD behind and carried the burden of a recent divorce and a drinking problem cross-country to Paradise, Massachusetts. He is offered the job of police chief there—much to his surprise, since he was drunk at the interview. He soon finds out why, when he's caught between corrupt town leaders, a local militia group, and a murderer on the loose.

But Stone just might surprise his bosses—and do the job he was hired to do. Because he may have left his entire life behind in California. But he didn't leave his soul . . .

"A fast-paced, character-driven tale that practically reads itself."
—*The Raleigh News & Observer*

"Marvelous characters and a wonderful sense of place . . . Jesse seems intended to return. Hope it's soon."
—*The Toronto Globe & Mail*

"Parker's debut thriller featuring Jesse Stone will leave you looking forward to the second installment."
—*The Atlanta Journal-Constitution*

"[A] strong first entry in a projected series . . . [Jesse is] appealingly flawed."
—*The New York Times Book Review*

"Not for nothing is Parker regarded as the reigning champion of the American tough-guy detective novel, heavyweight division. Over a twenty-five-year career, the man has rarely composed a bad sentence or an inert paragraph. His thirtieth novel, which features brand-new protagonist Jesse Stone . . . proves no exception."
—*Entertainment Weekly*

continued on next page . . .

... And for Robert B. Parker's previous novels

"Parker's brilliance is in his simple dialogue, and in Spenser. Here is a character who is fearless, honest and clever but never preachy. He's self-deprecating, sometimes sensitive; hard-boiled but never boorish. And he doesn't take himself too seriously."

—*The Philadelphia Inquirer*

Small Vices
Spenser tries to prove the innocence of a murder suspect—but when a man with a .22 puts him in a coma, the hope for justice may die along with the detective ... "POWERFUL."

—*The New York Times Book Review*

Chance
Spenser heads to Vegas to find the missing husband of a mob princess—but he's not the only one looking ... "THE WORLD'S MOST PERFECT PRIVATE EYE ... The dialogue is as brisk and clever as always."

—*Los Angeles Times Book Review*

Thin Air
Spenser thought he could help a friend find his missing wife. Until he learned the nasty truth about Lisa St. Claire ... "FULL OF ACTION, SUSPENSE, AND THRILLS."

—*Playboy*

Walking Shadow
An actor's murder sends Spenser and Hawk behind the scenes of a shabby waterfront town ... "FAST-MOVING AND WITTY ... ONE OF HIS BEST!"

—*The Denver Post*

Paper Doll
Spenser searches for the killer of a "model wife and mother"—and finds some shocking surprises ... "IT TAKES ROBERT B. PARKER EXACTLY TWO SENTENCES TO GET THE TENSION CRACKLING."

—Christopher Lehmann-Haupt, *The New York Times*

continued on next page ...

Double Deuce

Spenser and Hawk wage war on a street gang . . . "MR. SPENSER IS AT HIS BEST . . . TENSE . . . SUSPENSEFUL . . . DARKLY POETIC."

—The New York Times

Pastime

A boy's search for his mother forces Spenser to face his own past . . . "EMOTIONALLY TENSE . . . GRIPPING . . . VINTAGE HARD-CORE SPENSER!"

—Kirkus Reviews

Stardust

Spenser tries to protect a TV star from a would-be assassin . . . "CLASSIC SPENSER . . . BRILLIANT!"

—The New York Times Book Review

Playmates

Spenser scores against corruption in the world of college basketball . . . "A WHOLE LOTTA FUN . . . KICK BACK AND ENJOY!"

—New York Daily News

Perchance to Dream

Robert B. Parker's acclaimed sequel to the Raymond Chandler classic *The Big Sleep*, featuring detective Philip Marlowe . . . "A STUNNING, DROP-DEAD SUCCESS . . . DAZZLING."

—Publishers Weekly

Poodle Springs

Raymond Chandler's unfinished Marlowe thriller—completed by today's master of detective fiction, Robert B. Parker . . . "A FIRST-RATE DETECTIVE NOVEL WITH ALL THE SUSPENSE, ACTION, AND HUMAN DRAMA THAT WE HAVE COME TO EXPECT FROM THE BEST."

—Playboy

Titles by Robert B. Parker

SMALL VICES
CHANCE
THIN AIR
WALKING SHADOW
PAPER DOLL
DOUBLE DEUCE
PASTIME
PERCHANCE TO DREAM (a Philip Marlowe novel)
STARDUST
POODLE SPRINGS (with Raymond Chandler)
PLAYMATES
CRIMSON JOY
PALE KINGS AND PRINCES
TAMING A SEA-HORSE
A CATSKILL EAGLE
VALEDICTION
LOVE AND GLORY
THE WIDENING GYRE
CEREMONY
A SAVAGE PLACE
EARLY AUTUMN
LOOKING FOR RACHEL WALLACE
WILDERNESS
THE JUDAS GOAT
THREE WEEKS IN SPRING (with Joan Parker)
PROMISED LAND
MORTAL STAKES
GOD SAVE THE CHILD
THE GODWULF MANUSCRIPT

SUDDEN MISCHIEF
Available in hardcover from G. P. Putnam's Sons

Night Passage

Robert B. Parker

JOVE BOOKS, NEW YORK

NIGHT PASSAGE

A Jove Book / published by arrangement with
the author

PRINTING HISTORY
G. P. Putnam's Sons edition / September 1997
Jove edition / November 1998

The Penguin Putnam Inc. World Wide Web site address is
http://www.penguinputnam.com

ISBN: 0-515-12349-8

A JOVE BOOK®
Jove Books are published by The Berkley Publishing Group,
a member of Penguin Putnam Inc.,
375 Hudson Street, New York, New York 10014.
JOVE and the "J" design are trademarks
belonging to Jove Publications, Inc.

PRINTED IN THE UNITED STATES OF AMERICA

10 9 8 7 6 5 4 3 2 1

For Joan:
Anywhere you are
is Shangri-La

Chapter 1

At the end of the continent, near the foot of Wilshire Boulevard, Jesse Stone stood and leaned on the railing in the darkness above the Santa Monica beach and stared at nothing, while below him the black ocean rolled away toward Japan.

There was no traffic on Ocean Avenue. There was the comfortless light of the streetlamps, but they were behind him. Before him was the uninterrupted darkness above the repetitive murmur of the disdainful sea.

A black-and-white cruiser pulled up and parked behind his car at the curb. A spotlight shone on it and one of the cops from the cruiser got out and looked into it. Then the spotlight swept along the verge of the cliffs and touched Jesse and went past him and came back and held. The strapping young L.A. patrolman walked over to him, holding his flashlight near the bulb end, the barrel of it resting on his shoulder, so he could use it as a club if he needed to. The young cop asked Jesse if he was all right. Jesse said he was, and the young cop asked him why he was standing there at four in the morning. The cop looked about twenty-four. Jesse felt like he could be his father, though in fact he was maybe ten years older.

"I'm a cop," Jesse said.

"Got a badge?"

"Was a cop. I'm leaving town, just thought I'd stand here a while before I went."

"That your car?" he said.

Jesse nodded.

"What division you work out of?" the young cop said.

"Downtown, Homicide."

"Who runs it?"

"Captain Cronjager."

"I can smell booze on you," the young cop said.

"I'm waiting to sober up."

"I can drive you home in your car," the young cop said. "My partner will follow in the black and white."

"I'll stay here till I'm sober," Jesse said.

"Okay," the young cop said and went back to the cruiser and the cruiser pulled away. No one else came by. There was no sound except the tireless movement of the thick black water. Behind him the streetlights became less stark, and he realized he could see the first hint of the pier to his left. He turned slowly and looked back at the city behind him and saw that it was almost dawn. The streetlights looked yellow now, and the sky to the east was white. He looked back at the ocean once, then walked to his car and got in and started up. He drove along Ocean Avenue to the Santa Monica Freeway and turned onto it and headed east. By the time he passed Boyle Heights the sun was up and shining into his eyes as he drove straight toward it. Say goodbye to Hollywood, say goodbye my baby.

Chapter 2

Tom Carson sat in the client chair across the desk from Hastings Hathaway in the president's office of the Paradise Trust. He felt uneasy, as if he were in the principal's office. He didn't like the feeling. He was the chief of police, people were supposed to feel uneasy confronting him.

"You can quietly resign, Tom," Hathaway said, "and relocate, we'll be happy to help you with that financially, or you can, ah, face the consequences."

"Consequences?" Carson tried to sound stern, but he could feel the bottom falling out of him.

"For you, and if necessary, I suppose, for your wife and your children."

Carson cleared his throat, and felt ashamed that he'd had to.

"Such as?" he said as strongly as he could, trying hard to keep his gaze steady on Hathaway.

Why was Hathaway so scary? He was a geeky guy. In the eighth grade, before Hasty had gone away to school,

Tom Carson had teased him. So had everyone else. Hathaway smiled. It was a thin geeky smile and it frightened Tom Carson further.

"We have resources, Tom. We could turn the problem over to Jo Jo and his associates, or, depending upon circumstance, we could deal with it ourselves. I don't want that to happen. I'm your friend, Tom. I have so far been able to control the, ah, firebrands, but you'll have to trust me. You'll have to do what I ask."

"Hasty," Carson said. "I'm the chief of police, for crissake."

Hathaway shook his head.

"You can't just say I'm not," Carson said.

"You don't make the rules in this town, Tom."

"And you do?" Carson said.

His face felt stiff as he spoke and his arms and hands felt weak.

"We do, Tom. Emphasis on the 'We.' "

Carson was silent, staring at Hathaway. The mention of Jo Jo had made him feel loose and fragmented inside. Hathaway took a thick stationery-sized manila envelope from his middle drawer.

"You aren't much of a policeman, Tom, and it was just a sad accident that you learned things. But you did, and you were right to come first to me. I've been able to save you so far from the consequences of your knowledge."

"What if I went to the FBI with this?"

"This is what I'm trying to forestall," Hathaway said. "Other people, people like Jo Jo, would prevail. And your family . . ." Hathaway shrugged and held the shrug for a moment, and sighed as if to himself, before he continued.

"But we both know, Tom, you are not made of that kind of stuff. The better choice for you, and I'm sure you recognize this, is to take our rather generous severance package. We've found you a house, and we've contributed some cash to help you in relocation costs. The details are in here.''

"What if I promise not to say a word about anything, Hasty. Why can't I just stay here. You'd have a chief of police that won't give you any trouble.''

Hathaway shook his head slowly as Carson spoke. He smiled sadly.

"I mean, you know, the next chief," Carson said, "might be harder to deal with.''

Hathaway continued his sad smile and slow head shake.

"I am trying to help you, Tom," Hathaway said. "I can't help you if you won't help yourself.''

"I'm no troublemaker," Carson said. "How can you be sure you won't just get a troublemaker.''

"We have already chosen your successor," Hathaway said. "He should be just right.''

He held the envelope out toward Tom Carson and, after a moment of empty hesitation, Carson reached out and took it.

Chapter 3

Jesse drove out Route 10 past Upland, where he picked up Route 15 and followed it north to Barstow, where he went east on Route 40. He didn't turn on the radio. He liked quiet. He set the cruise control to seventy and kept a hand lightly on the steering wheel and slowly settled into himself and allowed his feelings to seep out of the compacted center of himself. He no longer had a badge. He'd turned it in with his service pistol. There was no wedding ring on his left hand. He smiled without pleasure. Turned that in too. It made him feel sort of scared to be without a badge or a wedding ring. Not quite thirty-five and no official status anymore. With his right hand he fished in the gym bag on the front seat beside him until he found his off-duty gun, a short-barreled Smith & Wesson .38. He arranged it near the top of the bag, where it would be easy to reach, and he let his hand rest on it for a time. It made him feel less insubstantial. He stopped at a truck stop outside of Needles, sat at the counter and had orange juice, ham, eggs, potatoes, wheat toast, and three cups of coffee with cream and sugar. It made him feel good. The place was full of truckers and tourists, and he was alone among them. No one paid any attention to him. They were going where they would and he was on his way east. He went to the men's room and washed his hands and face. Back in the car, cruise control set, he felt a small freshet of excitement. It was afternoon now, the sun was behind him. Shining on what he had left. The road spooled out ahead of him, straight to the horizon, nearly empty. Freedom, he thought, and smiled again, no badge, no ring, no problem. You look at it the right way and that's freedom. He nursed the excitement as long as he could, trying to build on it.

He stayed the night in Flagstaff, 250 miles north of where he had been born, and went to the motel bar for supper. He ordered scotch on the rocks and a chicken breast sandwich on a croissant. There were a couple of guys in plaid shirts and those little string ties they wore in places like Arizona, the kind with the silver hasp where a knot should be. Both bartenders were women wearing white shirts and black ties and short red jackets. One was a fat blond woman, the other a more slender dark-haired Hispanic girl who would be fat in five more years. Beyond the bar was a room with tables and a dance floor, and the setup for a disc jockey. No one was in the room yet. An unlit piece of neon script over the disc jockey stand spelled out "Coyote Lounge." He sipped a little scotch, felt the cold heat spread from his esophagus. A tall well-built man in his thirties came into the bar wearing a big Stetson hat and earphones. He seemed to be bouncing slightly to music that only he heard. He had on a plaid shirt with the sleeves rolled up and tight jeans and two-toned lizard-skin cowboy boots. The tiny tape player was tucked into his shirt pocket and the slender cord ran up under his chin. He looked as if he'd just come from a shower and a shave and his cologne came into the bar ahead of him. Clubman, maybe. Jesse watched him. There was nothing particularly interesting about him except that Jesse watched everything. The cowboy ordered a nonalcoholic beer and when it was served he left the glass and picked up the bottle and carried it with him as he walked along the bar looking everything over.

"When's that dancing start?" he said to one of the bartenders.

He spoke loudly, perhaps because he needed to speak over the music in his ears. He drank his nonalcoholic beer from the bottle, holding it by the neck.

"Nine o'clock," the Hispanic girl said. She had no accent.

The cowboy looked around the bar at Jesse, at the two guys in plaid shirts drinking beer, at the two bartenders.

"Anybody know a happening place around here?"

One of the beer drinkers shook his head without looking up. Nobody else even acknowledged the question. Everybody knows it, Jesse thought. Maybe it's how loud he talks. Or how he looks like a model in one of those western-wear catalogs. Or the way he walks around in the little backwater bar, like he was strolling into the Ritz. Whatever it was, everyone knew he was a guy who, encouraged by an answer, would talk to you for much too long. The cowboy nodded to himself, as if his suspicions were confirmed, and walked into the empty dance hall and walked around it, looking at the caricatures of dapper semi-human coyotes hanging on the walls. Then he put his half-finished bottle of nonalcoholic beer on the bar, surveyed the bar again, and walked out.

"Takes all kinds," the blond bartender said.

A jerk, Jesse thought. A good-looking jerk, but just as lonely and separate as the homely ones. His sandwich came. He ate it because he needed nourishment, and drank two more scotches and paid and went to his room. Nothing was going to happen when they opened up the dance floor that Jesse wanted to watch.

In his room he got the travel bottle of Black Label out of his suitcase and poured some into one of the little sanitary plastic cups he found in the bathroom. The walk down the hall for ice seemed too long so he sipped the scotch warm. He didn't turn on the television. Instead he stood at the window and looked out at the high pines that rimmed the hill behind the motel. He'd grown up in Tucson when *The Brady Bunch* was hot, and while it was only four or five hours away, it could have been another planet. Tucson was sunlight and desert and heat, even in January. Up here they had winter. It was 7:45, getting dark. He was still in the same time zone. Jennifer would be home from work. Actually she'd probably be fucking Elliott Krueger about now. He let the images of his wife having sex roll behind his eyes as he stared at the now-dark windowpane and sipped his scotch. His reflection in the windowpane looked somber. He grinned at it, and raised his glass in a toasting gesture. Go to it, Jenn, fuck your brains out. It's got nothing to do with me. The bravado of it, buoyed with the scotch, made him feel intact for a moment, but he knew it was scotch, and he knew it was bravado, and he knew there was nothing behind the smile in the empty window.

Chapter 4

Hasty Hathaway had never really worked. His father had made a great deal of money in banking, and while he spent time in his office at the bank he'd inherited, he was mainly busy with being the most prominent citizen in Paradise, chairman of the Board of Selectmen, Commander of Freedom's Horsemen, and president of the Rotary Club. He stood now in his bedroom with the closet door open thinking about which jacket to wear. His wife lay in bed in her nightgown watching him.

"What about the blue seersucker?" he said.

"Blue looks good on you, Hasty," Cissy said.

"New chief of police is arriving this week," Hasty said, "from California."

"Didn't you meet him already?"

"Chicago. Burke and I went out to interview the finalists. Stayed at the Palmer House."

Hasty pulled out the blue seersucker and put it on and turned so Cissy could see him.

"Good," she said. "Are you going to wear that plaid bow tie?"

"You think I should?"

"It would go very nicely with that shirt and jacket."

"All right, then," Hasty said and took it off the tie rack on the back of the closet door.

"Is he a nice boy?" Cissy said.

"The new chief? Well, I hope he's more than that," Hasty said. "But he is young, and looks younger than he is. And he has a good record."

"And he'll fit in?" Cissy said.

"Yes, we were careful about that," Hasty said. "That was one of Tom Carson's problems, so we were all especially alert to that. He's one of us. Not wealthy of course, but the right background generally. College-educated, too."

"Really? What school?"

"Out there," Hathaway said. "One of the big ones, USC, UCLA, I can't keep them straight. Criminal justice. He took courses at night."

"It's always a shame, I think, when a young man can't get the full college experience. You know, not only classes, but football games and pep rallies, proms, intense discussions in the dorms."

"I know, but many young men are not as fortunate as we were. They have to make do."

"Yes."

As he did every morning Hathaway had a bowl of Wheaties for breakfast and two cups of coffee. Cissy sat across from him in her bathrobe with black coffee and a cigarette. He had quit twenty years earlier. They both wished she could quit, but she couldn't, and they had concluded that there was no point discussing it. She was a tallish woman with a youthful body. She rarely wore makeup, and if she did it was only lipstick. Her blond hair was starting to show silver and she wore it long. It looked nice with her youthful face.

"Well," he said, "have to run. Got a bank to run. Got a town to manage."

"Busy, busy," she said.

It was what she always said, because that was what he always said. She put her cheek up to be kissed. He kissed it and left, walking out the back door and down the driveway toward the town hall. His clothes always looked slightly unfashionable, as if he had spent money on them a long time ago and then outgrown them. The trouser cuffs were always too high. The jacket sleeves always showed too much shirtsleeve. His belt seemed too high and the waist of his suit coat always seemed a little pinched. Like her smoking, it was something put aside in the long years of marriage, under the heading "for better, for worse." She put his cereal bowl and coffee cup in the sink, poured herself another cup of coffee, and lit another cigarette and hugged her robe a little snugger around her and looked out at the flower garden which occupied most of her backyard. She'd been flattered to marry a man from such a good family. Later maybe she'd take a bath and shave her legs.

chapter 5

The first day's drive had been tan and parched, the hillsides littered with beige rocks. Every once in a while a tiny funnel of wind ran up a drywash and spiraled a handful of dust across the interstate. Jesse had seen no wildlife, and no vegetation other than the lifeless-looking desert scrub. He saw no water until he crossed the Colorado River near Needles. He was driving the Explorer. He'd left Jennifer the red Miata with the balloon note that she'd pay out of her first big break, she said. Now on his second day out, he was still in the mountains, east of Flagstaff. Green, clean, cool, full of evergreen trees. Very different from the southern Arizona of his childhood. The water bounded down gullies and gushed out of fissures in the rock face. The water ran with an abandon that Jesse had never seen, as if God had too much of it and had simply flung it at this part of the landscape. On cruise control, the car itself seemed to flow through the rich green personless landscape. He turned on the radio and pushed the scan button. The digital dial flashed silently as the radio sought unsuccessfully for a signal strong enough to stop on. One way to tell when you're in the boonies. It was clear in the mountains and still crisp. Even in late spring, there were still patches of snow, under the low spread of the biggest pine trees. Elliott had probably already screwed her under a tree. By the time he had reached Albuquerque he had dropped two thousand feet, though he was still high. It was impossible to drive across the country without imagining Indians and cavalry and wagon trains and mountain men, and Wells Fargo and the Union Pacific. Deerskin trousers and coats made of buffalo hide and long rifles and traps and whiskey and Indians. Bowie knives. Beaver traps. Buffalo as far as you could look. White-faced cattle. Chuck wagons. Six-guns with smooth handles. Horse and man seemingly like one animal as they moved across the great landscape. Hats and kerchiefs and Winchester rifles and the creak of saddles and the smell of bacon and coffee. East of Albuquerque he was back into sere landscape with high ground lying ominously in the distance, like sleeping beasts at the point where the vast high sky joined the remote landscape. At a rest stop the sign warned of rattlesnakes. He stopped for gas at an Indian reservation in New Mexico. He didn't know what kinds of Indians they were. Hopi maybe, or Pima. He didn't know anything about Indians. The gas was cheaper on the reservation and so were cigarettes because neither was subject to federal tax. Signs for miles along the interstate advertised the low price for cigarettes. A couple of Indian men in jeans and white tee shirts and plastic mesh baseball caps were hanging around the self-service pump. One of them eyed the California plates on the car.

"Where you headed," he said with that indefinable Indian accent.

"Massachusetts," Jesse said.

The two men looked at each other.

"Massachusetts," one of them said.

"All the way to Massachusetts?" the other one said.

"Yeah."

"Driving?"

"All the way," Jesse said.

"You got to be shitting me, mister. Massachusetts?"

Jesse nodded.

"Massachusetts," he said.

"Jeesus!"

The pump shut off and Jesse went into the tiny station to pay. There was some motor oil on a shelf. There was the electronic cash register on a tiny counter. There was a fat old Indian woman at the register in a red tee shirt that had "Harrah's" printed across the front in black letters. A cigarette was stuck in the corner of her mouth and she squinted through the smoke as she took Jesse's money and rang it up. The rest of the store was filled with stacked cartons of cigarettes.

"Cigarettes?" she said.

"Don't smoke."

She shrugged. As Jesse pulled away from the pumps he could see the two Indian men looking after him, talking excitedly. Massachusetts! There was nothing else in the shale and scrub landscape but the station and the two men. . . . The first time he met Jennifer she had blond hair. He had played basketball for an hour at Sports Club LA, where Magic sometimes worked out, against a bunch of former college players and one guy who'd spent a couple of years as the eleventh man on the Indiana Pacers. Showered and dressed, he was drinking coffee at a table for two in the snack bar during a crowded noontime when she asked if she could sit in the empty seat across from him. He said she could. It was a big part of why he came to Sports Club LA. He didn't really need to work out much.

At six feet and 175 it was as if he'd been born in shape and never really had to work at it. He'd been a point guard at Fairfax High School, the only white point guard in the conference, and he could climb a long rope hand over hand without using his feet. At the Academy he had been the fastest up the rope in his class. Mostly he came to Sports Club LA because he knew there would be many good-looking young women there in excellent physical condition, and he hoped to meet one. He played some handball, some basketball, and drank coffee in the snack bar where, had he wished to, he could have had a blended fruit-and-yogurt frappe or some green vegetable juice. Jennifer set her tray down and smiled at him.

"My name's Jennifer," she said.

"Jesse Stone."

"What are you having?" she said.

Her eyes were blue, the biggest eyes Jesse had ever seen, and the lashes were very long. She was wearing cobalt-and-emerald spandex and her fingernails were painted blue.

"Coffee."

"Wow," Jennifer said. "Here in the health food bar?"

Jesse smiled. Jennifer had some kind of sandwich with guacamole on whole wheat bread. When she took a bite the guacamole oozed out of the edges and dribbled on her chin. She giggled as she put the sandwich down and wiped her chin with a napkin. He liked the way she giggled. He liked the way she seemed unembarrassed by slobbering her sandwich on her chin. He liked the way her green headband held her hair back off her face. He liked the fact that her skin was too dark a tone for her blond hair, and he wondered momentarily what her real color was.

"So, you in the business?" Jennifer said.

"I'm a police officer," he said.

"Really?"

"Yes."

"God, you don't look like one."

"What do I look like?" Jesse said.

"Like a producer, maybe, or an agent. You know, slim, good haircut, good casual clothes, the Oakley shades."

Jesse smiled some more.

"You carry a gun?" Jennifer said.

"Sure."

"Really?"

Jesse opened his coat and turned his body a little so that she could see the nine-millimeter pistol he wore behind his right hip.

"I've never even picked up a gun," Jennifer said.

"That's good."

"I'd love to shoot one. Is it hard to shoot one?"

"No," Jesse said. The gun nearly always worked. Unless they were sort of late-age hippies and then it turned them off. "I'll take you shooting sometime, if you'd like."

"Is there a big kick?"

"No."

Jennifer ate some more sandwich and wiped her mouth.

"If I'd known I was going to eat with someone I wouldn't have ordered this sandwich," she said.

Jesse nodded.

"You don't say much, do you?"

"No," Jesse said. "I don't."

"Why is that, most guys I know around here talk a mile a minute."

"That's one reason," Jesse said.

Jennifer laughed.

"Any other reasons?"

"I can't ever remember," Jesse said, "getting in trouble by keeping my mouth shut."

"So what kind of cop are you? You a detective?"

"Yes."

"LAPD?"

"Yes."

"Where are you, ah, stationed? Are cops stationed?"

"I am a homicide detective. I work out of police headquarters downtown."

"Homicide."

"Yes."

Jennifer was silent for a moment thinking about the gap between the world she lived in and the one he worked in.

"Is it like, what? *Hill Street Blues?*" she said.

"More like *Barney Miller,*" he said.

It was his standard answer, but it was no truer than any other, just self-effacing, which was why he used it. Being a homicide cop wasn't like anything on television, but there wasn't much point in trying to explain that to someone who could never know.

"You an actress?" he said.

"Yes. How did you know?"

It was another thing he always said. He had a good chance to be right in Los Angeles, and even if he were wrong, the girl was flattered.

"You're beautiful," he said. "And you have a sort of star quality."

"Wow, you know the right things to say, don't you."

"Just telling the truth," Jesse said.

"Right now I'm working at the reception desk at CAA," Jennifer said. "But one of the agents has noticed me and says he's going to get me some auditions during pilot season."

"You done any work I might have seen?"

"Mostly nonspeaking parts, crowd scenes, things like that. I'm in a play three nights a week just down the street here. It's a modern version of a Greek tragedy called *The Parcae*. I play Clotho."

"Sounds really interesting," Jesse said. "I'd like to come see it."

"I can leave a ticket for you at the box office. All you have to do is let me know the night."

"How about tonight?" Jesse said.

"Sure."

"Maybe have a bite afterwards?"

"That would be very nice," she said.

"Good," Jesse said. "I'll meet you afterwards in the lobby."

She smiled and stood and disposed of her tray.

"If you don't like the play, don't arrest me," she said.

"I'll like the play," Jesse said.

He watched her as she walked away. He knew he'd hate the play, but it was part of what he was willing to pay in order to see that body without the Lycra. . . . At Santa Rosa he crossed the Pecos. It was a pretty ordinary-looking little river to be so famous. What the hell made it so famous? Was it Judge Roy Bean? The law west of the Pecos? Small things pleased him as he drove. He liked seeing the towns that had once marked Route 66: Gallup, New Mexico, Flagstaff, Arizona, Winona. He liked seeing the occasional wind-driven tumbleweed that rolled across the highway. He liked seeing road signs for Indian reservations and places like Fort Defiance. Past Santa Rosa he pulled off of the interstate to get gas and a ham-and-cheese sandwich at a gas station/restaurant in the middle of the New Mexico wilderness. It was the only building in sight with views in all directions to the empty horizon. He pumped his own gas, and a skinny girl with pale skin and a tooth missing took his money and sold him a sandwich. He sat in the car and ate the sandwich and drank a Coke and thought about how alone the skinny girl was and wondered about what she did when she wasn't working the gas station and selling the pre-wrapped sandwiches. Probably went someplace and watched television off a dish. The sense of her aloneness made him feel a little panicky, and he put the car in gear and drove away, finishing his sandwich on the move. As he drove he ran the ball of his thumb over his wedding ring, in a habitual gesture. But of course there was no wedding ring, only the small pale indentation on his third finger where the ring had been. He glanced at the indentation for a moment and brought his eyes back to the road. The sun was behind him now, the car chasing its own elongated shadow east. He wanted to make Tucumcari by dark . . . The play had been incomprehensible, he remembered. A lot of white makeup and black lipstick and shrieking. He took her up to a place on Gower called Pinot Hollywood that was open late and featured a martini bar. They drank martinis and ate calamari and talked. Or she talked. She chattered easily and without apparent pretense. He listened comfortably, glad not to talk too much, pleased when she asked him a question that he could answer easily, aware that though she talked a lot she was quite adroit at talking about him. After the bar closed he drove her to West Hollywood where she had an apartment on Cynthia Street above Santa Monica Boulevard. It was 2:30 in the morning and the street was still. At the door she asked if he'd like to come in. He said he would. The apartment was living room, kitchen, bedroom, and bath. It had been built into one corner of the building so that all the rooms were angular and odd shaped. The living room overlooked the street. The bedroom allowed a glimpse of the pool.

"Would you like a drink, Jesse?"

"Sure," he said.

She was wearing a little black dress with spaghetti straps

and backless high-heeled shoes. She put her hands on her hips and smiled at him. Maybe a little theatrical, but she was an actress.

"Let's have it afterwards," she said.

Her bedroom was neat. The bed freshly made. She had probably planned, this afternoon, to ask him in. He watched her undress with the same feeling he used to have when, as a small boy, he unwrapped a present. She folded her dress neatly over the back of a chair and lined her shoes carefully together under it. She squirmed out of her underpants and dropped them into the clothes hamper in her closet. She wiped her lipstick off carefully and dropped the tissue in the wastebasket. They made love on top of the bedspread, and lay together afterward in the dim bedroom listening to the comforting white noise of the air conditioning.

"You're very fierce, Jesse."

"I don't mean to be," he said.

"No, it's fine. It's exciting in fact. But you seem so, um, so still, on the outside and then, you know, wow."

"You're pretty exciting," he said. He didn't know what else to say. He didn't like to talk about his emotions.

"I try to be," she said.

They lay quietly on their backs. His arm under her neck. Her head on his right shoulder.

"I wouldn't want to make you mad," Jennifer said.

"You won't."

They lay quietly for a while longer, then she got up and put on a longish tee shirt and made them a drink. He felt like a fool sitting naked, but he didn't want to be so formal as to get fully dressed. He settled for putting his pants on, and leaving his gun holstered on top of her dresser. They sat on stools at the tiny counter that separated her kitchen from her living room, and sipped white wine.

"How'd you get to be a cop, Jesse?"

"I was going to be a baseball player," Jesse said. "Shortstop. Dodgers drafted me out of high school, sent me to Pueblo. I was doing okay and then one night a guy took me out on a double play at second base. I landed funny, tore up my shoulder, ended the career."

"Oh, how awful," she said. "Does it bother you still?"

"Not if I don't have to throw a baseball."

"Couldn't you have played where it didn't matter?"

"No. I hit okay for a shortstop, but I was going to make it on my glove."

"Glove?"

"I was a much better fielder," Jesse said, "than I was a hitter."

"And you couldn't just field?"

"No."

"How old were you?"

"Nineteen," Jesse said. "I came home, worked construction for six months, joined the Marines, got out, took the exam for fire department, police, and DWP. Cops came through first."

"Do you miss baseball?"

"Every day," Jesse said.

"Isn't it kind of depressing being a policeman?" she said. "You know, seeing all that awfulness."

Again he was aware of how skillfully she turned the conversation to him. He enjoyed her interest, but more than that he admired her skill.

"I like police work," he said. "You're with a bunch of guys, but the work is mostly one on one. Sometimes you get to help people."

"And the awful things?"

"There's not as much as you think," he said.

"But there is some," she said.

"Sure."

"What about that."

"That's just how it is," Jesse said.

"That's all?"

"What else," Jesse said. "Life's hard sometimes."

"So you don't let it bother you."

"I try not to," Jesse said.

chapter 6

Jo Jo Genest first got into the money business through a guy named Fusco that he met at the gym in Somerville.

"Guy I know," Fusco said, "is looking to smurf some cash."

Jo Jo was sitting spread legged on the floor doing lat pull-backs.

"Whaddya mean smurf?" he said.

"You know, go around to banks," Fusco said. "Deposit cash for him so he can wire transfer it later."

"Why?"

"Why what?"

"Why the whole thing," Jo Jo said.

His movements as he pulled the cables and raised the weight were smooth and appeared effortless. His muscles moved like huge serpents under his pale skin.

"Man, where you been," Fusco said.

"I been around," Jo Jo said. "Maybe I'm being smart. Tell me the deal."

Fusco sat on a weight bench with a towel over his thighs.

His stomach pushed against his tank top. His thin legs were very white and hairy in blue sport shorts.

"Guy I know makes a lotta money in ways that maybe he shouldn't, you unnerstand? Lotta money. He needs to wash it, you unnerstand, launder it, so the government can't find it and if they do, they can't trace it to him."

Jo Jo let the cable go slack on the lat pull machine and mopped his face with a hand towel, waiting for the lactic acid to drain from his muscles.

"So he needs to get the dough into banks so that he can transfer it around, maybe overseas."

"Like to a numbered Swiss bank account," Jo Jo said.

"Sure," Fusco said, "like that. Anyway what you do is go around with a sack full of cash and buy cashier's checks or money orders for amounts small enough so they don't get reported."

"What happens then?"

"You give them to me."

"What do you do with them?"

"None of your business."

"Aw, Fusco, come off it. You know I'm all right or you wouldn't have told me this much. What happens to the checks and money orders, they get sent to a Swiss bank?"

Fusco grinned. "You really like them Switzers, don't you," he said. "Usually it's the branch of some South American bank in Florida."

"So don't they get reported?"

"No. It's not a cash deal. CTRs are required only for cash."

"CTR?"

Jo Jo had begun a second set, holding his upper body still, isolating the muscles. His voice showed no sign of strain.

"Cash Transaction Report."

"So you change the cash into something else and you don't have to report it," Jo Jo said.

"Bada bing," Fusco said, shooting at Jo Jo with his forefinger. "You want some?"

"How much?"

"Half a percent," Fusco said. "Everything you smurf. Plus expenses."

Jo Jo pulled the bar toward him and moved a huge stack of iron plates up by means of a cable-and-pulley arrangement. He held the bar tight against his stomach, then very slowly let it down. Fusco watched him with admiration.

"You gotta focus on the muscle," Jo Jo said. "You got to be thinking about it when you work it. On this one it's the lats, nothing else, just think about the lats, Fusco."

"Half a percent," Fusco said again. "You interested?"

"Sure," Jo Jo said.

Chapter 7

In Tucumcari Jesse stopped at a Holiday Inn just off the interstate on old Route 66. There was a gas station across the street, and a field where horses and one mule grazed, and nothing else. He had a club sandwich in the motel restaurant and got some ice and went to his room where he sat with the door open and sipped scotch and watched the few people still using the pool in the courtyard. There was a couple with two children using the pool. The children were unpleasant—unkind to each other, demanding of their parents. The father looked awkward in his ill-fitting bathing suit, white-bodied, hairy, and soft. The mother was bottom-heavy and knew it, wearing a bathing suit with a tiny skirt in a useless attempt to conceal her disproportion. Her parents were with them. The grandmother was a thin old woman in matching beige pants and blouse. Her hair was evenly gray and curled tightly to her head. Whenever the mother spoke sharply to one of her children, the grandmother would intervene. The grandfather looked like he might once have done heavy labor. His forearms were still thick and there was a hint of muscle pack in his sloped shoulders. But his stomach was big and his white legs in their pink polyester shorts were blue-veined and rickety-looking. The grandfather had a grim look, as if the family trip had not been his idea. Jesse imagined the man's dismay at his family. Still it was family, three generations of it. Jesse felt remote as he sat, as if he were viewing himself from far away, a tiny figure, diminished by distance, dwindling as he sat. . . . In the morning he was on the interstate before seven and crossed into the Texas panhandle before eight. There were signs for Big John's Steak House in Amarillo. A seventy-two-ounce steak. Eat it in an hour and get it free. By ten he was in Amarillo. Big John was not alone. The highway was suddenly beset by motels and fast food, car dealers and steak houses and gas stations. Then he was out of Amarillo and back onto the plains. The Big John's signs faced the other way now, luring the westbound travelers. On each side of the highway the open range reappeared, dotted occasionally with cattle grazing on the unappetizing brown grass. Once in a while there would be a gate, usually made of iron piping, with a sign indicating a cattle baronage. But he never saw any houses, or any cowboys, mostly just brown grassland beyond the wire fencing that lined the highway, and now and then a water cistern. The grass did not look nourishing. He had the cruise control on seventy, but the distances were so great and the sky so high and the horizon so distant that the car seemed in the ulteriority of his imagination a beetle scuttling without measurable progress beneath a limitless sky across an uncomprehending plain . . . They'd been married a month when they had dinner at a table in the rear at Spago with Elliott Krueger. He had been across the street from Spago once, at 2:35 in the morning, on the crime-scene team, when a Chicano coke dealer named Street Duck had been killed by somebody who shot him five times in the stomach at close range with a nine-millimeter pistol. No one had seen the shooting. Elliott was about fifty. His thick black hair was touched with gray, his short careful beard was touched with more. He was medium height, medium build. He didn't look like he exercised. He had on an unconstructed linen jacket with the sleeves pushed up over his forearms. He wore a Rolex watch. It had been Jesse's experience that people who really had a lot of money didn't waste it on Rolex watches. In the bad neighborhoods, on the other hand, a Rolex watch on a kid meant he was so tough that no one dared to take it away from him. Elliott had a girlfriend with him. Her name was Taffy. She seemed about sixteen, but she might have been twenty. Wearing a flowered dress with a very short ruffled skirt, she sat silently beside Elliott like an obedient spaniel waiting for a command.

"It's my business to know this sort of thing," Elliott said to Jesse. "And your wife here has the goods."

Jesse nodded.

"Oh, Elliott," Jennifer said. "I'll bet you say that to all the girls."

"My right hand to God," Elliott said, and put his right hand in the air. "I see twenty girls a day. All of them are good-looking. Everybody out here is good-looking, you know? But none of them come alive through the lens like you do, Jennifer."

Jesse sipped the tall scotch and soda he'd ordered.

"What are you working on now, Elliott?" Jennifer said.

"Got a thing in development at Universal," Elliott said. "Absolutely amazing story about a plastic surgeon, got an Oedipal deal going with his mother. Women come to him for a makeover and he does a surgical reconstruction so that they look like his mother, then he kills them. Great vehicle for Tommy Cruise.''

"I love the concept," Jennifer said. "Do you love it, Jesse?''

"Love it," Jesse said. Tommy Cruise.

"Maybe I can bring you aboard, Jesse, you know, you being a cop and all, could use a little professional consult on this. You ever dealt with psychopathic killers?"

"Not my job to decide if they're psychopaths," Jesse said.

"Oh, Jesse," Jennifer said, "you know what he means.''

"Well, you murder somebody," Jesse said, "probably something wrong with you.''

"Well, I may give you a ringo, soon as I teach this idiot writer I'm working with how to write a screenplay.''

"He's never written one?" Jennifer said.

"No, he's a damn novelist, you know?''

"The worst.''

"You got that right," Elliott said. "Can't tell them shit.''

He sighed thoughtfully for a moment, looking around the room, then he patted his chest over his shirt pocket, and frowned, and took a twenty-dollar bill out of his pants pocket and handed it to his girlfriend.

"Taffy," he said, "go get me some cigarettes.''

Taffy took the money and headed for the bar near the waiting area out front.

"I like it back here," Elliott said. "Lotta people like it out front where everyone can see them. Real Hollywood, right? I'm not into that.''

"Don't blame you," Jesse said. He knew Jennifer liked him to talk around industry people.

"I'm a blue-collar guy, you know, Jesse. I make pictures.''

Jesse had never heard of any picture that Elliott had

made. But he didn't pay much attention to movies. He thought they were boring, except for westerns. Of which there weren't many new ones. Taffy came back with the cigarettes. The waitress brought them another round of drinks.

Elliott said, "Lemme tell you a little more about this picture, Jenn."

Jesse took a long pull on his scotch and soda, feeling the cold thrust of it down his throat, waiting for the good feeling to follow. . . . In Oklahoma City he turned northeast, toward St. Louis. He was in the central time zone now. He could remember listening to Vin Scully broadcasting the games from St. Louis, right at suppertime. It was as if he knew St. Louis, the ballpark glowing in the close summer night, the Mississippi running past. Bob Gibson, past his prime but still ferocious. Bake McBride, Ted Simmons. It was how he knew much of the country: Scully's effortless voice from Wrigley Field and Three Rivers and Shea and Fulton County Stadium, a kind of panoramic linkage under the dark skies of the Republic. He'd listened to Vin Scully all his life. Vin Scully was authority, containment, certainty. Vin Scully was home. He reached St. Louis in the late afternoon with the rush-hour traffic clogging the interstate. He crossed the Mississippi and pulled off the interstate and found Busch Stadium, near the river. In front, a statue of Stan Musial. Jesse sat in the car for a moment and stared at the statue.

"Stan Musial," he said.

Jennifer would never have understood. Maybe no one could who had not played. The feel of it. The smell of the field, the way the skin of the infield felt under your spikes. The way your hands and arms and upper body felt when you hit the ball square, on the fat part of the bat. Maybe you had to have played to hear the oral poetry of chatter and heckling, the jock humor that lingered at the poles of arrogance and self-effacement, the things umpires said every time they defended a call, the things the first baseman said every time, out of the corner of his mouth, while he watched the pitcher, if you reached first on a lucky blooper. They didn't know that when you were in the field waiting for the pitcher to throw, or that when you were at bat trying to pick up the spin of a curve ball, you didn't hear the crowd or the coaches or anyone else. They didn't know that you were in a place of silence that seemed unregulated by time. Though they were men and they often spent time in the company of men, Jennifer's friends didn't have any feel for men in groups. Many of them seemed more at ease with women . . . after a cocktail party in the interests of Jennifer's career they had a fight about it.

"Why were they so boring?" Jennifer said.

"They don't know anything that matters," he said.

"They are successful people in the business," Jennifer said.

"Nobody in the business knows what matters," Jesse had said.

"For Christ's sake, they talked with you about baseball all night."

"They don't know anything about baseball," Jesse said. "They just knew the names of a bunch of players."

"Oh, fuck you," Jennifer said.

As he left St. Louis it began to rain, spitting at first, and then more of a steady mist. He stayed the night in a motel in Zanesville, Ohio, and when he came out to the car in the morning it was still dark after sunrise and the rain was coming steadily. He pulled into the Exxon station next to the motel, a half block from the interstate ramp. Most people weren't up yet in Zanesville. The empty roadways gleamed in the rain reflecting the bright lights of the gas station. He pumped his own gas and when he went in to pay bought himself coffee and two plain donuts in the convenience section. The man behind the counter had a shiny bald head and a neat beard. He wore a crisp white shirt with the cuffs turned back and there was a small tattoo on his right forearm that said "Duke" in ornate blue script.

"Early start," the man said.

"Long way to go," Jesse said.

"Where you heading?"

The man made change automatically, as if his hands did the counting.

"Massachusetts."

"Long way is right," the man said. "Never been there myself."

Jesse pocketed his change and took his coffee and donuts.

"Safe trip," the man said.

There were places like this all across the country, dependent on the interstate, open early, bright, smelling of coffee, not unfriendly. The interstate was an entity of its own, a kind of transcontinental neighborhood, filled with single people, who hung out in the neighborhood places. He swung up onto Interstate 70 and drove east into the rain, drinking his coffee. . . . He still didn't know exactly when she started sleeping with Elliott Krueger. He knew she was out more and later. He would stand sometimes at the window, looking out at North Genesee Street and thinking maybe the next car will be her. He was embarrassed with himself about that, but it seemed as if he had to do it. Sometimes when they were having dutiful sex, a voice in his head, which seemed not even his, would say, This isn't the first time today she's done this. The voice was not uncertain. The voice knew. He knew. But then he didn't know. Despite the passion of their courtship, she had become perfunctory about sex. He couldn't imagine her being so consumed by desire that she would cheat on him. And he couldn't imagine that she would even if she were. She wouldn't do that to me, his own voice would say in his head. She wouldn't do that to me. As he drove through the wet gray morning toward West Virginia he smiled at himself. It wasn't about me. It was about her, about what she needed, about being an actress. She needed to be an actress more than she needed to be a cop's wife. He wondered sometimes what he needed from her. A kind of richness, maybe. The palpability of her, the odd combination of intellect and ditz that she balanced so beautifully. Maybe it made no sense to try to figure. Could anyone list the reasons they loved someone? Probably not. He crossed the Ohio River at Wheeling, the rain dimpling the iron-colored surface of the wide water below the bridge. He liked rivers. They always hinted to him of possibility. The interstate was uphill now in West Virginia, and it curved around the slopes. The big trailer trucks roared through it, sending up a sheet of water as they passed him on the down slopes. On the next hill they would slow, and he would either have to slow to their speed or pass them, only to have them roar past him again as they made up the time on the downgrade. Time was money to truckers. He sympathized with that. But, especially in bad weather, trucks were a pain in the ass. It was part of his own problem, he thought, that he understood Jennifer's behavior only in terms of himself. She wouldn't do that to me. But it was human. He didn't condemn himself, though his one-wayness, too, embarrassed him sometimes when he thought of it. He'd been a cop too long not to understand the limits on human empathy. I thought she didn't like sex anymore, when in fact, she didn't like sex anymore with me. Even the sex she liked, as he thought about it, had, maybe, been about getting what she wanted, which, at one time, had been him. Maybe she never really liked sex as much as she seemed to. Maybe once she had used it to catch what she was fishing for, she didn't enjoy it anymore. Because she liked fishing didn't mean she had to like fish. The rain came now so thickly that it nearly overwhelmed the wipers. He shifted the Explorer into four-wheel drive as the gleaming interstate wound slickly through the hills. She denied Elliott when she left him, saying she had to get away and wasn't leaving him for anyone. It was probably meant as a kindness. It probably was a kindness at the time, and by the time she dropped the other shoe and talked about Elliott, he had already begun the process of shoring up his self and could hear it. The night she left and he was alone in the house he looked at his service pistol and picked it up and thought about where to shoot himself. A lot of cops shot themselves. They had the means at hand, and they knew how. Put them ahead of the general populace, he thought, in suicide efficiency. Probably putting the muzzle in his mouth and shooting up and back would be the way most likely to take him out instantly. Cops called it eating your gun. He sat on the bed and hefted the gun and felt comforted by it. If he couldn't stand her leaving, if she didn't come back, it was always there. It was a comfort to know it was there. Like booze. If it got bad enough he could always drink. He put the gun back in the drawer by his bed and went and looked out the window. . . . The rain was a constant. Sometimes it intensified as he drove through the north spur of West Virginia. It was never gentle and sometimes it was intense, and Jesse drove mostly by focusing on the taillights of the car ahead. He had a momentary fantasy of a ten-mile-long line of cars, each driver following the taillights ahead of him going one by one over a cliff as the first driver in the long line missed the turn. . . . After she had left and he decided to at least postpone shooting himself, he found that it was bad enough to drink. At first nobody noticed much. Then his partner, a fifty-two-year-old guy named Ben Romero, talked to him about it. Jesse listened and shrugged and went about his drinking. After an incident at night when Jesse couldn't seem to get the handcuffs on a perp, Romero asked for a new partner.

"I got five kids," Romero said. "Two of them in college. I can't risk it with you anymore, Jesse."

Jesse nodded and shrugged. Romero shook hands with him, opened his mouth to say something, and closed it, and shook his head and walked away. When his new partner quit him in less than a week, Jesse was transferred inside to records. When he started not showing up for work, Cronjager called him in and talked to him and sent him to the police doctor. The doctor got him to AA. He thought the meetings were full of self-satisfied assholes, and he hated the higher power crap. After the second meeting he went home and drank nearly a fifth of scotch and slept through most of the next day. The day after that Cronjager offered him the chance to resign or go through the firing process. Jesse resigned. And went home and sat in his small kitchen with ice and scotch and found himself without connection or purpose. I'll drink to that. He sat and drank scotch and the tears ran down his face.

Chapter 8

Her sister had agreed to take the kids for the night,
and Carole Genest had the house to herself. Before she
went to dinner with Mark she had changed the bed linens.
She and Mark had had two margaritas and a bottle of white
wine with dinner and they were laughing as Mark pulled
the BMW sedan into her driveway and parked under the
big maple tree near her side door.

"You better lock the car," Carole said when they got
out. "I don't think you'll be leaving for a while."

As Mark beeped the lock button on his key ring, and the
power locks clicked in the car, Jo Jo Genest loomed out of
the shadows by the side door.

Carole said, "Jesus."

"Where's the kids?" Jo Jo said.

"Get out of here, Jo Jo," Carole said.

"You gonna fuck this pipsqueak?" Jo Jo said.

"Watch your mouth, pal," Mark said. But he didn't say
it with conviction. Hulking before them in the half light,
Jo Jo looked like a rhinoceros.

Jo Jo put his huge hand against Mark's face and slammed his head back against the roof of the car. Mark's legs buckled and he staggered but remained upright, leaning on the car, clasping his head with both hands, rocking slowly from one side to another.

"Get outta here," Jo Jo said.

Mark went around the car, still holding his head, got into it, and backed down the driveway, the car running off of one side of the driveway and then the other as he overcorrected, going too fast backward in the dark.

"You son of a bitch," Carole said. "I got a court order on you. I'm going to put you in jail, you bastard."

"Kids are at your sister's, aren't they? You stashed them there so you could come home and fuck that faggot."

"And if I did, what's that to you. Don't you get it, you jerk. We're divorced, D-I-V-O-R-C-E-D."

She unlocked the side door as she talked and pushed past him into the house. He followed her.

"Get out of my house," she said.

"Your house? Your fucking house? You paid for it?"

Jo Jo kicked the side door shut with his heel.

"I'm calling the cops," Carole said.

"No," Jo Jo said. "No. I came here to talk. Lemme talk with you."

"Nice start to a talk," Carole said. "Smacking my date against the car."

"I'm sorry," Jo Jo said. "I just can't stand seeing you with somebody, you unnerstand? I can't. You and me are forever, Carole. I can't stand it, you're with somebody else."

"Well, you better get used to it, Jo Jo, because that is how it is."

Jo Jo felt frantic. She was killing him. How could she kill him like this.

"I was hoping maybe, we could, you know, have sex, just one time, for old times' sake, you know?"

"Are you crazy? You come up here, two years we been divorced, you beat up my date and push in here and tell me you want to have sex? Get the hell out of here, Jo Jo. I'm calling the cops."

"Carole, please, I need it. I'm going crazy without it. Please."

She turned toward the phone and Jo Jo pushed her away. She tried to step around him and he grabbed her arm. She hit him with her free arm, a wild swing punch with her fist closed. He shoved her backward, away from the phone and onto the couch.

"Please," he said. "Please."

She was trying to hit him, but he held her wrists as he forced her down. She kicked at him, but it seemed to have no effect.

"Please," he said. "Please."

Her skirt was up over her thighs. He tore at her hose. His mouth pressed against hers. She tried to twist away. She punched, she kicked, she tried to bite him. But he was so oppressively strong, so irresistibly huge, that her struggles had no impact. His face was pressed against hers. She could smell liquor on his breath, or maybe it was liquor on hers. He had gotten most of her clothing out of the way. His weight pressed her helplessly back and his hands were on her and she could barely move and barely breathe and she thought oh, God, what's one more time, and gave up.

Chapter 9

The rain stayed with Jesse into western Pennsylvania. It had eased when he stopped on the Pennsylvania Turnpike, west of Pittsburgh. He got a cheeseburger in the restaurant, and a cup of coffee. He ate at the counter looking at the scattering of travelers around him. A lot of truckers, a lot of old people, retired probably, who'd arrived in their RVs. See the country: Trailer parks where you could get water and electrical and sewage hookups. Gas stations where you could fill up on gas and buy a pre-made sandwich wrapped in Saran Wrap, places like this where you could sit among your fellow adventurers and not look at them. They all looked like they'd eaten too much white bread. When he finished eating, he went to the men's room, and washed, and came out and walked to his car. The rain was firm now, and pleasant. Standing beside his car with one hand on the door, Jesse took off his baseball cap and turned his face up to the rain. He stood a long time letting the hard rain soak into him. He didn't know why he was doing it, and he stopped only when he became aware that other people were watching. His wet clothes were uncomfortable to drive in and when he reached the next rest stop he got some dry clothes out of his suitcase and changed into them in a bathroom stall. He bought a large coffee at the rest stop, and back in the car added a lot of scotch to it. He sipped the laced coffee as he crossed the Delaware River north of Philadelphia and picked up the Jersey Turnpike. He was in the east now, but it wasn't yet the east he imagined. This part of the east looked like Anaheim. Except for the rain. This was eastern rain. No sudden outbursts, no scudding clouds, no interruption for sunshine before another downpour, no bright colors made more brilliant by the wetness. Eastern rain was steady and unyielding and gray. . . . What confused him most was that Jennifer would neither embrace him nor let him go. He was a self-reliant guy. He had spent most of his life staying inside, playing within himself. He was pretty sure he could still do that, but there had to be some sort of completion between them. Having been her lover, he was quite sure he could never be her friend and nothing more. In the early days of his dismay he had thought maybe he could share her. He had, after all, in the last year or so of their marriage been sharing her involuntarily. But in a while he understood that he could not. And so he sat one evening in their kitchen, on one of their high stools at the breakfast counter, with a United States road atlas, a police help-wanted listing, and a bottle of scotch, and decided where he would go to look for peace. He had to work and all he knew was cop. Of the possible jobs the one in Paradise, Massachusetts, was the farthest away. With a lot of scotch inside him, which made him ironic rather than sad, he imagined the salt spray and the snowy streets at Christmastime and the cheery New Englanders going steadfastly about their business and decided to try Paradise first. Now as he approached the

George Washington Bridge he was maybe two hundred miles away from it and he felt as remote and unconnected as if he were adrift in space. There were other ways to get to New England, but he wanted to do it this way. He wanted to drive over the Hudson River across the George Washington Bridge. New York City stretched along the river to his right looking the way it did in all the pictures. Not to be confused with Los Angeles, he thought. He'd been in Chicago once looking for a guy who'd killed a process server in Gardena, and again for the Paradise job interview. He'd arranged several at a law enforcement convention in the Palmer House. But he assumed he wasn't getting a glowing recommendation from the LAPD, and Paradise was the only one to offer him a job. He remembered the march of Chicago cityscape along the lake front, but the New York skyline was different. Chicago had been exuberant. This congregation of spires was far too reserved for exuberance. There was nothing exultant in their massed height. There was something like contempt in the brute grace of the skyscrapers standing above the river.

The memory of the interview embarrassed him. He had been drinking scotch in the bar downstairs and his memory was the embarrassing memory of all drunks, he thought, the struggle to seem sober undercut by the half-suppressed knowledge that you were slurring your words. What bothered him even more was that he had needed to drink even though he knew it would jeopardize the job. His face felt hot at the memory. But they hadn't noticed. The two interviewers, Hathaway, the selectman, and a Paradise police captain named Burke, seemed oblivious of the times when he couldn't stop slushing the s's in Los Angeles. It was late afternoon. Maybe they'd had a couple before the interview themselves. They'd talked in a one-bedroom suite that Hathaway was in. The police captain had a single room

down the hall. Jesse remembered the room being too hot.
And he remembered that Burke hardly spoke at all, and
that Hathaway didn't seem to be asking the right questions.
He'd had to excuse himself twice to go to the bathroom,
and each time he had splashed cold water on his face from
the sink. But drunk is drunk, as he well knew, and cold
water didn't change anything. Hathaway had sat in front of
the window eleven stories above the loop with a manila
folder in his lap, to which he occasionally referred. Hathaway asked about his education, his experience, his marital
status.

"Divorced," Jesse said.

He didn't like saying it. It still seemed to him somehow
a shameful thing to admit. It made him feel less.

Hathaway, if he thought it shameful, made no sign.
Burke was silent in the shadow near the window to Hathaway's left.

"What do you think, Jesse," Hathaway said, about fifteen minutes into the interview, "about the right to keep
and bear arms?"

"Constitution's clear on that, I think." Jesse had trouble
with all the t's in *constitution.*

"Yes," Hathaway said, "I think so too."

They talked a bit about Jesse's life in the minor leagues
and how it was too bad that he couldn't make the throw
anymore. They talked of how many cases he had cleared
in L.A.

"Nobody clears them all," Jesse said with a smile, trying
to enlist Burke, who remained silent, his arms folded.
Clears came out *clearth.*

"We talked with your Captain Cronjager," Hathaway
said, referring to his folder.

Jesse waited. Cronjager was a decent enough guy, but he

believed in police work and he might not recommend a cop who drank on duty.

"He speaks very well of you, though he said you might have been developing a drinking problem when you left."

Jesse made a minimizing gesture with his right hand.

"I probably went off the deep end there for a bit during the time my marriage was breaking up," Jesse said. "But I'm fine now."

He had started to say *I am,* and then wasn't sure he could transit between the two vowels, and changed it to *I'm.* Did they hear the stutter?

"All of us like a drink," Hathaway said. "And in times of personal anguish, many of us need one. When one sees a man with your record applying for a job like this one, questions occur. I think I can speak for Lou when I say it is a relief really to hear that you maybe drank a little too much at a time when most of us would. I don't have a problem, do you, Lou?"

Burke's heavy voice came from the shadow where he sat.

"No problem, Hasty."

And that had been it. They had hired him on the spot and brought out a bottle and had drinks to seal the bargain. It had worked out fine. But I shouldn't have been drinking, Jesse thought as he went down the circular ramp off the bridge. Especially I shouldn't have needed to be drinking.

Jesse turned north along the Henry Hudson Parkway. He drove over the Harlem River Bridge and through the Bronx, where the city was already beginning to green. He followed the parkways, as he had planned, into Connecticut and up Route 15 feeling almost disembodied. He picked up Route 84 in Hartford, crossing the Connecticut River, with the cluster of small-city skyscrapers off to his left. It was dark by the time he crossed the line into Massachusetts and stopped for the night in Sturbridge. He could have driven the last seventy-five miles or so, but he didn't want to. He wanted to arrive in Paradise in the morning. He didn't know why, anymore than he knew why he had stood on Ocean Avenue and stared at the Pacific before he left. But after Jennifer left he had decided that if he was going to be alone, he probably ought to pay attention to what he wanted, even if he didn't always know why he wanted it. In his motel room he poured the almost ritualized drink and sat in the one chair in the silent room with his feet up on the bed. He'd read somewhere that two drinks a day were thought to be good for your heart. That was not bad, two drinks a day. It would give him something to look forward to every evening. It wouldn't scramble his mind. He thought that two drinks a day was about right for him. When he'd been with Jennifer he had tried to pay attention to what she wanted. If she's happy, he always said to himself, I'm happy. It wasn't true. But he had thought at the time that it ought to be true, and he insisted on trying to make it true, no matter how unhappy it made them both. He shook his head sadly in the small room. He was a cop, a guy who took pride in seeing evidence, on making judgments on what was really there. And he failed entirely to do that in his own life.

"What an asshole," he said.

His voice seemed so loud in the quiet room that he wondered if someone next door could hear him talking to himself. When you start talking to yourself . . . He smiled and sipped his scotch. He could see himself in the full-length mirror on the wall beside the bed. He raised the glass at himself. Get a grip, Jesse. Then he leaned back in the chair, holding the whiskey in both hands, and closed his eyes and thought about the next day. Maybe three drinks a day.

Chapter 10

Jo Jo Genest was always alert when he went to the South End. There were a lot of fags down there and he was ready to retaliate if one of them was flirtatious. Jo Jo could bench-press five hundred pounds. At six feet, he weighed 283 and, under the pressure of his latissimus dorsi, his arms stuck out as he walked. He crossed with the light at Clarendon Street near the Cyclorama, and went a half block west on Tremont, and went down three stairs to a basement-level storefront in one of the old brownstones. In black letters on the big glass window of the store was written Development Associates of Boston. He opened the door and went in. A good-looking young man with dark curly hair and a diamond earring sat at the reception desk, sorting mail. He looked up when Jo Jo entered.

"Is it Tarzan or one of the apes," the young man said.

The young man was always saying stuff like that to him, and he never liked it. If he didn't have business to do here, he'd slap the little faggot upside the head. Maybe someday.

"Gino back there?" he said.

"Sure."

Jo Jo nodded and went past the young man through the open archway into the back room. Gino Fish was sitting at a round antique table, in a high-backed antique chair. He was tall and thin with gray hair. Along the right-hand wall, a little behind Fish, sat Vinnie Morris with his chair tipped back and balanced on its back legs. Vinnie was listening to earphones from a small portable tape player clipped to his belt.

"How's it going, Gino," Jo Jo said.

"Fine," Fish said.

"Vinnie," Jo Jo said, "how they hanging?"

Vinnie Morris always made Jo Jo a little uneasy. The uneasiness puzzled Jo Jo. He weighed a hundred pounds more than Vinnie. But there was something about Vinnie's stillness. And when Vinnie moved he moved with such quickness and economy. And he had heard that Vinnie could shoot better than anyone in Boston. And Vinnie always seemed a little scornful of Jo Jo, which didn't make any sense because Jo Jo could have broken him in two like a twig, and Vinnie better not try anything with him, or he would.

There were two big suitcases on the floor next to Vinnie. Fish nodded at them.

"Two million," Fish said, "and change."

"No sweat, Gino."

"I'm sure," Fish said.

"Thing is, Gino, I been getting three and a half on it, and I gotta split it with some people. Makes the math a little complicated. I was looking to get four even on this one, if I could."

Fish sat silently and looked at Jo Jo, his hands resting on the table, his long fingers interlaced. Fish pursed his lips while he thought about this.

"We could cut it to two," Fish said. "That would sim-plify the math even further."

Jo Jo laughed.

"I know you're kidding, Gino. But I'm coming cheap at four percent. Not many guys can move two million, three for you bang bang like that, you know?"

Again Fish was quiet, pursing his lips. This time he was quiet for quite a while. It made Jo Jo nervous. He didn't like being nervous, and especially didn't like being made nervous by two guys he could crush like a couple of grapes. They should be nervous of me, he thought.

"What you say is true, Jo Jo," Fish said. "Not many men have your contacts in this. But that doesn't mean no one does. I'll give you the four, but I don't want you com-ing in next week and asking for five."

"Hey, Gino, I don't do business that way. I say four, it's four and that's it."

"Fine," Fish said, and nodded at the suitcases.

Jo Jo went and picked them up. Each of them weighed more than 120 pounds, but if they were too heavy Jo Jo didn't show it. The trapezius muscles bunched along the top of his shoulders and the triceps defined themselves more deeply along the backs of his arms.

"I'll take care of this today, Gino," he said.

"I'm sure you will," Fish said.

"Take it easy," Jo Jo said.

Neither Fish nor Vinnie spoke and Jo Jo left the office and went through the anteroom and out the front door. The good-looking young man came in with the mail and put it on the table in front of Gino.

"What do you think," he said. "Cute?"

Fish glanced up at him and snorted and began to open the mail.

"What do you think, Vinnie," the young man said.

"He's a jerk," Vinnie said. "He thinks muscles matter."

"Well, maybe they do to me," the young man said.

Vinnie shrugged and turned up the volume on his tape player. The young man went back out to the anteroom smiling.

Outside on Tremont Street, Jo Jo walked a half block back up the street, and, out of sight of Gino's office, put the bags down on the curb and waited for a cab.

Chapter 11

Jesse drove into Paradise at ten in the morning with the sun shining straight at him so that he had to put the sun visor down even with sunglasses on. He could smell the Atlantic before he saw it. Before he went to the town hall, he found the beachfront along Atlantic Avenue and parked and got out and walked onto the beach and looked at the eastern ocean. It probably had something to do with closing a circle. What circle it was, Jesse didn't know. But it did no harm to look at the ocean. He stood for a while, then got back in the car and drove slowly along Atlantic Avenue, following the directions they'd sent him, to the town hall. The east in Jesse's imagination had always been New England: village greens, and white steeples and weathered shingles and permanence. He had always liked to imagine it in winter when the clear virtuous cold was antipodal to the hot desperation of Los Angeles. It wasn't winter when he arrived. It was late June and the narrow streets were dappled by the sunlight shining through the full-foliaged arch of old trees. It wasn't clean and cold, but it was clean and warm and he liked it.

He met the town, or as many members of the town as were interested, including most of the police department, in the auditorium of the brick town hall. The Board of Selectmen sat on stage in folding chairs. Jesse stood, while the chairman of the Board of Selectmen introduced him from a lectern, reading into an insensitive microphone from a sheet of paper with his remarks typed out on it.

"It gives me great pleasure, ladies and gentlemen, to present Paradise's new police chief, Jesse Stone."

The chairman of the board was named Hasty Hathaway. He wore a pink shirt and a plaid bow tie and a seersucker jacket that appeared too small for him. Jesse wore his dark suit with a white banded-collar shirt and no tie. He wore the short .38 in a black holster in back of his right hip. Hathaway handed Jesse the new badge that said "Paradise Police Department" around the outside, and "Chief" across the center.

Jesse slipped it into his shirt pocket.

"As most of you know, Chief Stone comes to us from Los Angeles, California, where he is a ten-year veteran of the Los Angeles Police Department, serving most recently as a homicide detective. He holds numerous departmental citations, and was once featured in *Parade* magazine's list of America's Top Cops. Chief Stone was selected for this post after an exhaustive search from a field which included a number of very viable candidates. I'd like to thank all the members of the search committee who gave unsparingly of their time, and my thanks also to Lou Burke, who served us so well as interim chief. I know he and all the men, and women, of the Paradise Police Department will continue to serve with the devotion to duty that has marked this department since its inception. Chief Stone, would you care to say a few words?''

"I'm glad to be here," Jesse said into the microphone. "Right now, everyone in the room knows more about the town than I do. I'll need your help. Thank you."

He stepped away from the microphone. Hathaway looked as if he were hoping for more. But he rallied.

"Okay," he said, "let's give Chief Stone a round of applause."

Everyone clapped. Jesse went upstairs with Hathaway and the town legal counsel, whose name was Abby Taylor, and signed several papers. While he was signing them he noticed that the town counsel was wearing a nice-looking pale yellow suit, with a short skirt.

Then he went next door to the brick wing where police and fire were housed and sat down in the swivel chair in his new office. Lou Burke came in with a Sig-Sauer nine-millimeter pistol.

"The one Tommy Carson turned in," Burke said, "when he got fired."

"Thanks," Jesse said. "I've got my own gun."

Burke shrugged and put the pistol on the desk.

"Belongs to the department," he said. "Goes with the job."

Jesse picked up the gun and put it in the right-hand drawer of the desk.

"Have a seat," Jesse said. "I might as well start learning."

Burke sat. He was a compact man with dark skin and an advanced case of male pattern baldness. What hair remained along the sides of his head was black and cut very close.

"Is this a first-name department?" Jesse said.

"Has been."

"Good. How you feel about them bringing me in from the outside, Lou?"

Burke sat quietly for a moment as if thinking about the question.

"Relieved," he said finally.

"You didn't like being chief?"

Burke shook his head.

"Why not?"

"Pay's not worth the aggravation," Burke said.

"Tell me about the aggravation," Jesse said.

"You're used to a big force," Burke said. "Big city. Lotta cops, lotta people, you get to keep some distance from the civilians. Here you're a town employee. Everybody knows everybody. The civilians are in our face twenty-four hours a day. For crissake you have to attend Rotary Club meetings."

"Rotary Club?"

"Yeah. They didn't mention that to you? Chief of police here is automatically a member of the Rotary Club, meets every Wednesday at the Paradise Inn."

"How's the food?" Jesse asked.

"You like chicken pot pie?"

Jesse shrugged.

"That's how the food is," Burke said.

"Well," Jesse said, "we'll see about Rotary."

A big yellow cat came silently into Jesse's office and jumped up onto the window ledge and curled up on himself and went to sleep in the sun.

"Who's this?" Jesse said.

"Captain Cat," Burke said. "Wandered in here five years ago. We feed him."

"Cop house cat," Jesse said.

Burke nodded.

"Tell me about the town legal counsel," Jesse said.

"Abby? She works for the firm in town. Big firm for a small town, ten, twelve lawyers. Real estate, wills, estate planning, that kind of stuff. Gives the town about ten hours a week pro bono."

"You like her?"

"Sure."

"What do you like best about her?"

"She's got a nice ass," Burke said.

"I noticed."

"And she's usually got a hair across it."

Jesse grinned.

"You're not too careful, are you?" Jesse said.

"No," Burke said. "I ain't."

"Good," Jesse said.

"You didn't ask me about Hathaway or any of those people," Burke said.

"Thought that might be pushing you a little hard this early in the game," Jesse said. "I'll find out about them myself."

Burke nodded.

"Selectmen get elected by the town," Burke said. "Town and the police don't always agree on how things get done."

"Lou," Jesse said, "no cop counts on elected officials."

Burke grinned.

"Well," he said. "You ain't as young as you look."

"Maybe I'm not," Jesse said.

Chapter 12

Lou Burke sat with Hasty Hathaway on the bench outside the meeting house on the town common. Hathaway had a bag of popcorn which he was feeding to some pigeons that had gathered.

"You got any pets, Lou?" Hathaway said.

"No."

"I'd like to have some animals, but Cissy . . ." He shook his head and held out a piece of popcorn on his upturned palm. A pigeon circled it, hesitated, feinted once, then darted in and grabbed the corn. "I guess Ciss just isn't an animal person."

"Sure," Burke said. "They're not for everybody, I guess."

"You know Ciss, used to having her house just so. God knows what she'd have been like if we'd had kids."

"Easy to get set in your ways," Burke said.

The common was a small green triangle at the intersection of three streets. There was a white eighteenth-century meeting house set on it, where at Christmas, the women's auxiliary of something or other, Burke had never really known what, sold greens and fruitcake and handmade satin bows.

"So what do you think of Stone?" Hathaway said.

He took a handful of the popcorn and scattered it on the grass in front of the bench.

Burke was silent a moment, watching the pigeons hop and flutter after the popcorn.

"Well," Burke said finally, "it's too soon to say, I guess."

"I realize that, but what's your impression."

"He might not be the answer," Burke said.

"Really?" Hathaway seemed surprised. "Why do you say so?"

"I don't know exactly, there's just something . . . he's got more iron in him than I was expecting."

"Lou, he's a lush," Hathaway said. "He was fired for drinking on duty. His personnel file said he was unfit for police work."

"Yeah, I know," Burke said. "But he doesn't give me that feeling. He was a homicide cop in L.A., remember."

"And he was half gassed when we interviewed him in Chicago," Hathaway said.

Burke shrugged.

"Well, let's keep our eyes open," Hathaway said. "What we don't want is some born-again straight arrow poking his sober nose in where it shouldn't go."

Burke nodded.

"I still don't see why you wouldn't take the job, Lou," Hathaway said. "It would have worked out so well."

"No," Burke said. "I'm a lot more effective if I'm not in charge. I'm the chief and things go bad, everybody lands on me. I'm just a cop following orders and no one pays me much attention. I know as much as I would being chief, and I'm a lot less visible. I do us more good where I am.''

''Things aren't going to go bad, Lou.''

''I like to plan for what's possible, not what's likely,'' Burke said.

''Sure, Lou, I understand, just would have been nice if we'd been clearer on this before Tom left.''

''He'd have had to leave anyway.''

''Yes, I guess so,'' Hathaway said.

The pigeons still fluttered and strutted, their heads bobbing like mechanical contrivances around him, but the popcorn was gone.

''And maybe I'm wrong,'' Burke said.

Hathaway nodded enthusiastically.

''Yes,'' he said. ''I think you probably are. He seems pretty harmless to me.''

Chapter 13

Jesse was renting a condo in a waterfront development called Colonial Landing. It was a series of contiguous town houses painted gray with white shutters. Jesse's had a living room, kitchen with dining area, and a half bath on the first floor, two bedrooms and a full bath on the second. The living room faced the ocean and there were wall-width sliding doors that led out onto a small deck over the water. The place was new and had an unused quality to it which Jesse felt worked with his circumstances. He stood on the little deck and drank scotch on the rocks and watched the brisk chop of the Atlantic prancing in against the rust-colored stone below him. It had been a month yesterday since he'd leaned on the railing in Santa Monica late at night and watched the black Pacific and said goodbye.

His glass was empty. He went back in to add some ice and splash in some more Black Label when the phone rang. His short-nosed Smith & Wesson in its black holster lay on the table beside the phone.

"Jesse?"

"Yeah, Jenn."

"You didn't give me a number," Jennifer said. "I had to call information."

"Here I am," Jesse said.

"You didn't say goodbye."

"No."

"You don't sound glad to hear from me."

"I guess I don't."

Jesse took a drink of scotch.

"You miss me?"

"Less."

"I don't know if I like you missing me less, Jesse."

"I'm trying not to worry too much about that."

"Whether I like something?"

"Yeah."

"You all right?"

"Sooner or later," Jesse said.

"You like the new place?"

"Too soon to say."

"You meet anybody?"

"Met a lot of people."

"No," Jennifer said, "you know what I mean. You ought to get out more, Jesse, you ought to date, make friends. You met any nice girls?"

"I think they call them women here, Jenn."

"Well did you?"

"Day at a time, Jenn."

"What time is it there?"

"Eight-forty-five in the evening."

"It's quarter to six here."

"That would have been my guess."

"I got a nice audition tomorrow, new series on Fox. I think I'm just right for the part."

"I'm sure you are," Jesse said.

He twirled the small revolver aimlessly as he talked to her, the phone hunched between his left shoulder and his neck. With his right hand he swirled the ice in his glass for a moment, then drank some more scotch.

"You drinking, Jesse?"

"Couple."

"You need to be careful of that."

"Sure."

"You still mad at me about Elliott?"

Jesse kept his voice flat.

"Elliott and everything else," he said.

"I don't want to lose you, Jesse."

"You don't show it much," Jesse said.

"I know. It sounds crazy. I mean here I am with another man and we're divorced and yet I don't want to look at my life and think 'No Jesse.' I can't imagine my life without you in it, Jesse."

"Un huh."

"Am I losing you, Jesse?"

"There's some danger of it, Jenn."

"Oh God, well I can't talk now. I got to work out, I have to get my hair done. Can I call you again, soon?"

"If you want to, Jenn."

"I do, Jesse."

"Fine."

After he hung up Jesse continued to stand at the table looking at the phone, slowly twirling the Smith & Wesson in its holster. Then he stopped and went back to the sideboard and made himself another drink. He carried the drink to the refrigerator and looked in. There was half of a mushroom-and-green-pepper pizza there on the second shelf, wrapped neatly in Saran Wrap, left over from Monday night's supper. He got it out, unwrapped it, and put it in the microwave. When it was hot he slid it onto a dinner plate and took it out onto the deck and ate it, sitting in a folding chair, drinking scotch between bites, looking out at the lights across the harbor on Paradise Neck.

"I guess I don't want to lose you either, Jenn," Jesse said aloud, "but maybe I'll have to."

Chapter 14

The call came in to the dispatcher at 2:43 in the afternoon. She put it through to Jesse.

"It's Simpson, Jesse. DeAngelo and I are at Thirteen Sylvan Road. People named Genest. Domestic dispute. I think you need to come over."

"Do I need the siren?" Jesse said.

"I think you should get over here quick," Simpson said.

"Here I come," Jesse said.

The house was a big white one, back from the street and up a slight rise. It was white clapboard with dark green shutters, and a very big maple tree shaded much of the front of it. A Paradise cruiser was parked in the driveway. Jesse shut the siren off as he pulled in behind it and got out. The Chief of Police badge was pinned to his white uniform shirt. He wore pale amber Oakley sunglasses, and no hat, the short .38 on his right hip. The side door of the house stood open and he went in without knocking. In the den to his right were his two officers, a woman, and a bodybuilder with longish blond hair combed back like Kirk Douglas, and a nice tan. The woman was crying.

The bodybuilder's name was Jo Jo Genest. The woman was Jo Jo's ex-wife.

"For crissake," Jo Jo said. "The chief. Nice shades, chief, very L.A."

Jesse stared at him without any expression at all.

"Don't we have a restraining order on you, sir?" Jesse said.

"It ain't working too good, is it?" Jo Jo said.

"What's the story?" Jesse said to Simpson.

Suitcase Simpson was a sturdy kid with fair skin and red cheeks. He'd been a tackle in high school. He was twenty-two. His partner was Anthony DeAngelo.

"This is Carole Genest," Simpson said. "She called us. Alleges her husband forced his way into the house and threatened her."

"That right, ma'am?"

She nodded. Her eyes were red, and her nose was running. She sniffed.

"The bastard," she said in a thick voice, "is going to kill me someday."

Jesse nodded.

"Kids?" he said.

"I sent them upstairs," Carole said. "They're frightened of him too."

"Anthony," Jesse said. "You got kids?"

DeAngelo nodded.

"Three," he said.

"Okay, go upstairs and find the kids and do what you can to make them feel safe."

"Hey, you got no right talking to my kids," Jo Jo said.

Jesse paid no attention to him. He nodded at DeAngelo and DeAngelo headed for the stairs.

"Did he say he was going to kill you, ma'am?" Jesse said.

"He says that all the time. And he's not my husband. We're divorced."

"Maybe you're divorced, slut, I'm not," Jo Jo said. "You're my wife until I say you're not."

"Can't you people do anything about him?" Carole said.

"Yes, ma'am," Jesse said. "We can. Did he hit you or otherwise assault you?"

"Not this time. I called the cops the minute he showed up."

"Did you invite him in?"

"No fucking way," Carole said. "I tried to lock him out but he's still got a key."

"It's my house," Jo Jo said. He was smiling like a man patiently indulging some children. "It's my wife. I'll come and go as I fucking please."

"Did he force his way in?"

"Yes. I tried to hold the door, but he's—look at him— what am I supposed to do against him?"

"You did what you should have done, ma'am," Jesse said.

"How about you, Slim?" Jo Jo said to Jesse. "What are you supposed to do against me?"

"But he didn't assault you?"

"Not this time. He didn't have time. He beat the shit out of me last time he came. He raped me once. I shoulda gone to the cops then, but we weren't divorced yet, and . . . you know conjugal rights . . . and the kids . . . I mean how do they feel, everybody talking about how their father raped their mother?"

Her voice trailed off.

"There was no rape and you know it, a husband can't rape his wife," Jo Jo said. "You didn't go to the cops because you loved it."

As they argued, Jesse nodded, almost absently, as if he were thinking of something else.

"We probably don't have an assault charge here," Jesse said to Simpson. "We might get forced entry, even though he had a key. We obviously have him for violating the restraining order."

Jo Jo laughed.

"Big fucking deal," he said. "Restraining orders don't mean shit and you know it."

"Yes, sir," Jesse said. "I know."

"I go to court with my lawyer. They issue a new restraining order. I walk out of court twenty minutes later."

"That's how it usually works, sir," Jesse said pleasantly, "especially if you've got some money."

"Which I do," Jo Jo said. "And some clout and I can come in here and grab her crotch, or whatever else I want to grab, anytime I goddamned want to."

"Is that right?" Carole said to Jesse.

Jesse shook his head.

"Oh?" Jo Jo said. "You just admitted you couldn't do shit about it."

"No, sir," Jesse said. "I said the restraining order probably wouldn't work."

"Same thing," Jo Jo said.

"Not really," Jesse said, and kicked Jo Jo in the groin.

The movement seemed casual. But it was a very quick movement. And hard. Jo Jo gasped and doubled up and fell over and lay on the pale blue flowered carpet of the den and moaned. Jesse bent over him with a look of blank disinterest and grasped Jo Jo's hair with his left hand and held his head up and put his face very close to Jo Jo's and spoke to him.

"You're all mouth and show muscle," Jesse said gently. "If you come near this woman again, or if anything happens to her or her kids, no matter what, and no matter whose fault it is, I will kick you around town until you look like roadkill. And if you are annoying, like you were today, maybe I'll shoot you." Jesse tapped Jo Jo on the bridge of the nose with the muzzle of his revolver. "Right here . . . capeesh?"

Jo Jo was still moaning.

"Answer me, Jo Jo," Jesse said. "Or I will kick you in the balls again. Capeesh?"

Jo Jo squeezed the word "capeesh" out between moans.

Jesse let Jo Jo's head go and it thumped on the rug. Jesse stood up.

"Suitcase, you and Anthony stay here until Mr. Genest has gone," Jesse said. "Ma'am, you should probably get those kids to a shrink."

Carole's eyes were wide and bright. There was a flush of color on her cheekbones, as if she had a fever.

"What if he comes back," she said.

"I don't think he'll come back," Jesse said.

He turned and walked out of the house and down the driveway to his car.

Behind him he heard Suitcase Simpson say, "Jesus Christ!"

Chapter 15

Jesse sat in his office in the early evening with Abby Taylor.

"The selectmen have asked me to talk with you," she said.

"Good," Jesse said.

She was wearing a black suit with a long jacket and a short skirt. At least she didn't have on one of those frilly neck pieces that some professional women wore like a pretend necktie; her white blouse was open at the neck. Her briefcase was on the floor leaning against the leg of her chair. She wore black high-heeled shoes. Jesse thought her ankles were very nice.

"I'm speaking now as town counsel," Abby Taylor said carefully.

"Yes, ma'am."

"May I call you Jesse?"

"Of course, Abby."

She smiled automatically.

"Now, I know," she said, "that you are new not only to this job, but to this environment."

Jesse smiled helpfully.

"But whatever the circumstances of your police work in Los Angeles, this is a town in which everyone's civil liberties are important."

Jesse nodded. He seemed interested.

"May I be frank with you?" Abby Taylor said.

"Sure."

"You cannot go about beating people up," she said. "It leaves the town vulnerable to lawsuit. I understand the provocation. And I certainly am sympathetic to Carole Genest's situation. But we cannot permit you to take the law into your own hands. It is not only illegal. It simply is not right."

Jesse nodded thoughtfully.

"Let me ask you a question," he said.

"Of course."

"You asked me if you could call me Jesse, and I said you could. But you didn't."

"Excuse me?"

"You never used my name."

"What the hell has that got to do with you brutalizing Mr. Genest?"

"Just seemed odd to me," Jesse said.

"Well, if it does, it does," Abby Taylor said. "I'm not going to be sidetracked."

"Course not, Abby."

"Do you have anything to say about the matter of your assault on Mr. Genest?"

"Not really," Jesse said.

"I'm afraid there has to be more than that," Abby Taylor said.

"The restraining order wasn't working," Jesse said. "Think of me as implementing it."

"You really have to take this seriously," Abby Taylor said.

" 'You have to take this more seriously, Jesse,' " he said.

Abby Taylor smiled.

"You have to take this more seriously, Jesse."

"No I don't, Abby."

"You don't make it easy . . . Jesse."

He nodded and leaned back a little in his chair. His blue uniform shirt was tailored and carefully pressed. He had nice eyes, she noticed, with small wrinkles at the corners as if he had spent a lot of time squinting into the sun.

"Jo Jo Genest should be kicked in the balls once a day," Jesse said. "He's terrorizing his ex-wife. He's frightening his children. When Anthony went up there the youngest two were under the bed. There's a restraining order in place. He paid no attention to it. It was necessary to get his attention."

Abby was silent for a time, frowning, as she thought about his answer. He watched her think. He liked the way the small vertical wrinkle appeared between her eyebrows when she frowned.

"The selectmen are aware of the provocation," Abby said. "And they are prepared to go forward from here. But they would like your assurance that something like this will not occur in the future."

"It might," Jesse said.

"God," Abby said. "You don't give a damn inch, do you?"

Jesse smiled.

"Since you drew it up," Jesse said, "you know that my

contract here provides recourse to the selectmen if they are dissatisfied with my performance."

"So, you're saying the ball is in their court."

"Yes."

They looked at each other. Abby held his look, feeling challenged by it. Then she smiled.

"God, you are so much harder than you look."

Jesse smiled again.

"And what's my name?"

"Jesse."

They laughed. Abby sat back in her chair and crossed her legs.

"I mean you look like a history teacher," she said. "Who might coach tennis on the side."

Jesse didn't say anything. He was looking at her legs.

"And yet you handled Jo Jo Genest."

"Experience is helpful," Jesse said.

"Have you had that much experience with people like Genest?"

"In L.A. I worked South Central," Jesse said. "People in South Central would keep Jo Jo for a pet."

"No one ever confronted him before like that."

"Guess it was time," Jesse said.

"You won, but don't misjudge him. He can be very dangerous."

"Anybody can be very dangerous, Abby."

"I believe he has mob connections."

" 'Jesse.' "

She smiled.

"Jesse," she said.

"Good. You married?"

"I don't see what that has to do with the issue before us," she said.

"Me either," Jesse said.

"I'm happily divorced," Abby said. "Five years."

"Taylor your own name?"

"Yes."

They were silent again. Outside his office he could hear the sporadic murmur of the dispatcher's voice. The occasional sound of a door opening and closing. It was a lulling sound, it went with quiet summer nights and green space in the center of a small town. The office itself was very spare. Jesse's desk was bare except for the phone and a pair of gold-tinted Oakley sunglasses. There was a window behind his chair which looked out at the driveway of the fire station. A green metal file cabinet stood to the right of the window. There was no rug on the floor. No pictures of anyone.

"Have you ever been married?" Abby said.

"Yes."

"But you're not married now."

"No."

"Divorced?"

"Yes."

"Jesse, one of the rules of conversation is that when asked a question you don't give a one-word answer."

Jesse looked at his watch.

"Okay," he said. "It's suppertime, want to have dinner with me?"

Abby opened her mouth and closed it. She had come in to reprimand this man and he didn't seem reprimanded.

"I . . . I don't . . . certainly," she said. "I'd love to."

Chapter 16

Driving toward Gillette on Route 59 north of Bill, Wyoming, Tom Carson felt alien in the rolling landscape. Pronghorn antelope appeared here and there in the hills, grazing in herds, strung out along a stream drinking. Buffalo grazed too in the gently undulant pastures. They weren't wild herds, he knew. They were ranch buffalo, healthful, destined to be slaughtered and sold in specialty stores. He'd never been anywhere very much until he moved to Wyoming. Lived all his life in Paradise, and his parents too. His mother taught seventh grade at Paradise Junior High. His father ran the Gulf station. The only gas station in the downtown area. He had no military experience. He hadn't gone to college. He'd joined the cops after working three years for his father. The complete townie, he'd married a girl from his high-school class and lived with her in a house his parents helped him buy, near Hawthorne Park on the hill above the harbor. Along the empty roadway, he saw several mule deer, nervous and gangly as they grazed and looked up. More skittish than the prong-

horns, he thought. Always looking over their shoulder.
Now he was marooned here, vastly alone with his family
in an emptiness of grass and rolling hills over which the
huge blank sky hovered comfortless. He'd been proud to
be a policeman, proud of the right to carry a gun. It hadn't
been very hard. Life in Paradise had been largely law-
abiding. He had been polite to the selectmen, and firm with
the high-school kids who used to congregate on the stone
wall around the historic cemetery across from the common.
He had taken courses in criminal justice at Northeastern
University in the evening, and he had practiced regularly
at the pistol range, in case he ever had to use the gun, which
he hadn't. He wasn't spectacular, maybe, but he hadn't
done anything wrong either and when he was appointed
chief he felt it an achievement which he had earned. He
wasn't much with budgets and finance, but Lou Burke was
able to take care of that end of things for him, and he got
along well with the men in the department. The townspeo-
ple liked him. He was genial and nonthreatening, and he
looked pretty good in dress uniform at the Memorial Day
parade. He liked the weekly Rotary Club meetings, where
he got to fine people for various violations of Rotary procedure, and to participate in the general bonhomie. He collected the fines every week in a chamber pot. Now that was
over. His wife was neither understanding nor forgiving of
the move to Wyoming. His children went miserably to a
regional grammar school with the children of plainsmen
and miners. He could not explain to any of them why they
were here and they badgered him angrily about it nearly all
the time. He was ashamed to have been sent away, ashamed
that he hadn't stood firm and seen justice done. Often he
thought of going to the FBI office in Cheyenne. It was the
closest one. He'd looked it up in the phone book. But he
was afraid to. Afraid for his wife and children, and, he had

to admit it, afraid for himself. But every day here became
more bitter. He missed the ocean, the faces on the evening
news, the closeness of the horizons back home where you
could only see as far as your neighbor's house across the
street. He missed the sense that he was enveloped by the
civilization as old as the country. Out here he felt vulnerable and exposed. He felt skittish. He was afraid to act, but
he hated his inaction and he hated the life he was leading.
He hadn't found a job yet in this wilderness and he was
running out of the money they gave him. He didn't dare
ask them for more. There was something about the steeli-
ness in Hasty's prissy eyes ... But he couldn't go on like
this, his family miserable, all of them lonely, himself frightened in addition. He spoke aloud in the cab of the new
Dodge pickup they'd provided.

"Sooner or later," he said. "Sooner or damn later."

He drove on toward Gillette, alone in the big prairie, no
one else in sight on the narrow road. The only other car, a
maroon Buick behind him, had turned off at Bill. He felt
exhilarated by the thought that he might do something to
change things. As long as he could think about it without
actually doing it, he felt excited, and possible. He'd felt it
before, but he was not introspective and he didn't think
much about the difference between thinking it and doing
it, or how often he'd thought it before without doing it.
When he actually began to imagine doing it, what he would
say to the FBI agent in Cheyenne, what he might do if he
had to go back to Paradise and testify, the bottom of himself got watery and loose, and his throat narrowed so it was
difficult to swallow. But he wasn't thinking of that now,
he was thinking about how he would face the problem
someday, and he was feeling as good as he was able to feel
in his exile when the Dodge exploded beneath him. The
hood of the truck, and part of the dashboard, and some bits

of Tom Carson, went a hundred feet in the air and landed thirty yards from the roadway, sending two mule deer into a terrified run. The remainder of the truck, and of Tom Carson, was an impenetrable ball of flame in the empty roadway that burned unobserved as the deer, their white tails flashing, disappeared over the hillcrest.

Chapter 17

They were outside the Gray Gull Restaurant, on the deck overlooking the harbor. Abby had an Absolut martini, up, with several olives. Jesse had a beer. He didn't look like the beer type to her. Her father had been a beer drinker, burly, red-faced, tending to fat as he got older. He always said he didn't have a problem as long as he drank beer. But he had drunk a lot of beer, and she knew he had a problem. She wondered sometimes if she did. Originally she had switched from white wine to martinis because she liked white wine too much and felt that martinis would be something she could sip through an evening. She smiled to herself with some sadness as she sipped this one. She had learned to like martinis very much and, sometimes, if her self-control slipped, would sip four or five during an evening.

"What's a lobster roll?" Jesse said as they looked at the menus.

"A lobster roll?"

"Yes. Is it a kind of sushi or what?"

Abby smiled.

"God, you California kids," she said. "A lobster roll is lobster salad in a hot dog roll."

"Oh," Jesse said. "Actually I wasn't a California kid. Didn't move there until I was fifteen."

"Where'd you grow up before then?"

"Around Tucson. My father was with the Pima County Sheriff's Department."

"Ah," Abby said. "Second generation."

"Un huh."

"Why'd you move?"

"My father was working paid detail with a film crew in Tucson, and he got friendly with one of the stars and took a job as the star's driver, personal assistant, bodyguard, whatever. So we moved."

"So do you know a lot of famous movie people?"

"Nope, my father lasted about a month and got fired and took a job at Hughes."

"Oh my," Abby said. "Who was the star?"

Jesse shook his head.

"Why not?" Abby said.

"Old news," Jesse said.

"Well, aren't you private," Abby said. "Your folks still alive?"

"No."

"Brothers? Sisters?"

"Brother."

"Where is he?"

"I don't know. He and my father didn't get along. He took off."

"And you don't know where he went?"

"No."

She drank the rest of her martini. The waitress stopped by at once. The profit here was on drinks. Abby nodded yes, she'd have another one, and she noticed that Jesse had another beer.

"I wouldn't have figured you for a beer drinker," Abby said.

"I'm not. I'm a scotch on the rocks drinker, but I didn't want to get drunk on our first date."

"Do you get drunk?"

"I have some trouble stopping when I start," Jesse said.

"You're open about it," Abby said.

Jesse shrugged.

"I have trouble too," she said.

"Stopping?"

"Un huh. My father was a boozer." She smiled. "Drank only beer."

"In my house it was my mother."

"What did she drink?"

"Port," Jesse said.

Abby wrinkled her nose.

"Ugh," she said.

The waitress came back and took food orders. It was a noisy crowd out on the deck. Young men and women, many of them from the same condo complex where Jesse was renting, single, well employed, affluent, stylish, and loud. They were drinking things like Long Island iced teas and tequila sunrises. As Abby looked across the table at him, Jesse seemed to her a figure of stillness in the midst of turbulence, as if he were the only boat with an anchor. He sat perfectly still, his hands resting on the tabletop. When he moved it was for a reason, to pour beer, to drink beer, to pick up the menu. He wasted no energy. It was hard to imagine him drunk and out of control. It was hard to imagine him kicking Jo Jo Genest in the balls, too. Though her official position required her to disapprove, she was glad he had. No one deserved a kick in the balls more than Jo Jo Genest, she thought. Her martini was gone. She could handle one more, all right. She loved the feeling of integration and certainty the drinks gave her. He would be an interesting guy to have sex with. See how contained and steady he was then.

"I'm going to go ahead and order another martini," she said to Jesse. "If you want to order a scotch, go ahead. Our cards are on the table, I'm willing to risk it, if you are."

Jesse smiled and ordered a Black Label on the rocks.

"You have any children, Jesse?"

"No. You?"

"No, we tried and couldn't seem to. I guess I'm barren."

"Or he is," Jesse said.

The drinks came. Jesse was barely able to stifle a sigh as he took some of his scotch in and felt the ease begin to seep through him. Abby smiled at him over the rim of her martini.

"Good times," she said and held the glass out. He clinked it with his. Each of them drank again.

"Can a man be barren?" Abby said.

"You mean is it a word you can use about men?"

"Yes."

"I don't know," Jesse said. "But if the two of you couldn't have children, it doesn't mean you were the one that couldn't. You do any testing?"

"He refused," she said.

Jesse nodded as if his point had been made. There was something about his eyes, she thought, as if he saw the world in a funny way and was quietly amused. He had on a blue blazer and a white shirt open at the neck and his skin had a healthy out-of-doors look to it. He was clean-shaven, his dark hair was cut close, and the sideburns were neatly trimmed.

"How long were you married?" Abby said.

"Five years."

"What happened?"

"She was, is, an actress. She started sleeping with a guy, maybe guys for all I know, who could help her in her career."

"Did you know?"

"Not at first."

"Did you suspect?"

"Eventually."

"And that was the end?"

"Yes, I think."

"You think?"

"Well, at first I sort of denied it, and then I increased my drinking and finally, in fact, she left me. I got fired in L.A. for drinking. It had to be in my record. Hell, I was sort of drunk when I interviewed for this job."

"Did they know?"

"I don't know how they could have missed it," Jesse said. "I must have smelled like a rum cake."

"And they hired you anyway?"

"Yes."

"I'll be damned. They must have seen something in you."

"Maybe."

"Well, so far you seem to have justified their faith in you."

"Maybe," Jesse said.

"Why the maybes?" Abby said.

"Maybe they wanted a lush for a police chief."

She frowned.

"Why on earth would they?"

"Don't know. Maybe they didn't want a good cop in town."

"That's crazy," she said. "I think you're too hard on yourself."

"I try not to be," Jesse said.

The food came, and another drink apiece.

"The lobster's in a damn hot dog roll," Jesse said.

"I told you."

"I didn't think you meant an actual hot dog roll."

They ate quietly for a few moments. The moon made a long shimmer on the harbor water. There was no wind. The salt smell was strong.

"You still feel connected to her," Abby said.

"Yes. I'm working on it, but I still do."

"She with someone else now?"

"She's still living by herself, I think. But she's in another guy's bed a lot."

"And that hurts," Abby said.

Jesse nodded.

Abby smiled at him and drank from her martini. She wondered if he were passionate, if someone, herself for instance, could get past the containment.

"Maybe it would help if you got even a little," she said.

Her eyes were very bright, and her body, so neatly and professionally clad, seemed somehow kinetic as she sat across the table.

"Couldn't hurt," he said.

Chapter 18

Charlie Buck got out of his Ford Bronco and walked across Route 59 toward the burned-out truck. A portly man with a pleasant face, receding hair, and rimless glasses, he was a detective from the Campbell County Sheriff's Department. Yellow crime-scene tape defined the place. Half a dozen county vehicles were parked haphazardly around the perimeter of the tape, and more than half a dozen county employees were in the area.

"How many dead?" he said to Ray Vollmer.

"Coroner thinks only one," Vollmer said. "Remains are a little scrambled."

"Infernal device?" Buck said, looking at the twisted metal skeleton.

"I'd say," Vollmer answered. "No sign that he ran into anything. Got some bomb-squad people coming in from Casper."

Buck nodded, looking at the scene along the empty roadway. Occasionally a car would appear and slow to look at the crime scene only to be waved on by one of the deputies stationed on the road for that purpose. Most of the time, however, they were alone with the silent wreckage under the high sky.

"No reason for him to have stopped here," Buck said.

Vollmer shook his head.

" 'Less he stopped to take a leak," he said.

"Even so," Buck said, "be hard for someone to rig a bomb on your car while you were pissing."

"Coulda driven by and thrown it," Vollmer said.

"Which would mean they were following him with a bomb waiting for the moment."

"Yep."

"More likely it was rigged earlier, with a timing device."

"Could be," Vollmer said. His eyes were wandering over the other deputies who were crisscrossing the area looking for anything that might be useful.

"If it was, would they have any way to know where he'd be when it went off?"

"They must have had a way to know he'd be in the car," Vollmer said.

"Yeah. You can rig it to start when the ignition goes on. But what if his wife drove it. Could be a matter of weight."

"So what if the wife and some kids got in."

"Could be rigged for weight in the driver's seat."

"And what if it went off in the middle of Cheyenne, or in Gillette, next to a school bus?" Vollmer said.

"Maybe they didn't care," Buck said.

"Nice people."

"Or maybe somebody trailed him at a distance," Buck said. "And when he got out in the middle of an empty stretch they beeped the bomb like you'd open a garage door."

"The technology's there for that," Vollmer said.

"Yeah. What's up there."

"Piece of the truck," Vollmer said, "and maybe some bits of the driver." He made a face. "M.E. scraped most of that up and took it with him."

Buck nodded.

"I'll take a look," he said.

He and Vollmer walked up the hill where the mule deer had grazed and looked at the twisted hood and part of the foam-plastic dashboard. He squatted on his heels and looked more closely at the dashboard. Riveted into it was a metal band bearing the serial number of the truck.

"A little luck," he said to Vollmer, and nodded at the band.

"Take a while to trace it," Vollmer said.

"We got a while," Buck said.

Chapter 19

Lou Burke came into Jesse's office with two cups of coffee. Captain Cat was asleep on top of the file cabinet. He didn't stir when Burke came in. Burke put one cup down on the desk for Jesse, and took his to the window and looked out.

"Anthony's cruiser," Burke said. "He took it home last night after work and parked it in front of his house. Somebody spray-painted the windshield."

Jesse got up with his coffee and came to the window and stood beside Burke. In the parking lot below was one of the Paradise cruisers. Clumsily sprayed in blue onto the windshield was the word SLUT.

"I had it towed in," Burke said. "It wouldn't look good to have Anthony drive it in peeking around the graffiti."

Jesse sipped some of the coffee and stared down at the cruiser.

" 'Slut,' " Jesse said. "Maybe it's personal."

Burke shrugged and didn't say anything.

"Have Perkins go over it," Jesse said. "Probably won't

find much, but it'll be good practice for him.''

Burke nodded.

"And ask Anthony to come talk to me," Jesse said.

Burke nodded again and left the office. Jesse stood for a while at the window drinking his coffee. He watched as Peter Perkins, the crime scene specialist, came out with his kit. While Jesse watched, Perkins took pictures of the car and dusted it for prints. He scraped a small sample of the paint off the windshield and dropped it into a small envelope. Probably a hundred people had had access to the cruiser in the last month, Jesse knew. The prints, to the extent there were any usable ones, would mean almost nothing. Still, the department had an evidence specialist; if he didn't go over the car, what was he getting paid for?

Anthony DeAngelo came into the office and Jesse turned from the window.

"You wanted to see me, Jesse?"

"Yeah. What can you tell me about the paint job?"

"Nothing much. I parked it outside my house, you know where I live, up on Archer Ave, after I got off at eleven last night. We always take the cruiser home on that shift unless we're turning it over."

"I know," Jesse said. "That's no problem."

"Anyway I went in, my wife made me a sandwich, and I had a beer and watched the end of the Sox game from Seattle and hit the rack. In the morning I went out and there it was."

"Talk to any of the neighbors?" Jesse said.

"No, I, to tell you the truth I was a little embarrassed."

"Yeah, I can see why you would be. On the other hand, be less embarrassing if we catch the perp," Jesse said. "Could it be personal. I mean, 'slut' is sort of a funny thing to spray on a police cruiser."

"You saying it could be about my wife or something?"

"No. I'm asking. Your wife got any enemies?"

"No. And she's no slut either."

"Had to ask, Anthony."

"Sure. Probably some kid mad at me for rousting him off the wall, or something. You know what assholes kids are."

Jesse nodded.

"Ask around," he said. "See what you learn."

"Sure, Jesse, I'm sorry it happened."

"Not your fault," Jesse said, and DeAngelo left the room.

Talking to Anthony hadn't told him anything. He hadn't thought it would. Asking around probably wouldn't tell him anything either. They would probably never know who sprayed their car, anyway. Hardly the crime of the century. Still, all the buttons had to be pushed, otherwise what were the buttons there for? Lot of motions to go through in police work, Jesse thought. He picked up Captain Cat from the top of the file cabinet and held him in his arms and scratched him thoughtfully behind the ear.

" 'Slut,' " he said to the cat. "What the hell does that mean, Captain?"

chapter **20**

Abby Taylor had done this before. She seemed calm as she undressed and hung her clothes up in his closet. She was careful when she wiped off her lipstick, and she was relaxed when she came to the bed and he put his arms around her. Then she gave herself to the experience. The lovemaking absorbed her. She was inventive and adroit, but most of all, he noticed even at the highest pitch that she was genuine. She pretended to nothing, and kept nothing in. She liked this. They made love for a long time and finished and lay together on their backs with her head resting in the crook of his arm.

"Whatever she didn't like about you," Abby said, "it couldn't have been the sex part."

Jesse smiled in the darkness. The sex part had been one of many things Jenn didn't like. He wasn't sure what all of it was that Jenn had liked or not liked. Right now she appeared to like Elliott Krueger.

"Some guy said once that war was the extension of politics," Jesse said.

"That's an answer?"

"Sex is probably the extension of relationship," Jesse said.

"Why can't it just be sex?" Abby said.

As she talked she raised her head and leaned it on her elbow; her naked body was damp with the recent effort. She seemed not to notice that she was naked. Jenn, who had always flaunted her tightly clothed body, seemed oddly ill at ease when her clothes were off . . . at least with him.

"I don't know," Jesse said.

"Wasn't that what this was? A good time was had by all?"

"Yes."

"So how does that fit with your theory?"

"We don't have a relationship."

"That's cold, Jesse."

"I didn't mean to be," he said.

"No, I don't think you did," Abby said.

"I'm just saying we don't come to bed with any arguments to finish, you know?"

"So the key to perfect happiness is wham-bam-thank-you-ma'am?"

"Well, I don't think I was saying that," Jesse said.

"Oh?"

Jesse was silent for a time. He did not normally spend much time thinking about matters like this, and with her lawyer's mind she had raced ahead of him.

"I think Jenn didn't have sex for the pleasure of the sex," he said. "I think she did it to start a romance or keep one going or because she was in a marriage and it was like her responsibility to have sex, you know?"

"Didn't she like it?" Abby said.

"I don't think she disliked it, except maybe at the end, with me. But I don't think the question of liking or disliking really has much to do with sex for Jenn. It's like an instrument of policy, if you follow what I'm saying."

"Yes," she said.

"When we were feeling good, sex was what we did to prevent us from not feeling good. When we were feeling bad, sex was the way we said we were mad."

"That's pretty thoughtful for a guy who recently kicked Jo Jo Genest in the balls."

"I know. I'm a little surprised myself."

"Still, it would be depressing to think that the longer the relationship, the worse the sex."

"Maybe we need to research it," Jesse said, "develop a relationship and see what happens."

"Day at a time," she said.

"Easy does it," he said.

They both laughed.

"Both been to meetings, I guess," Abby said.

"I had a little trouble acknowledging a higher power," Jesse said.

"I don't know you very well," Abby said. "But why am I not surprised."

chapter 21

Sitting at the rustic pine conference table, under the glass-cased boat models, in his office at the bank, with the door closed, Hasty Hathaway counted the stacks of small bills that Jo Jo took from the suitcases on the floor beside the table.

"People don't realize," Hathaway said, "how troublesome cash is to deal with."

"Yeah, and it's no picnic lugging it around in suitcases," Jo Jo said.

Hathaway nodded, his hands moving expertly among the bills.

"Lucky you're so strong, Jo Jo."

The counting continued. The bills were stacked and banded and put aside as Hathaway counted them.

"I started as a teller," he said as he counted. "You never forget."

"Yeah, yeah. I'm telling you, I counted already. There's two million three hundred and twelve thousand, eight hundred and fifty-four dollars there."

"I have a fiduciary responsibility," Hathaway said.

"How come you started as a teller?" Jo Jo said. "Your father owned the fucking bank."

Hathaway smiled without answering and continued to count.

"I hear you had a dispute with Jesse," Hathaway said. "We were surprised at the outcome."

"Son of a bitch blindsided me," Jo Jo said.

"It makes us worry a little," Hathaway said, carefully slipping the band over a stack of twenty-dollar bills, paying great attention to the process, "about our judgment."

"Don't worry," Jo Jo said. "He ain't that good."

"I hope he isn't. He was certainly hired on the assumption that he wouldn't be. What also concerns us is that we hope you are better than the encounter suggests."

Jo Jo stopped taking bills from the suitcase and rose to his feet.

"You ever been kicked in the balls?" he said.

Hathaway shook his head and looked mildly contemptuous. People of his caste did not receive kicks in the balls.

"He suckered me once, he won't do it again."

"We hope not," Hathaway said.

Jo Jo stood looking down at him, feeling the anger surge along his latissimus dorsi. He could pick the little twerp up and strangle him like a chicken. It annoyed him that Hathaway was not more aware of that.

"Look at me," Jo Jo said. "Look at him, next time you see him. You think I'm not going to even it up?"

"Not directly," Hathaway said.

"Whaddya mean?"

"He's the chief of police," Hathaway said.

As he spoke he continued to count.

"So fucking what?" Jo Jo said. "Anyone screws around with me, has to pay."

"You are a valuable member of our team, and we can't compromise the team mission for petty personal reasons."

"Hey," Jo Jo said. "I'm not anybody's team, you unnerstand, I'm just me, Jo Jo. I do what I goddamned please."

Hathaway stopped counting and looked up at Jo Jo silently with his pale blue eyes.

"We want you to avoid any confrontation with Jesse Stone," Hathaway said.

"And maybe I do it anyway."

Again the silence while Hathaway looked at him, and Jo Jo felt a little tingle of fear inside the protective muscle layers.

"We'll have to insist," Hathaway said.

Jo Jo held his look for a long moment and then shrugged and crouched and began to take money from the open suitcase. The little pussy was going to get his someday too, but there was no point arguing with him now. He was still useful. They finished the count in silence.

"I get two million, one hundred and fourteen thousand, nine hundred and five dollars," Hathaway said when the money was counted. "Do you want to recount it?"

"Hell no," Jo Jo said. "I'll take your count."

"Fine," Hathaway said. "You get four percent?"

"Yeah."

Hathaway tapped on a calculator for a moment.

"Eighty-four thousand, five hundred and ninety-six dollars and twenty cents," Hathaway said. "If we'd used your count it would have been more like ninety-two thousand."

"Don't matter," Jo Jo said. "Plenty more coming."

"Fine."

Hathaway counted out Jo Jo's percentage.

"Keep the twenty cents, too," Jo Jo said and laughed.

Hathaway made no response except to shrug slightly.

"Would you like that in an envelope?" Hathaway said.
"Sure."

Hathaway folded it neatly, put it in a plain brown envelope, and handed it to Jo Jo. He put it back in one of the suitcases, picked up both of them, and started for the door.

Hathaway said, "Why don't you have a seat while I get this deposited and get you a receipt."

Jo Jo tried to look like he didn't care, although in fact, he had been in a hurry to get out of Hathaway's office and had forgotten that he needed a receipt to show Gino. He sat and looked at the boat models while Hathaway and two tellers deposited the cash.

Hathaway returned when it was gone and gave Jo Jo a deposit slip.

"What do you get outta this?" Jo Jo said.

Hathaway looked at him blankly without answering. Jo Jo shrugged, tucked the deposit receipt in his shirt pocket, picked up the suitcases, and walked out of the office, waddling a little under the pressure of his vast thighs.

chapter 22

Two target sites at the firing range of the Paradise Rod and Gun Club on the north edge of town were set aside on Thursdays for the members of the Paradise Police Department. Jesse required everyone on the force to fire service pistol and shotgun once a month. Fifty rounds pistol, ten shotgun. This Thursday it was Jesse's turn, and Suitcase Simpson's. Jesse brought both the nine-millimeter service pistol that came with the job, and the short .38 revolver that he usually carried. Both men put on the earmuffs, and Simpson shot first, two-handed, in the crouch that everyone used. He scored well enough, but Jesse could tell that he didn't like shooting very much, that he was controlling a flinch. When it was his turn Jesse fired two clips from the nine-millimeter, and put all but three rounds into the bull's-eye.

"Jesus, Jesse, you can shoot."

Jesse read his lips and nodded. He put down the nine, drew the revolver, and put all five rounds into the black.

Then he stepped back, reloaded the revolver, holstered it, and took off his earmuffs.

"How in hell did you get to shoot like that?" Simpson said.

"Practice," Jesse said.

They each fired the shotgun, taking turns with it. When they were through Jesse handed the shotgun to Simpson.

"You get to clean it," Jesse said.

" 'Cause you're the chief?"

"Of course," Jesse said.

Simpson nodded.

"But I'll buy you coffee," Jesse said. "Prove I'm a regular guy."

They sat in Simpson's cruiser outside the Salt Air Doughnut Shop behind the supermarket in the town's only shopping center, and ate some donuts and drank coffee.

"You married, Suit?" Jesse said.

"Not yet," Simpson said. "I'm still playing the field, you know?"

"Plenty of time," Jesse said. "What's your real name?"

"Luther. My mother teaches Sunday school, she's a very religious person, named me after some famous religious guy."

"Un huh."

"Gym teacher started calling me Suitcase when I was in the fourth grade, and it stuck."

"Better than Luther," Jesse said.

"Yeah, I guess so. I never did know why he called me Suitcase."

"After the ballplayer, don't you think?"

"Ballplayer."

"Harry Simpson," Jesse said. "Cleveland, KC, the Yankees."

"Never heard of him," Simpson said. "Why'd they call him 'Suitcase'?"

"Big feet, I suppose."

Simpson ate half a donut.

"I never knew why he called me that," Simpson said, "and I didn't want to seem stupid, so I never dared ask."

"So how come you asked me?" Jesse said.

Simpson paused and frowned for a time, which he did, Jesse knew, when he was trying to think.

"I dunno," he said finally, "you don't seem like you think things about people."

"It's a good way for a cop to be," Jesse said.

"Not thinking things about people?"

"Something like that," Jesse said.

Simpson frowned again and drank some coffee. They were quiet watching the junior high school kids, ill at ease and full of pretense, cutting through the parking lot to hang out in front of the shopping center.

"Man," Simpson said finally, "you can really shoot."

chapter 23

When Jennifer called, Jesse was on his third drink, sitting on his tiny deck overlooking the harbor with his chair tilted back, balancing with one foot on the deck rail.

"I need to talk," she said when he answered.

"Okay," Jesse said.

He added some ice to his glass and poured more scotch over it. He took the drink and the portable handset back out onto the deck, and sat down again, and hunched the handset between his shoulder and neck, and drank some scotch.

"I'm through with Elliott," Jennifer said.

"Un huh."

"Are you glad?"

Jesse took another drink. Across the harbor, the lights on Paradise Neck seemed untethered in the thick night.

"I'm trying to get to a place where what you do doesn't make me glad or sad," Jesse said.

"You're drinking, aren't you, Jesse," Jennifer said. "I can hear it in your voice."

"Or you can hear the ice rattle in the glass when I take a sip," Jesse said.

"Don't you want to know why I broke up with Elliott?"

"He and Tommy Cruise decided to make the picture without you?"

"There's no need to be hateful, Jesse."

"Maybe there is," he said.

Jennifer was silent for a time. When she spoke it was with a kind of desperate dignity.

"I can't just sit here on the phone and let you beat up on me, Jesse."

"No," Jesse said, "you can't. I'll try not to."

"Thank you."

"So how come you broke up with Elliott," Jesse said.

"And I don't need to be humored, either," Jennifer said.

"Jenn," Jesse said, "I didn't call you. You want to talk, I'll listen."

There was a pause. He heard the clink of glassware and realized she was drinking too. Probably white wine. Couple of lushes, Jesse thought, three thousand miles apart. . . . Better than drinking alone, I guess.

"Do you remember that ridiculous girlfriend Elliott had with him when we had dinner once at Spago?" Jennifer said.

"Taffy."

"Yes, that's right. God, Jesse, you always remember stuff. She was like an ornament, you know, like his Rolex."

"A way to look successful," Jesse said.

"That's right, well, I suppose everyone wants to look successful, but . . ."

"There's better ways," Jesse said.

"Like being successful?" Jennifer said.

"That's one," Jesse said.

She wasn't stupid. She was ditzy enough so you could

think she was, but she wasn't. She understood a lot, when she permitted herself to think.

"Well, he was starting to treat me like Taffy. You know?"

"I'm shocked," Jesse said.

"Don't make fun of me, Jesse. It's too easy to do."

"Yes," Jesse said. "You're right. I'm sorry."

"So I called him on it. I told him I wasn't, you know, like a new hat he could wear around and hang up when he wasn't using it. And he got really mad, and said he was sick of getting used by all the stupid starlets that he tried to help and a lot of other things . . . and I started to cry and told him to go fuck himself and got up and walked out of the place."

"Good for you," Jesse said.

"I feel like an asshole for crying," Jennifer said.

"Everybody cries," Jesse said. "The important thing is you didn't let him use you."

"Thank you," Jennifer said.

They were silent across the continent while each of them drank.

Then Jennifer said, "But now what am I going to do?"

"What are you going to do about what?" Jesse said.

"I don't have a job," Jennifer said. Her voice was shaky and he knew that she wasn't far from crying. "My career is going nowhere. I'm alone, and I've lost the only decent thing that ever happened in my life."

"Meaning me?"

"Yes."

"It's not like we're enemies, Jenn."

"Oh, Jesse, I want to see you."

"Until the next producer comes along?"

"Don't, Jesse. I need to see you."

"Not right now, Jenn. Let things settle. Get yourself organized a little before you decide what you need. Maybe you might get some help, a shrink or somebody.''

"I have some friends in therapy," Jennifer said.

"If you do get help, Jenn, try to get real help. Not some nitwit that reads your aura or does crystal therapy.''

"You think I'm a dreadful fool, don't you, Jesse.''

"I think you do foolish things, sometimes, Jenn. I don't think you're dreadful.''

They drank. Jesse's glass was empty; he got up, holding the phone, and refilled his glass with ice and scotch.

"Have you met anyone, Jesse?''

"Yes.''

"Do you love her?''

"Not yet," Jesse said.

"I still love you, Jesse.''

Across the harbor the lights were fewer now as people went to bed. And the ones that still glowed in the black night were more separate and much farther apart.

"Do you still love me, Jesse?''

"I'm trying not to, Jenn.''

"I know, I don't blame you. But I . . . I don't like to think about life without you.''

Again Jesse was silent, looking at the disconnected pinpoints of light in the overreaching darkness.

"Can I see you sometime, Jesse?''

"Sure," Jesse said. "But right now we both need to be a little separate so we can get our heads back in order, I think.''

"Can I call you again?''

"Sure, Jenn. You can call me anytime.''

"I still love you, Jesse.''

"Take care of yourself, Jenn. Don't do anything impulsively. It's time to go slow and think things through. If you feel crazy, call me up.''

"Are you succeeding?" Jennifer said.

"Succeeding?"

"You said you were trying not to love me, Jesse. Are you succeeding?"

Jesse took a long breath and let it out and drank some scotch. In the harbor, invisible in the darkness, a bell buoy sounded.

"Not so far, Jenn."

chapter 24

Jesse was sitting in the middle booth at the Village Room restaurant a block from the town hall having lunch with Abby Taylor.

"Jenn called me the other night," Jesse said.

"Oh?"

"She broke up with Elliott."

"The producer?"

"Yes."

"So what does that mean?" Abby said.

"I don't know."

"Well, what does it mean to us?" Abby said.

"Us?"

"Us. You know, you and me, who have been sort of dating and sleeping together and stuff like that. Us."

"I don't know."

"Christ!" Abby said. "Think about it. Does it mean you're going to annul the divorce?"

"No. Can you do that?"

"No. Does it mean you are going to dash back to L.A. and move back in with her?"

"No."

"See, you can think about this. Do you still love her?"

The waitress came to the booth.

"Who gets the tuna?" the waitress said.

Jesse pointed at Abby. The waitress set the plate down in front of her.

"And you must get the club."

Jesse nodded. The waitress put it down in front of him and went off. Jesse picked up a wedge of sandwich.

"Do you?" Abby said.

"Still love her?"

"Un huh."

Jesse put the sandwich wedge back down on the plate and leaned back in the booth.

"I don't know where it will go with Jenn," Jesse said. "I don't even know where I want it to go."

"That's comforting," Abby said.

"What I know is that I'm not a good basket to put all your eggs in at the moment, you understand. I don't know if I love Jenn or not right now. I don't know if I can love anybody but Jenn right now. I like you, and we have fun together, but I don't know what it will be like between us next week or next month. Until I get myself clear about Jenn . . ." He didn't finish the sentence because he didn't know how to. So he let it hang unfinished. Abby met his look for a moment and took a deep breath and let it out slowly. Her eyes glistened. Then she looked down at her sandwich.

They were quiet for a time neither talking nor eating.

Then Abby said, "Well, consider myself warned, I guess."

She looked up at him and smiled very brightly.

"Doesn't mean we can't eat lunch," she said and her voice was as bright as her smile. Jesse didn't feel very hungry at the moment, but he started on his sandwich because he didn't know what else to do.

Jo Jo Genest came into the restaurant and took a seat at the counter. He was wearing a sleeveless black tee shirt and his arms bulged obscenely. He swiveled on the counter stool and rested his back and elbows against the counter and looked at Jesse. Jesse finished chewing a bite of his sandwich and looked back at Jo Jo. He was a city cop, and he had long ago mastered the dead-eyed city cop stare. Jo Jo's stare was more of a smirk, Jesse thought. They held the stare for about a minute, which to Abby, sitting in the booth watching them, seemed like an hour. Then Jo Jo wheeled slowly around on his stool and faced the counter and ordered a steak sandwich.

"Doesn't he scare you?" Abby said softly.

Jesse shrugged.

"Like hell," Abby said. "No shrugging. I asked you a question I want you to answer."

Jesse didn't like her tone and it showed in the look he gave her. But Abby held his look.

"Talk about yourself, Jesse. I want to know you."

"What's to know?" Jesse said.

"Well, for instance, are you scared of Jo Jo Genest?"

Through his nose Jesse took a long inhale and a long exhale, and pursed his lips. His right hand rested on the tabletop and he tapped it several times, as if listening to music that Abby couldn't hear. She waited.

"On the one hand," Jesse said, "Jo Jo's big and strong and stupid and mean and he's mad at me. I'd be an idiot not to be scared of him. On the other hand, if I have to, I can shoot him just as easy as if he were small and weak and smart and kindly."

"And you'd be willing to do that?" Abby said.

"I'd be willing," Jesse said.

"You ever shoot anyone?"

"Yes."

"Kill him?"

"Yes."

"Will you tell me about it?"

Jesse shifted uncomfortably.

"He had a machete," Jesse said. "Nine years ago."

"You would have been, what? Twenty-six?"

Jesse nodded. Abby waited. Jesse didn't continue.

"So you shot him dead?" Abby said.

"Yes."

"Did you mean to?"

"Yes."

"You didn't try to wound him, you know, shoot him in the leg or something?"

"You shoot, you always shoot to kill. It's not the movies. You're in a crisis situation, you got about a half second to do what needs to be done. Your heart's pounding, you can't swallow. It feels like you can't get your breath and you got some guy with a machete. You aim for the middle of the mass and you try to remember not to jerk the trigger."

Abby nodded slowly as she watched his face.

"Listening to you talk," Abby said. "It's in there."

"What exactly?" Jesse said.

"I don't know exactly. I sensed it when we made love. I guess I thought of it as, you know, 'My he's strong,'" Abby said. "But that wasn't really it."

"Jenn said I was very fierce."

Abby nodded. "Something like that. I suppose you need to be that way if you're a policeman."

"Maybe I'm a policeman because I'm that way," Jesse said.

"And that's why you're not scared of Jo Jo."

Jesse smiled.

"It is prudent to be scared of Jo Jo. It would also be prudent of Jo Jo to be scared of me."

chapter 25

Pat Sears found Captain Cat when he got off the eleven-to-seven shift and parked the cruiser out front and went in to log off. There were three steps up to the front door of the police station. The cat was on the bottom step, dead, with a small sign hanging around its neck. On the sign was written SLUT in black Magic Marker. By the time Jesse got there most of the police had heard about Captain Cat and several of them had come in, though they weren't on duty. Nobody said much. He was after all, only a cat. But he had been their cat and they liked him and they all could see that his death was about them.

"I find the little punk asshole that did this," Suitcase Simpson said, and realized he didn't quite know what he'd do and so didn't finish the sentence. But his round face was bright with anger.

"What the hell does 'slut' mean?" Pat Sears said. "For crissake he's a male cat."

Jesse picked up the cat and his head flopped loosely.

"I'd say his neck is broken," Jesse said.

He put the cat back down.

"Peter," Jesse said to the evidence officer, "when you've done what you can do here, take the cat down to the vet and see what he died of. And dust that tag on him."

Perkins nodded. Jesse stood and went into the police station. He closed his office door and sat in his chair and put his feet up on the desk. "Slut" again, he thought. It didn't fit with spray painting the cruiser, and it doesn't fit with killing the cat. But of course it was not about the cruiser, Jesse knew that, or about the cat. It was about the police department and about somebody's private connection to the word "slut." Is it the whole department? Is it one cop? Is it me? Jesse laced his hands behind his head and let his mind go empty, letting the problem drift at the periphery of his consciousness, looking at it obliquely. He was still sitting, hands behind his head, feet up on the desk, lips pursed slightly, when Peter Perkins knocked on the door.

"Vet says the cat's neck is broken," Perkins said. "Says he would have died immediately."

Jesse nodded.

"There's a little trace of dried blood on the cat's claws," Perkins said. "Not enough really to do me much good, but I figure Captain scratched the guy."

"Can you get a blood type?"

"Not enough," Perkins said. "It's microscopic."

"How about state forensic?"

"For what," Perkins said. "A felinicide?"

Jesse smiled slightly.

"Might be a little embarrassing, I guess."

Perkins stood without speaking in front of Jesse's desk.

"You find anything else?" Jesse said.

"No."

Jesse waited.

"I," Perkins started and stopped, looking for what he

wanted to say. "I don't like this thing, Jesse."

"What thing?"

"The slut thing. The cruiser, now the cat. It's an escalation."

"Yes," Jesse said. "It is."

"Maybe this isn't some kid."

"Maybe not," Jesse said.

"Maybe it's serious," Perkins said.

"Maybe you need to take the microscopic blood samples into state forensic," Jesse said.

"It's still on the cat's claws," Perkins said.

"So take the cat."

"Jesus, Jesse."

"I'll call over there," Jesse said. "Sort of smooth the way for you."

Perkins nodded. He was not happy.

"You think it could be important, Jesse?"

"I got no idea, Pete. I'm just trying to accumulate data."

Perkins nodded. He wanted to say something else. But there wasn't anything else to say. He hesitated another minute, then turned to leave.

"I'll get right on it, Jesse."

Perkins went out and closed the door quietly behind him. Jesse leaned back again with his feet up and his lips pursed and his mind relaxed and laced his hands behind his head.

chapter 26

Freedom's Horsemen were practicing squad maneuvers in the wooded area along the railroad tracks in back of the high school.

In full battle dress, camouflage fatigues with a white-handled .45 revolver in a shoulder holster, Hasty Hathaway directed his troops through a bullhorn.

"I want first squad along the track embankments to the right."

His voice amplified by the bullhorn had lost its human sound.

"I want second squad on the high ground back here under those trees."

The mechanized voice sounded odd in the leafy margin where the tracks went out through a low salt marsh.

"You spread out," the voice boomed, "under the trees so the helicopters can't see you, and you lay your field of fire down, so it'll intersect with first squad, the way we laid it out. Noncoms stand by your men, and await my command."

The late-summer afternoon buzzed with the low hum of locusts, and the sound of a bird's odd cry which was more like hiccup than song. The salt marsh supported a large number of flying insects with big translucent wings who hovered close to the surface of the brackish water between the salt hay hummocks. Bobbing on the water among the clumps of sea grass were several bright beach balls.

The mechanical voice over the bullhorn spoke again.

"Commence firing."

And a fusillade of small-arms fire snarled over the salt marsh. The beach balls exploded as the bullets tore through them, and the water between the clumps of marshland spurted and roiled as the bullets sloshed into it. The gunfire was mixed. There was the crack of pistols and the harder sound of rifle fire and the big hollow sound of shotguns.

After a few moments of sustained fire, the mechanical voice boomed, "Cease firing," and the marsh, ringing with the memory of sound, was now entirely silent, devoid even of the odd hiccupping song and the locust buzz. No insects flew over the surface of the marsh, and the beach balls had vanished from the waterways. Only the bright scrap of one clinging to a reed remained as evidence that they had been there.

"Assemble on me," the bullhorn voice said. And the men dressed up like soldiers came out of the woods and from behind the railroad embankment and gathered around Hathaway, who stood on a pile of railroad ties, a hundred yards down the track from the football field behind the high school. He put the bullhorn to his mouth again and the voice spoke.

"Fellows, first let me congratulate you. Had this been the real thing, and not an exercise, we would have prevailed entirely. The fields of fire interlocked, the firing discipline was maintained, each of you did his job and I'm proud of every one of you.''

The men stood in a semicircle around him, thirty-one of them, carrying a variety of shotguns, hunting rifles, modified military weapons, and side arms.

''And make no mistake about it, men, one day it will be the real thing. And men like us will be what stands between the one-worlders and this White Christian Nation. We who have remained true. We who abide by the constitutional mandate for a well-regulated militia. We who exercise our constitutional right to keep and bear arms. We will keep safe the heritage of this country. And if someday we must die to serve this cause, well, then, it will be a good day to die.''

Hathaway handed the bullhorn to Lou Burke, who was standing on the ground beside the pile of ties. Then he turned back toward the assembled men and came to attention and saluted them. They returned the salute and Hathaway yelled, his voice much smaller without the bullhorn.

''Dismissed!''

The men broke their ranks and wandered down the tracks toward the parking lot near the commuter station off Main Street. They stowed their guns in trunks and backseats and drove home in their Toyota sedans and Plymouth Voyagers to take off their uniforms and watch television until bedtime.

The parking lot had been empty for several minutes and the insect buzz and birdsong had resumed around the salt marsh and along the railroad tracks when Jesse Stone walked out of the woods, cut through the high-school football field, and walked back toward the town hall in the lavender twilight.

Chapter 27

Cissy Hathaway lay facedown on the bed, her face buried in the pillow, holding on to the white iron head-board, while Jo Jo Genest spanked her naked backside quite gently with a hand the size of a catcher's mitt. Each time he struck her she made noise into the pillow and her body twisted as if trying to get her grip loose from the headboard.

The room was small and spotless. The walls were white. The floor was polished oak. There was no rug. Opposite the foot of the bed was a chest of drawers painted white, and on the wall beside it was a full-length mirror with a white plastic frame. There was no night table, no lamp. The overhead light was very bright above them. Jo Jo's naked body under the bright overhead glistened with sweat. The muscles and veins were so prominent, stretched so tight against his white skin, that he seemed an anatomy specimen as he sat beside her on the edge of the bed, hitting her gently while she sobbed and moaned into the muffling pillow.

Finally she twisted, releasing her hold on the headboard

for a moment as she rolled onto her back, her body arching toward him. She gripped the headboard again and raised her knees and he eased his huge body onto her.

"You've got me now," she gasped. "You've really got me."

Later, standing on a chair at the foot of the bed, Jo Jo aimed carefully through the Polaroid camera at Cissy Hathaway, naked on the bed. Jo Jo snapped six pictures and placed them carefully on the top of the dresser while they took form. He stared at himself for a moment in the mirror. Then he brought the pictures to the bed and held them up for Cissy to see. She looked at them intently.

"Take more," she said and assumed a different pose. "Different."

"Boy, you are some sick bitch," Jo Jo said.

His pale body seethed with muscles, the veins in his arms distended from steroids. He crouched at the foot of the bed and took some pictures. Then he stood, and reloaded the camera, and went to the far side and took some pictures. He continued to move around her, snapping pictures and letting them cure on the bureau top while he took more. As he snapped, Cissy arched her body into different positions. Finally he ran out of film. He went and stared down at the twenty-four pictures of Cissy that lay faceup on the top of the dresser. He picked one up and touched it to see if it was dry. It wasn't quite, so he blew on it and put it back down.

Behind him on the bed, Cissy said, "Show me."

Jo Jo turned and looked at her for a moment, and shook his head, and brought the pictures to the bed. Sitting on it while she lay back against the pillows, he held the pictures up one at a time. She studied each one carefully, her eyes shiny, her breathing shallow.

"Hard to figure," Jo Jo said, "how you ended up marrying a geek like Hasty."

"I don't feel comfortable," she said, "that you have those."

"You want to keep them at your house?" Jo Jo said.

"No, you know I don't dare do that."

"Want me to burn them?" Jo Jo said.

"No."

"Then I guess you'll just have to be uncomfortable, huh?"

Cissy nodded. She seemed disoriented. Her manner was vague. Her eyes were wide and her pupils were so dilated that she seemed almost to have no iris. She got off the bed and began to dress while he carefully stowed the pictures of her in the top drawer of the dresser.

"See you next Thursday," he said.

She didn't answer.

"Your old man ever wonder where you go on Thursday nights," Jo Jo said.

"No," Cissy said. "Hasty always conducts field training on Thursday nights. I'm home before he is."

"He ever wonder why your ass looks so red?"

Cissy hated it when Jo Jo talked so coarsely. But she tried not to show it. If she showed it she knew he'd just do it more.

"He rarely sees me undressed," she said.

"Well, ain't that a trip," Jo Jo said. "Everybody else in town sees you that way."

"Must you?" Cissy said.

"Well," Jo Jo said with a wide grin, "maybe not everybody, but I'll bet I ain't the only one, am I right?"

Cissy shook her head without answering.

"Well, I'm not," Jo Jo said. "One guy once a week ain't enough for you. Maybe you do different things.

Maybe Thursday's your night for rough trade. But I'm not the only guy.''

A flush smudged along Cissy's cheekbones. She took her small straw purse from the top of the dresser, put her lipstick in it, closed it carefully, and then, without looking again at Jo Jo, went out of the bedroom. Jo Jo made no move to go with her.

Jo Jo said, "Good night, slut," but she was probably too far down the stairs to hear him.

He closed the door, and began to strip the bed. He put the sheets and pillowcases in the old-fashioned wicker laundry hamper in the bathroom, and remade the bed with clean sheets. When he was done he went into the bathroom and took a long shower. After he got out and toweled dry, looking at his muscles in the mirror, he rubbed a little Neosporin ointment into the scratches on his hand.

chapter 28

Lou Burke always looked as if he were ready for inspection. His uniform was tailored and pressed. There were military creases in his shirt. His badge shined. His shoes were spit-shined. His pistol belt and holster gleamed with polish. What little hair he had left was always freshly cut. He was carefully clean-shaven, and he smelled faintly of cologne.

"So tell me about this militia group you belong to," Jesse said.

Burke shrugged. Carefully, Jesse thought.

"Freedom's Horsemen?" Burke said.

Jesse nodded.

"Just a bunch of guys, like to shoot, like to stay ready," Burke said.

"Ready for what?"

"For whatever comes. You know, like the Constitution says, a well-regulated militia."

Jesse nodded.

"Everybody got paper for the guns?"

"Sure," Burke said. "Mostly F.I.D.'s. Guys with handguns got carry permits."

"And discharging a firearm within town limits?"

Burke smiled.

"No problem. Selectmen made that legal, four, five years ago, look it up, as long as it is not done in a way to endanger life or property," Burke said. "Besides, even if it were illegal, you going to arrest half the town government, including the head selectman?"

"Not me," Jesse said. "Any automatic weapons?"

"Nope. These guys wouldn't know where to get one. Hunting rifles mostly, some shotguns, couple old M1's, couple of M1 carbines that fire semi only."

"Hasty the commander?"

"Yeah. He's real serious about it."

"Any talk of, you know, white supremacy, Jewish conspiracy, that kind of stuff?"

"Hell no, Jesse. We're a self-defense force that enjoys getting together one day a week and doing some maneuvers. You know I wouldn't be a part of anything that wasn't straight."

"Any blacks in the self-defense force?"

"No, but hell, there's no blacks in town, are there?"

"Good point," Jesse said.

"Probably why a lot of people move here, get away from what's going on in Boston."

"What's going on in Boston?"

"Aw, come on, Jesse. You worked in L.A. You know you get a bunch of blacks you get crime and drugs and guns and the neighborhood goes to shit. It's not prejudiced to say that. It's just reality."

"Who finances the Horsemen?"

"What's to finance? The guys buy their own uniforms, supply their own weapons and ammo. We have a couple parties a year. I think Hasty pays for them.''

Jesse nodded slowly. He tapped the fingers of his left hand softly on the desktop, and pursed his lips in a facial gesture that Burke had seen before. It meant Jesse was thinking. Burke felt a bit uncomfortable.

''You got a problem with any of this, Jesse?''

Jesse continued to purse his lips and drum gently on the desk. Then he stopped, and grinned at Burke.

''No. Hell no, Lou. I got no problem with any of it.''

Burke did not feel entirely reassured. Sonova bitch doesn't miss much, Burke thought.

Chapter 29

The apartment was very still when Jesse got home. The small sounds of a functioning building only underscored the silence. Jesse walked to the sliders that opened onto the little deck, and looked out at the harbor. There was still enough light to see all the way across to the Neck. A single lobster boat came in toward the town dock, otherwise the boats that bobbed on the calm surface of the harbor were moored and empty. Jesse liked the silence. It was comforting. He stood for a while looking at the quiescent harbor and let the silence sink in. Then he went to the kitchen and got the bottle of Black Label from the cabinet and poured some over ice. He let it sit for a moment while he hung his coat on the back of a chair. Then he picked up the glass and walked into the living room and looked out the window and took his first drink. First one at the end of a day was always a home run. He sat down on one of the armchairs that had come with the apartment, and put his feet up on the coffee table. He sipped again. The silence made him feel strong. And the whiskey made him feel strong. He tried to simply feel the strength and let his mind go, let it be part of the silence and the whiskey and not think about Jenn. He felt strong about Jenn. Right here at least. Right now. The prospect of life without her seemed for the moment filled with possibility. He drank again and got up and added some ice and poured some more scotch. He took the drink back to the window and looked out again. He could think about who killed Captain Cat, but he tried not to. He pushed the thoughts over to the periphery of his mind, let them drift there with thoughts about Freedom's Horsemen. They would work on their own if he didn't force them into the center of his consciousness and hold them too tightly. He swallowed some whiskey. The evening had come down upon the harbor. The Neck was no longer visible. Only the lights from some of the houses shone across the dark water. The lobster boat was docked now, nearly motionless against the dock in the bright mercury lamps of the town landing. Abby made things easier. He drank more whiskey. He liked her. But he knew better than to go from one monogamy to another. Abby would be the first of many. He liked the idea. He drank to it. His glass was empty. He got up and got more ice, holding the glass under the ice dispenser in the refrigerator door. He poured scotch over the ice. He looked at the bottle. There was an encouraging amount still left in the bottle. Happiness is a jug that's still three-quarters full. It was exciting to go out with a woman and be talking pleasantly and maybe having lunch and knowing that in a few hours, or maybe next week, after another date, that you'd see her with her clothes off. It was nice. He remembered the frantic scuffle of his adolescent dates. As an adult there was a calmness and friendliness to it all. Adults made love. How soon depended on circumstance. But all concerned knew it would happen and it took all the desperation out of the procedure. Jesse hated desperation.

Life, if he could make all the rules, would proceed in a stately manner. Dating as an adult was sort of stately. Stately. He liked the sound of it.

"Stately," he said.

His voice seemed loud and not his in the thick silence of the almost empty apartment. He took his drink to the kitchen and made himself a ham-and-cheese sandwich and ate standing at the counter, sipping his whiskey between bites. When he was done he made a fresh drink and walked back to the living room and sat back down. He tried to count how many he'd had.

"More than two," he said.

Again his voice was loud and alien. Stillness was the norm here. He tipped his head back against the chair. Stately, he thought. I like things to be stately.

He fell asleep and woke up in the hard darkness of late night, feeling thick and stupid. He went to bed and didn't sleep well and got up at daylight with a hangover.

Chapter 30

It was the first week after Labor Day and it still felt like summer except that the kids were back to school. Jesse was glad he wasn't a kid as he walked past Paradise Junior High School on his way to Carole Genest's house. Every once in a while one or two leaves on an otherwise green tree would show yellow as he walked along Main Street. There were adults, mostly female, moving about in front of the shopping center, and there was a back-to-business quality that seemed to settle in on a town once school was in session. Jesse had hated school, always. It had something to do with hating to be told what to do, he supposed. On the other hand he'd liked playing baseball and being in the Marines and being a cop in L.A., all of which entailed being told what to do. Maybe he didn't like being told what to do indoors. Or maybe he didn't like being instructed. But he didn't mind being coached . . . He couldn't figure it out, but it was not a problem he needed to solve, so he put it aside. The big oak tree that loomed over Carole Genest's driveway was entirely green. Jesse paused under it and looked at the bright lawn that rolled down to Main Street from the big white house. Ten rooms maybe, and a big yard in the middle of town.

Only the youngest Genest kid was home when Carole let Jesse in. He was in the den with some coloring books and some crayons and some little wooden figures scattered about, watching a home shopping show as if it were a performance of *King Lear*.

"Want some coffee?" Carole said.

"Sure."

Jesse followed her through the long formal dining room into the big kitchen, paneled in pine, with shiny copper pots hanging from a rack over the stove. The big window at the back of the room looked out at more land behind the house, planted with flowering shrubs and shielded by white pine trees.

"Nice property," Jesse said. "How much land you got?"

"Three-quarters of an acre," Carole said. She put coffee into the gold filter basket of a bright blue coffeemaker and added water and turned it on, and sat down at the kitchen table opposite Jesse. She was a pretty woman, with an empty face and wide eyes which always looked a little startled.

"Been here long?"

"Ten years," she said.

The kid came from the den carrying a ratty-looking stuffed animal by the ear. It was too dilapidated for Jesse to tell what it had been. The child laid the upper half of himself over his mother's lap and, holding the stuffed animal tightly, started to suck his thumb. Carole patted his head absently.

"You get it as part of the divorce?"

"Yes. And he's supposed to pay me alimony every month but he doesn't."

"Must be tough to keep the payments up," Jesse said.

"I got to pay taxes quarterly, but at least there's no mortgage."

"No mortgage?"

"No. Jo Jo bought it for cash, when we got married."

"Cash? Really? When was that."

"Nineteen eighty-six," she said. "House cost a hundred and fifty-five thousand dollars. Probably worth five now."

"I should think so," Jesse said. "Where'd Jo Jo get the cash?"

Carole shook her head. The coffeemaker had stopped gurgling. She raised the kid from her lap and got up and poured them coffee.

"You take anything?" she said.

"Cream and sugar, please. Two sugars."

"Skim milk okay?"

"Sure."

She put the coffee down on the table and sat back down. The kid plopped back in her lap and sucked his thumb some more.

"What did you ask me?" Carole said.

"Where Jo Jo got the cash. Hundred and fifty-five thousand is a lot of money. It was even more in 1986."

"I don't know," she said.

Jesse nodded.

"Jo Jo come around since he and I had that talk?" Jesse said.

"No."

"How are the kids doing?"

Carole shrugged.

"You talk to a shrink at all?"

"How'm I supposed to afford a shrink," Carole said.

"My HMO pays a hundred bucks for counseling. You know how far that goes?"

Jesse nodded.

"How are you getting by, financially?"

Again Carole shrugged. It was a particular kind of shrug. Jesse had seen it often. It was not a gesture of surrender or even of defeat, those were long past. It was a gesture of numbness. It meant no hope.

"You got any family?"

"My mother's dead," Carole said. "My father's in Florida with my stepmother. My father sends me some money."

"If Jo Jo's not paying what he's supposed to you can take him to court."

"Sure, and pay a lawyer, and have the judge tell Jo Jo to pay and have him not pay, and maybe come around later and beat the shit out of me?"

"I don't think he'll do that again," Jesse said.

"Maybe not if you're around, he hasn't bothered me since that time. But how long you going to stay around here?"

"I don't know," Jesse said.

"How come he's scared of you anyway?" Carole said. "I mean, look at him. Look at you. How come he doesn't get you for slapping him around?"

Jesse looked at the little boy, sucking his thumb on his mother's lap. How much of all this did he hear? Probably all of it. How much did he understand? Probably too much of it. What could Jesse do about that?

"Well," Jesse said. "I'm a cop, which carries a little weight, and I carry a gun, which may have a lot of weight."

"Jo Jo's got a gun. He used to have two or three around here."

Jesse nodded.

"So what is it," Carole said.

Jesse looked at the boy again. Nothing to do about that.

"Jo Jo's a fake," Jesse said. "Alone at night, when he can't sleep, sometimes, for a minute he knows it. And he knows that I know it too."

"A fake?"

"Sure. He's strong, and he's cruel. And that's a dangerous combination. But he isn't really tough."

"And you are?"

Jesse smiled at her.

"Yes, ma'am. I am."

The boy straightened and whispered in his mother's ear.

"Okay," Carole said. "I'll take you."

She stood.

"Excuse us a minute," she said to Jesse and went out of the kitchen with her son.

For a drunk, Jesse thought as he sat in the quiet kitchen, I'm pretty tough for a boozer.

The television blatted in the family room. The kitchen faucet had a slow drip. He wondered if it needed a washer or if she just hadn't shut it off tightly. Jenn had rarely shut the faucet off tightly. He always had to firm it up when he had walked through the kitchen. She never closed the cabinet doors all the way either. When she had stopped coming home everything had been much more buttoned up.

Carole came back into the kitchen. She got a Fudgsicle from the refrigerator freezer and removed the wrapper and gave the Fudgsicle to the boy.

"More coffee?" she said.

"Sure."

Jesse held the cup out and Carole poured from the round glass pot.

"When does he start school?" Jesse said, nodding at the boy.

"Kindergarten next year," Carole said.

The boy showed no sign that he knew they were talking about him. He sat on his mother's lap, working on the Fudgsicle.

"Can you get a job then?" Jesse said.

Shrug.

"What did you do before you got married?"

"High school," Carole said. "Jo Jo knocked me up senior year. I never graduated."

"Maybe you could get some training," Jesse said.

"Sure."

"What does Jo Jo do for a living?" Jesse asked.

Carole shrugged. "He does some bodybuilder contests, I know."

"Can you make a living doing that?"

Shrug.

"What was he doing for a living when he bought this house for cash?"

"I don't know," Carole said.

Jesse allowed himself to look puzzled.

"I'm not very smart," Carole said. "I never learned anything in school. I didn't even graduate. Taking care of me was his job."

Jesse drank some of the coffee. It had gotten stronger sitting in the pot.

"I think it would be good if you didn't have to depend on Jo Jo."

"Sure," Carole said. "It's what my old man is always telling me. From Florida. So who's going to marry a woman with three small kids and an ex-husband like I got?"

"Maybe you don't need a husband to take care of you," Jesse said.

"Yeah," Carole said. "Right."

"So as long as you knew him, Jo Jo never had a regular job?"

"He tended bar once in a while. Worked as a bouncer."

"Where?"

"Club in Peabody. The Eighty-six Club."

"He work there much?"

"No."

Jesse stood and brought his coffee cup to the sink.

"Well, you need me, you know how to get me," Jesse said.

"Yes."

"Thanks for the coffee."

"Sure."

Jesse looked for a moment at the little boy, his face dirty with melted Fudgsicle. You don't have a prayer, Jesse thought. Not a goddamned prayer.

Chapter 31

Hasty Hathaway picked up a triangle of cinnamon toast and bit off a corner, and chewed and swallowed.

"I asked you to have coffee with me, Jesse, because I'm concerned about some of the things that have happened in town recently."

Hathaway held the now truncated triangle of toast delicately in his right hand and moved it slightly in rhythm to his speech. Jesse waited.

"I mean, I know they are not serious crimes. But the spray-painting of a police cruiser, and the killing of that police station cat . . . well, it's all around town."

Jesse had nothing to say to that, so he waited.

"Obviously someone wishes to embarrass the police department."

Jesse continued to wait.

"Do you agree?" Hathaway said.

"Yes."

"And," Hathaway said, "I'm afraid they're succeeding."

" 'Fraid so," Jesse said.

"Who might that be?" Hathaway said.

Jesse leaned back in his seat and turned his coffee cup slowly with both hands.

"We roust some of the burnout kids in town every day," Jesse said. "We arrest several drunks a weekend. We referee a domestic dispute about once a week. We stop people for speeding. We tow cars for being illegally parked. We're in the business of telling people no."

"So it could be anyone," Hathaway said.

"Could be," Jesse said.

"But isn't it more likely to be one person than another?" Hathaway said. "Don't you have any suspicions?"

"Sure," Jesse said.

"Perhaps you'd care to share them with me," Hathaway said. "I am after all the town's chief executive."

Jesse thought it an odd phrase to describe the selectman's job, but he didn't comment.

"I had to guess, I'd guess it might be Jo Jo Genest," Jesse said.

"Jo Jo?"

"I came down pretty hard on him for harassing his exwife a while ago."

"But you yourself say you deal regularly with domestic disputes."

"Yes."

"So it could be any of those people's man or wife."

"Feels like Jo Jo to me."

"That's pretty weak," Hathaway said.

"Yes it is," Jesse said. "If it were strong I'd arrest him."

"But you're still suspicious."

"Jo Jo's the right kind of guy. He'd need to get even for being embarrassed in front of his ex-wife, and he wouldn't have the *cojones* to do it straight on.''

"Cohonees?"

"Balls," Jesse said.

"You think Jo Jo Genest is afraid?"

Hathaway seemed genuinely amazed.

"Can't always judge a book . . ." Jesse said.

"No," Hathaway said. "No. I can't buy that at all. Jo Jo grew up in this town. If you did something to Jo Jo he might be angry. But if he were angry, God help you. He wouldn't sneak around killing cats."

Jesse turned his coffee cup a little more.

"Sure," he said. "Probably right."

"And you have no other theories?"

"No."

"Well, you better get some," Hathaway said. "There was a story about it in the *Standard Times* last night."

Jesse nodded without comment.

"It made the papers, in my view, because you sent the cat remains to the state laboratory, and they talked about it to someone."

"Could be," Jesse said.

"Isn't it a bit preposterous to send the remains of a dead cat to the state whatever-it-is lab?"

"Forensic," Jesse said.

"I'd prefer that next time you are tempted to seek outside assistance, you consult me first. Agreed?"

"Agreed," Jesse said without meaning it.

"This town does not wish outsiders sharing our problems," Hathaway said.

"Of course," Jesse said.

"We handle our own business here. Part of liberty is self-reliance."

"You bet," Jesse said.

Hathaway stood and put one of his long-fingered bony hands on Jesse's shoulder.

"Don't mean to come down too hard on you, Jesse. But I have a responsibility to this town. Call on me for anything you need . . . and let's keep our troubles in-house."

"Gotcha," Jesse said.

Hathaway patted Jesse's shoulder briefly and turned and left the restaurant. Jesse sat looking after him, turning his coffee cup slowly on the tabletop. I wonder what Hasty is actually worried about, Jesse thought. He looked at Hathaway's plate. He had eaten the center of his cinnamon toast and left the crusts. Cinnamon toast, Jesse thought. Jesus Christ!

chapter 32

The call from Wyoming came at nine o'clock in the morning eastern time. Jesse took it in his office.

"I got Paradise, Massachusetts?" Charlie Buck said.

"Yes," Jesse said.

"You the chief of police?"

"Yes. Jesse Stone."

"My name's Charlie Buck. I'm an investigator for the Campbell County Sheriff's Department in Gillette, Wyoming."

"Well, you're an early riser," Jesse said. "What is it there, about seven?"

"Seven oh three," Buck said. "I'm interested in a man might have lived in Paradise at one time, man named Thomas Carson."

"He was the chief before me," Jesse said.

Buck grunted.

"Well, he was driving a Dodge truck up along Route 59 north of Bill a while back, when it blew up and him with it. Took us this long to trace what was left."

"In Wyoming?"

"Yeah, north of Bill, heading toward Gillette."

"You establish why it blew up?" Jesse said.

"Bomb."

"So it's a homicide."

"You might say so."

"You have any leads?"

"We was hoping you'd be the lead. If the bomb hadn't tossed the truck's serial number couple hundred feet away we wouldn't even know who he was."

"Considerable bomb," Jesse said.

"Considerable," Buck said. "Figure it was supposed to pulverize everything so we couldn't I.D. the victim. How long you had the job?"

"Got hired in May," Jesse said. "Didn't actually start until June."

"You know when Carson left?"

"Before May," Jesse said. "Sometime in the spring, I think. Until I took over, guy named Lou Burke was acting chief."

"Where were you before you took this job?" Buck said.

"L.A. Homicide."

Buck grunted again.

"Might be useful," he said.

"I'll try," Jesse said.

"Carson got any next of kin out there?"

"Not that I know of, but I'll find out, let you know."

"Wish you would," Buck said. "Friends, close associates?"

"Let me look into it," Jesse said. "I'll get back to you."

"Sure," Buck said.

"You know what detonated the bomb?" Jesse said.

"No. Best guess, someone trailed him and beeped it from

a distance. Pretty empty stretch of road along where it went off.''

''Makes sense,'' Jesse said. ''If you wouldn't mind, I'd like it if you talked only to me about this.''

Buck grunted.

''If you wouldn't mind,'' Jesse said.

''Hell no,'' Buck said. ''Your town, your department. Who'd you say you worked for in L.A.?''

''Homicide, Captain Cronjager.''

''Un huh. Well, I'll go ahead and see what I can do at this end. Maybe you can give me a ring in a couple days, tell me what you know.''

''Glad to,'' Jesse said.

''If I don't hear,'' Buck said, ''I'll give you a ring.''

''You'll hear,'' Jesse said.

chapter 33

Jo Jo Genest sat in Gino Fish's storefront office waiting for Gino, trying to impress Vinnie Morris.

"So I got this suitcase," Jo Jo said, "with seven hundred large, you know, small bills. Thing weighs a freaking ton, and I'm supposed to take it to a bank in New York City, down around Wall Street someplace. You know New York?"

Morris nodded. He was sitting with his chair tilted back. He had a Walkman clipped to his belt and he was listening to music through the earphones.

"Guy I know arranged I could make the deposit in an account under a fake name, no questions asked," Jo Jo said. "So I got this rental car and I'm trying to get there, and the traffic is out of control, you know. And when I finally get there I can't find a place to park, and I'm riding around the block down by the World Trade thing, and the freaking bank closes. You believe it. I got a dirty seven hundred thousand in a suitcase and the bank closes while I'm riding around like a dildo looking for a parking space."

Morris was looking at Jo Jo with no expression, his heels hooked in the bottom rung of his chair, his arms folded over his chest.

"You hear me okay?" Jo Jo said.

Morris nodded.

"Well, I figure the money's okay, I mean, who's going to mug somebody like me, you know? But I still gotta get it deposited, so I haul it back to the hotel. I'm staying at the Marriott in Times Square, and I ditch the car and next morning I get a cab and haul the money back downtown and it's dandy. Cabbie drops me off right in front of the bank. I take the stuff in, go to the desk, and ask for the name they gave me, who's going to count the cash and take care of the deposit and he ain't there. He's at another branch in freaking Queens, they gave me the wrong branch. So I go out with the suitcase, which is lucky I'm big and strong, because it's getting heavier every minute and I try to find a cab and I can't, so I get on the subway. I got a suitcase full of cash and I'm riding the freaking subway, and I'm boiling. And I go back to the hotel and get a cab there. You can always get a cab at a hotel, and I go over to Queens hauling the dough, and the guy is there, but he's in a meeting. So I tell the slut at the desk that they better get his ass out of the meeting or else and she says, real preppy, 'Excuse me?' And I said get this guy's ass out here, now. And I give her a real hard look and she gets up and goes in back and in a little while my guy comes out, and he's nice as freaking pie. 'Oh, sir, so sorry to keep you waiting, come right in to one of our conference rooms, blah, blah.' And I got the money deposited. But is that a kick or what, I'm chugging around freaking New York with three-quarters of a million in cash for two days trying to get somebody to take it."

"Scared hell out of that bank lady, huh?" Morris said.

Jo Jo didn't much like the way Vinnie said it. He could never tell whether Vinnie was putting him on or not. Hard to figure Vinnie. He didn't seem interested in anything. He never seemed in a hurry. He never had any reaction to anything, except to say things like "scared hell out of that bank lady," which Jo Jo could never quite figure out.

Jo Jo thought maybe he ought to grab Vinnie someday and slap him up against the wall. Get his freaking attention. But there was something about Vinnie . . . Jo Jo stopped thinking about it. He sat straight upright on the other straight chair. He would have liked to cross his legs, but they were too thick. He probably ought to do more stretching, loosen everything up a little. Gino Fish came into the room, nodded at Vinnie, walked past Jo Jo, and got behind his desk.

"Sorry I'm late," Fish said.

But he said it in a way that sounded to Jo Jo like he didn't care if he was late or not. He could use a little shaking up too, Jo Jo thought. Involuntarily he glanced at Vinnie, as if Vinnie could know what he was thinking. Vinnie looked blankly at him or past him or through him. Jo Jo could never be sure.

"No problem, Gino. Been talking with Vinnie."

Fish smiled without amusement.

"So what have you got for me, Jo Jo?" Fish said.

"Guy I know is looking for guns."

Fish was quiet for a moment, his gaze heavy on Jo Jo.

"Who is this guy?" Fish said finally.

"He'd like to remain anonymous," Jo Jo said.

"Wouldn't everyone," Fish said. "Is he IRA?"

"No, nothing like that."

"Zealots are not good people to do business with," Fish said.

Jo Jo wasn't exactly sure what a zealot was. But he knew Hathaway wasn't IRA.

"Can you do something for us?" Jo Jo said.

"What are you after?" Fish said.

"Automatic weapons, machine guns, mortars, handheld rocket launchers, grenades."

There had been other things on the list, but Jo Jo hadn't wanted to carry the list. It would be bad if he got caught with it, and he wanted Gino and Vinnie to think he knew more about guns than he did.

"In what quantities?" Fish said.

"Enough to outfit a regiment," Jo Jo said. It was what he had been told to answer.

Fish smiled again without warmth.

"When I was of an age for the military," he said, "I was in a different kind of government service."

"I didn't know you did government work, Gino."

"I was in jail," Fish said.

Jo Jo felt hot. He hated to look stupid in front of Vinnie.

"I knew that, Gino," he said. "I was kidding you."

"Well, don't," Fish said. "Vinnie, do you know what kind of weapons order you'd need to outfit a regiment?"

"Yeah."

"Do we know anyone who could supply that amount?"

"Sure."

Fish looked at Jo Jo.

"There," he said. "Now what?"

"Can you get me a price?"

"Supplier will set the price," Fish said. "I'll add my commission."

"Sure, Gino, of course. These are just, ah, whaddycallit, preliminary talks, you know."

"So tell your principals it'll be a few days, and I'll be

in touch with you. Before we go too much further, though, I will want to meet the principals.''

"They won't like that, Gino.''

"I don't care, Jo Jo. That's the way it will have to be. I don't do this kind of business with people I don't know.'' He smiled his joyless smile again. "I have had all the government service I care for.''

Jo Jo flushed again, feeling foolish about misunderstanding government service. He glanced sideways at Vinnie. Vinnie seemed oblivious.

"I'll talk to them,'' Jo Jo said.

"Fine. Now if you'll excuse us . . .''

Jo Jo stood up, too quickly. He wished he had reacted slower.

"I'll wait to hear from you,'' he said to Fish.

He made a little punching gesture at Vinnie with his clenched fist, and went out of the office. When he was gone, Fish turned to Vinnie Morris.

"What do you think,'' he said.

"Some homemade patriot group,'' Morris said.

"Why do you think that?''

"Because the only contact they got is a jerk like Jo Jo.'' Fish nodded.

"And the only contact he has is us,'' Fish said. "Do you have any idea how to arm a regiment?''

"Not a clue,'' Morris said.

"Do you have any contact with international arms dealers?''

"Piece I'm carrying I bought from a guy named Ralph,'' Morris said. "On Dorchester Ave.''

"Do you suppose he could arm a regiment?''

"Ralph works out of his car.''

"Yes, of course,'' Fish said. "Very efficient.''

"I could ask around,'' Morris said.

"Um hmm."

Fish seemed to be thinking of something else. Morris looked at him and came as close to smiling as he ever got.

"Or you could figure out a way to skin them," he said.

Fish didn't answer for a time, as if he had to finish a thought and return to the subject at hand.

"If they wish to give us their money," he said finally, "I see no reason why we shouldn't encourage them in that course."

chapter 34

Tammy didn't really like to see him with his clothes off. He was stringy, the sparse hair on his chest was white, and there were small wrinkles inside the bend of his elbow. He didn't look at all rich and powerful. In fact he didn't look anywhere near as good as Bobby had, and Bobby had been a loser for sure.

"Come to bed," she said.

And she was glad when he got in bed and was under the covers. He always got under the covers. The first time they had done it and he got under the covers she had almost laughed. Would he wear pajamas next time? With feet on them?

He put his arms around her and clamped his mouth against hers. She had to help him a bit, as she always did, to get it up, but as soon as it was up he rolled over on top of her and proceeded. While he was on her he whispered how much he loved her and called her his darling. He was through before she was even aroused. And like always he rolled off her and lay on his back beside her silently, with the covers up to his chin. Still, it didn't take him long, and there were other men, Saturday-night men, who would give her excitement.

"If you love me so much," she said, "how come you don't get rid of your wife and marry me?"

"I can't do that," he said. "We've been married twenty-seven years. I'm the leading figure in the town."

"But you know she's fucking other men," Tammy said.

"You know I don't like you to talk that way about my wife," he said.

"Well, it's the god's truth," Tammy said.

"We . . . have . . . our understanding," he said.

"Yeah, sure," Tammy said. "And where does that leave me."

"I give you money," he said. "I buy you things. We have our time together every week."

"Yeah, you sneak in here and bang me, and sneak out. You know what that makes me feel like?"

"Tammy, please, we've had this talk before."

"Well, we're having it again. I deserve more than that. I deserve to be out of the damn closet here. I deserve to be married and going to the Yacht Club with you, instead of her."

"God, no," he said.

"God, yes," Tammy said. She sat up in bed, and the motion pulled the bedclothes nearly off him. He struggled to keep covered. "I mean it. I got a right to be more than your whore once a week. I want to live in that house. I want to go to the Yacht Club dances and run a table at the Harvest Fair and have an account at Saks. I want you to marry me."

"It's not possible," he said.

"Maybe I'll make it possible," Tammy said.

She was angry, and she felt strong when she was angry.

Her anger had always worked with Bobby, and when she got angry enough it had driven him from the house. What a loser Bobby was.

"You will?" he said.

The anger was working with him too. He was very meek.

"If I have to. I'll go public with this. I'll tell your wife, I'll tell everybody. You'll have to marry me just to shut me up."

"Don't do that," he said.

His voice was so quiet. She almost smiled. Men were easy. Bobby had been strong as a blacksmith and all she had to do was get mad and he caved right in. Now it was working again. There he was with his money and his position and he was as meek as a little boy when she got mad.

"So think about it. Either you get rid of her and marry me, or I go all-out fucking public."

He nodded thoughtfully.

"Yes," he said. "Of course. I can see how you'd feel. Just give me a little time. I'll make it right. I care about you a great deal."

"And I care about you. But you gotta treat me right."

He nodded again.

"Yes," he said. "It'll take a little while for me to arrange everything. But I'll do the right thing, Tammy. I promise."

She laughed with pleasure and leaned over and kissed him.

"Will you give me an engagement ring?" she said. "A big engagement ring with a big diamond and maybe little emeralds on either side?"

"As soon as I can," he said. "As soon as I can get this all fixed. Just give me a little time and you'll get everything you want."

"Yes," she said and lay back on the bed and watched

him while he got up and put on his clothes, and left. When he was gone she stayed in the bed, her hands clasped behind her head.

"Yes," she said out loud and her voice seemed very powerful in the quiet room.

chapter 35

Jesse sat in his office with the gun permit file up on the computer screen. In Massachusetts, permits to carry a handgun were issued by the local chief of police. The permits had to be renewed every five years. Fire Arm Identification cards, permitting the holder to keep a gun, but not to carry one, were issued once and good for the holder's lifetime. All the carry permits currently held therefore had been issued by Tom Carson. Some of the F.I.D.'s were much older. But only two had been issued prior to Carson's arrival fifteen years before. No one had applied for a gun permit since Jesse had taken the job.

Jesse got up and walked to his office door and opened it and spoke to Molly Crane, who was the dispatcher and ran the front desk. She was also the jail matron and the only female officer on the force.

Molly was on the phone.

"Trash pickup has been delayed a day because of Labor Day," she said into the phone. "No, ma'am. One day later . . . When's your usual pickup? . . . Then it'll be Thursday this week . . . Yes, ma'am. Glad to."

She hung up and smiled at Jesse.

"Suitcase due in this morning?"

"He's on shift," Molly said. "Seven to three. Want me to get him in here?"

"When it's convenient," Jesse said. "Nice job on the trash pickup dates."

"Lotta practice," Molly said. "They call after every holiday."

Jesse went back into his office and looked at the list of gun permits some more. He looked at them for a long time with his lips pursed, then he pushed the print button and watched as the sheets came silently from the laser printer. He was still watching them when Simpson knocked on his door and came in. He took off his hat and stood in front of Jesse's desk a little awkwardly. At twenty-two he was still not entirely comfortable being called into the chief's office. Even if the chief wasn't very old himself.

"Hi, boss."

"Close my door, Suit, and then sit down."

Simpson did as he was told. His shoulders looked tight.

"You're not in trouble," Jesse said. "I just need some help and you seemed the right guy to give it."

Simpson's shoulders relaxed. He put his hat on the edge of Jesse's desk and leaned back slightly in his chair.

"Sure, Jesse."

"You know about the militia group in town."

"Freedom's Horsemen, sure. Mr. Hathaway is the commander, I think. I never figured the name out, though, tell you the truth. There isn't a one of them can ride a damn horse."

"And you know most of the people in the group?"

"Oh sure. I lived here all my life, Jesse. I know about everybody in town."

"That's why I figured you were the right one for this, Suit."

Jesse reached into the printer catch basket and took out the permit list and handed it to Simpson.

"Go through this list," Jesse said. "Check off the names that are also Freedom's Horsemen."

"Sure. You want me to do it right now?"

"Yes, please."

Simpson took a ballpoint pen from the pocket of his uniform shirt and began to go slowly through the list. Jesse watched quietly. It took Simpson a long time to go through the hundred or so names on the list. When he finished he handed the list over to Jesse and capped his pen and put it carefully back in his shirt pocket. Most of the names were checked.

"I don't know who a couple of those people are," Simpson said. "I put a question mark beside them. And a couple people I'm not sure if they're in the Horsemen or not. So I put two question marks next to them."

Jesse glanced over the list. There were only twelve unmarked names.

"Most of them are Horsemen," he said.

"Sure," Simpson said. "It's always the gun guys join a militia."

Jesse nodded.

"Gun is probably a prerequisite," he said. "What I'm wondering is why so few non-Horsemen have permits."

"Most people are scared of guns."

Jesse didn't answer. He stared at the list for a time while Simpson sat and waited.

"How come you want to know this, Jesse?" Simpson asked finally.

"Just like to keep track, Suit. Militias have sometimes gotten a little hairy."

"Oh hell, Jesse, you take the Horsemen too serious. I known most of them since I been a little kid. They just like to shoot, hang around with each other. Drink beer after the meetings. Hell, Lou's one of the officers, for crissake."

"You're probably right, Suit. What I would like is if you kept it to yourself, though, be kind of embarrassing if Lou found out, or Mr. Hathaway, that I was checking them out."

"Oh sure, Jesse, no sweat. I won't say a damned word."

"And the other thing, Suit, if you know anybody that tried to get a gun permit and couldn't, could you let me know his name."

"That off the record too, Jesse?"

"Yes."

"Okay," Simpson said and his round pink face widened as he smiled. "Suitcase Simpson, Undercover."

chapter 36

The Strand movie theater in the old downtown section
of Paradise was left over from the time when every town
had a movie theater. There was a balcony. The ceiling was
high. And the screen was big, with maroon drapes gathered
at each side of it. Jesse didn't like the movie much. But he
liked the theater. And he enjoyed being with Abby.

"What'd you think," she said as they walked out onto
Washington Street.

"The computer broke, they'd have had no movie," Jesse
said.

He had the slightly disoriented lightness he always felt
coming out of a movie.

"Computer?" Abby said. "Oh, you mean all the special
effects."

"Un huh."

"But that's how film is made these days. I mean art is
partly about making use of the technology available."

"Art?" Jesse said.

There was a gym on the second floor next to the theater,

and coming out the front door of the gym and walking toward them was Jo Jo Genest. He had on a cutoff black tee shirt and gray sweatpants and a black headband. His long hair was wet with sweat. He was wearing the fingerless leather gloves that everyone wore in the movies. His face was dark with an unshaven beard. The tee shirt read, *I am an animal. I will eat you,* across the front.

"Hey, Chief Stone," Jo Jo said. "How you doing?"

Jesse looked at him without speaking.

"How you doing, little lady," Jo Jo said.

"Fine," Abby said.

"Closing in on that cat killer, chief?"

Jesse continued to look at him dead-eyed.

"Whatsa matter, you can't hear me?" Jo Jo said.

Some of the people coming from the movie slowed, looking covertly at the confrontation.

"You got an alibi for the time of the cat killing?" Jesse said. He was smiling, playing to the crowd, which was pretending not to notice as it moved around the scene.

"Sure do," Jo Jo said.

"How do you know when the cat was killed?" Jesse said.

"Huh?"

Jo Jo stopped smiling.

"You got an alibi for the time the cat was killed, you must know when the cat was killed. How do you know that?"

"Hey, don't be an asshole, Stone. I just meant whenever it happened, I didn't do it, so I'd have an alibi."

"Turn around," Jesse said.

His voice was flat.

"What?"

"Turn around. Put your hands flat against the wall."

"Wait a freaking minute, Stone."

"You disobeying the lawful order of a policeman?" Jesse said.

He unbuttoned his blazer jacket.

"What are you gonna do? Shoot me?" Jo Jo said.

"Hands on the wall," Jesse said in the same flat voice.

Abby had taken a couple of steps away from Jesse, moving closer to the passersby who paused and stared, or walked by as if nothing were happening, depending on their temperament.

"Oh for crissake," Jo Jo said.

He placed his hands flat against the building.

"Step away from the building, leaving your hands in place," Jesse said. "Spread your legs."

Jo Jo did as he was told. His face was flushed, and his breath was coming shorter. Jesse tapped his ankles with the edge of one foot, moving Jo Jo's feet farther apart. Then he patted him down. When he was through, he stepped back away from Jo Jo and stared at him without speaking.

"How long am I supposed to stand here?" Jo Jo said.

"Until I tell you to stop," Jesse said.

He continued to look silently at Jo Jo for another full minute.

Then he said, "Okay."

Jo Jo straightened and turned from the wall. He glared at Jesse without speaking. Jesse stared back at him.

Then Jesse spoke very softly. "We both know something, don't we, pal."

"Whaddya mean?"

"We both know," Jesse said again.

"Aw," Jo Jo said and made a push-away motion with his left hand, and stepped past Jesse and walked down the street away from them, trying to swagger.

Jesse stepped over beside Abby.

"Want to eat at the Rosewood?" Jesse said.

"Jesus Christ," Abby said.

chapter 37

"I don't like this," Hasty said to Jo Jo as they walked along Tremont Street.

"Gino says it's this way or no way," Jo Jo said. "He likes to see who he's doing business with."

"Why does someone like him care?" Hasty said.

Jo Jo shrugged.

"Gino's a strange guy," Jo Jo said.

They went down the stairs to the basement-level entrance and walked into Development Associates of Boston. The pretty young man behind the reception desk looked up at them.

"Well, Tarzan," he said with his infuriating smile. "And who's this, Cheetah?"

Jo Jo had a momentary image of himself yanking the little faggot from behind the desk and smashing his head against the white brick wall. But he didn't. This was business, and he was always aware of Vinnie Morris and his odd unnerving stillness, and how quick everyone said he was when he had reason to be.

"Gino's expecting us," Jo Jo said.

"Me check," the young man said. "You wait."

He stood and went back through the door behind the desk and into the back room. In a moment he came out and made a sweeping gesture of invitation like a maitre d' at a pretentious restaurant. Jo Jo could almost feel Hasty's disapproval. But Gino was Gino and he had to meet the client.

Hasty looked around the inner office. It too was white brick, with a vase full of flowers on the desk. A tall spare man sat behind the desk, and a compact efficient-looking man sat to Gino's left, tilting his straight chair back against the wall.

"I'm Gino Fish," the spare man said. "This is my associate Vinnie Morris."

Morris didn't make any sign that he even heard Gino. He simply looked at them without expression. Vinnie Morris made Hasty uncomfortable. He made him think of his new police chief, though he wasn't quite sure why. Something about potential unexpressed, maybe. The motionless implication that there would be more than what you saw, if you pushed beyond the stillness.

"How do you do," Hasty said.

Why was he so uncomfortable? He was meeting a couple of small-time crooks. He was the president of his own bank. He commanded a force of men that would liquefy these two thugs at his order. If one were to guess from the nance at the reception desk, Fish might even be a homosexual.

"You want some guns," Fish said.

"As many as you can get, small arms, heavy weapons. I'm sure Jo Jo has spelled all this out for you."

"Jo Jo couldn't spell cat," Fish said, "if you gave him the C and the A. What do you want the weapons for?"

"There's no need for you to know."

"I like to know," Fish said. "You want to do business

with me, you do it on my terms. What are you going to do
with the weapons?''

''We are a group of free men,'' Hasty said. ''Patriots.''

Fish smiled.

''I don't expect you to understand,'' Hasty said.

He could feel his face getting hot.

''Go on,'' Fish said.

''We know that the government is intent on destroying
us. We are ready for it. But we need weapons. Not only
for the moment but for the long struggle. We need to stock-
pile so that when they think they've confiscated our arms,
we can unearth a new supply and rise when they least expect it.''

Fish nodded slowly. He glanced once at Vinnie Morris,
and then back at Hasty.

''So, you're going to bury the guns?'' Fish said.

''Yes.''

Fish smiled.

''This got to do with an international Jewish conspiracy?'' he said.

''I know you're mocking, but you'll see. Jews, Catholics,
one-worlders, anybody who wishes us to give up our sov-
ereignty to a foreign power.''

''Like the Pope, or the UN,'' Fish said.

''Yes.''

Fish looked again at Vinnie Morris.

''See?'' Fish said. ''Didn't I say it would be worth it to
have him come in and see us.''

''That's what you said.''

Jo Jo didn't like the way this was going. He didn't have
any idea what Hasty was talking about. He never had
known why the Horsemen ran around in the woods with
guns. This was the first he'd heard about one-worlders,
whatever they were. But he knew Gino was having fun with

them, and it made him feel sweaty. For his part Hasty wasn't used to being laughed at. He wasn't sure how one was supposed to respond to being laughed at.

"Lot of unmarked UN helicopters hovering over, ah, where are you from again?"

"Paradise," Hasty said.

His face felt somewhat stiff.

"Ah yes," Fish said. "Paradise."

"I am doing business with you," Hasty said. His voice was hoarse and seemed hard to squeeze through his windpipe. "Admittedly. But you are also doing business with me, and goddamn it, if you don't want the business, just keep it up and I'll take my money somewhere else, where they don't have a damned fairy at the reception desk."

There was silence in the office for a long moment. Vinnie kept his blank stare on Jo Jo. Then Fish smiled slowly.

"He used the F word, Vinnie."

Vinnie Morris nodded without saying anything. His eyes steady on Jo Jo.

"Spunky devil, isn't he?" Fish said.

Vinnie shrugged.

"Well," Hasty said, hoarsely. "You want the business or not."

"Of course I do," Fish said. "Let's talk particulars."

chapter 38

Suitcase Simpson was blushing.

"Well, did you ever think of doing that?" Cissy Hath-away said.

They were sitting on the king-sized bed in a Holiday Inn in the middle of the afternoon drinking California champagne out of the little plastic glasses.

"Jesus, no," Simpson said. "Cissy, you got to understand, I haven't had that much experience, you know? I mean you weren't my first, but, well, I got a lot to learn."

"But you have youth," Cissy said. "And energy."

She drank champagne and refilled her plastic cup.

"Thank God," she said, "for energy."

Simpson blushed again and drank, as much to occupy his hands as any other reason. He didn't really like champagne. It was sour compared to Pepsi, and sweet compared to beer. He really liked beer better. Hell, he admitted to himself, he really liked Pepsi better. But sitting in a motel with a married woman you were about to screw, didn't seem the right time for Pepsi. Cissy was wearing a little black dress with thin straps over the shoulders and very high heels. She had gotten to the hotel first and he knew she had changed into these clothes. He could see the brown dress she'd worn hanging in the closet. The mirror in the bathroom was still misted so he knew she'd showered, which meant that she had put on the makeup just before he arrived. She'd brought the champagne too, and he knew she was paying for the room. He felt a little funny about not paying. But he didn't have all that much money, and she had tons. I guess my contribution is the energy, he thought.

"You love your husband?" he said.

Cissy widened her eyes slightly.

"Do I love Hasty," she said.

"I mean you sneak off with me every week. Maybe other people."

Cissy narrowed her eyes and smiled to suggest that maybe he was right.

"But you don't want a divorce or anything, right?"

"Divorce? No, I don't want to divorce Hasty. We have been together for twenty-seven years. He is worth a lot of money. We have a nice home. He is not demanding of my time, and we are comfortable with each other."

"So how come you cheat on him?" Simpson said.

He wished he hadn't said "cheat" as soon as it came out. But Cissy didn't seem to mind.

"Hasty is not passionate," she said. "I am."

"That's for sure," Simpson said.

Cissy smiled and looked at him sideways like Lauren Bacall.

"This week," she said, "I think we should experiment with positions."

He thought they'd already been doing that, but he didn't say so.

"Sure," he said.

chapter 39

They went north from Boston, over the Mystic River bridge, Hasty driving the big Mercedes, Jo Jo looming beside him. It was a high bridge and at the peak of its arch you could look east down the long harbor where the city seemed to rise directly from the water, or west, up the river where the vast Boston Edison plant sent white vapor into the bright blue air. Neither Hasty nor Jo Jo paid any attention to the view.

Jo Jo was worried about the way the meeting had gone with Gino. He was bothered by the crack about how he couldn't spell cat. It had been a mistake for Hasty to call the receptionist a fairy. He probably was. Gino was probably scoring him. But it wasn't smart to talk like that to a guy like Gino. He didn't like the way Vinnie Morris always watched him. He never looked at anyone else. Hasty had no idea what these people were like. If Gino simply nodded his head, Vinnie would have shot both of them dead. They always said with Vinnie at least it was quick. No lingering. No pain. One right between the eyes and sayonara. Hasty

didn't get that. Gino had laughed at them both. Jo Jo knew
that he had. But Hasty seemed to think he was some kind
of stand-up guy because he got to have war games behind
the high school every week or so. He wouldn't be so fucking stand-up if Vinnie put one right between Hasty's eyes.
Jo Jo didn't know what Gino would do, but he wasn't going
to let that fairy remark go. Jo Jo was willing to bet the
ranchos grande on that. He hunched the muscles in his
back, felt them swell and press against the fabric of his
shirt. He often did that when he was scared. Made him feel
impregnable. As if the wall of muscle he'd created could
keep him safe.

Hasty felt good about the way he'd stood up to Gino
Fish. You have to be firm. And he was pretty sure they
knew that he was firm. He wasn't just some suburban
banker in over his head. He commanded armed men. Once
they realized who they were dealing with, Fish had been
as nice as pie. Good meeting, Hasty thought. The arms deal
seemed firm and Freedom's Horsemen could at last be fully
combat-ready. He couldn't stave off what was to come,
perhaps, but, properly armed, he and his men could keep
their little piece of America safe and free. They went over
the crest of the bridge, where the toll booths had been before it was toll-free northbound, and sloped down toward
Chelsea. Hasty needed to clear Tammy Portugal from the
agenda. He could not have his life's work contaminated by
a mercenary woman, just as his life's work was to reach
fulfillment. He was a little worried about the new chief.
Jesse didn't seem to be what he was supposed to be when
Hasty hired him. He seemed to have his drinking under
control. He seemed to be a lot tougher and maybe a lot
smarter than they had thought he would be when he had
sat in the hotel room in Chicago smelling of booze, trying
not to slur his speech. But that wasn't clear yet, and aside

from manhandling Jo Jo, which Hasty had actually rather enjoyed, Stone hadn't gotten in the way, and maybe would not. If he did he could be dealt with. If one were steadfast, one could deal with what came along. It was the girl that needed tending. He knew it was as much his fault as hers, his own weakness, to throw himself into the arms of this cheap tramp, like he had. But he was a man, and a man needed things. Cissy seemed unable to give him those things. He didn't know why, and after a while had stopped thinking about it. Women were women. So he'd made a mistake, but he could rectify it.

He glanced over at Jo Jo sitting vastly in the passenger side of the big Mercedes. Someday, perhaps, when he was no longer of use, he might be rectified as well. But not yet. For all his loutish stupidity he was handy.

They reached the flat where the roadway curved through Chelsea before it split off to go north along Route 1 or east along the Revere Beach Parkway.

"Jo Jo," Hasty said. "I need you to fix something for me."

Chapter 40

Michelle Merchant was smoking dope with some friends on the low stone wall of the historic burial ground opposite the town common. They liked to sit there and freak out the adults. The adults retaliated through the selectmen who posted "No Loitering" signs and insisted that the Paradise police enforce them. Michelle was seventeen. She had dropped out of school after tenth grade and spent as much time as possible on the cemetery wall.

When Jesse Stone pulled his unmarked car up onto the grass beside them, the two boys Michelle was sitting with got up and moved sullenly away. Michelle did not. She took a last long drag on her joint, and dropped it in the street and scuffed it out with the heel of her red sneaker, looking all the time straight at Jesse as he got out of the car and walked toward her.

"You gonna bust me, Jesse?"

She put a heavy stress on the name, to remind him that she was not speaking respectfully to an officer of the law.

"Probably not," Jesse said.

He sat down beside her on the stone wall.

"How you doing?" he said.

Michelle snorted, as if the question were too stupid to answer. Jesse nodded as if she had answered. The kids who had moved sullenly off lingered now, near the shopping center, watching. The traffic was sparse at midmorning, and the bird noise was easily audible in the burial ground behind them. It was late in September and the leaves had just begun to turn on some of the early trees, showing a touch of yellow or red against the still predominant green. Jesse was quiet. Michelle looked at him sideways, puzzled, annoyed, and stubborn. She was a small girl with a thin face that would have been pretty had it not been so empty. There was a streak of lavender in her blond hair, and her fingernails were painted black. She wore jeans and red sneakers and a blue sweater with the sleeves too long so that only the tips of her fingers were visible. She had a small gold bead in one nostril.

She struggled to be as quiet as Jesse, but she couldn't.

"You going to run me off the wall or what?" she said.

"No," Jesse said.

"So how come you're sitting here?"

"I was thinking what a waste of time this deal is for both of us," Jesse said.

"What deal."

"You sit on the wall and smoke dope. I chase you off. You come back. I chase you off. You come back. It's a waste of my time and yours."

"I'm not wasting my time," Michelle said.

"Really?"

"Really. It's a free country. I should be able to do what I want."

"And this is what you want?" Jesse said. "Sit on the wall and smoke dope."

"You can't prove I'm smoking dope."

"Doesn't matter."

"So why don't you leave me alone then?"

"Why don't you go to school?"

"School sucks," Michelle said.

Jesse grinned.

"Babe, you got that right," he said. "You know that Paul Simon song, 'When I think back on all the crap I learned in high school/It's a wonder I can think at all'?"

"Who's Paul Simon?"

"A singer. Anyway, yeah, school sucks. It's one of the great scams in American public life. On the other hand, most people grind through it. How come you don't?"

"I don't have to, I'm seventeen."

"True," Jesse said.

They were both quiet for a time. Michelle kept looking at Jesse as covertly as she could.

"My sister says she sees you sometimes down the Gray Gull having drinks," she said.

"Un huh."

"So how come that's okay and smoking dope isn't?"

"It's legal and smoking dope is illegal."

"So that makes it right?" Michelle said.

"Nope, just legal and illegal."

Michelle opened her mouth and then closed it. She was trying to think. Finally she said, "Well, that sucks."

Jesse nodded.

"Lot of things suck," he said. "After a while you sort of settle for trying not to suck yourself, I guess."

"By pushing kids around?" Michelle said.

Jesse turned his head slowly and held her gaze for a moment.

"Am I pushing you around, Michelle?"

She shrugged and looked absently at the white meeting house across the street.

"What do you think you'll be doing in ten years?" Jesse said.

"Who cares?" Michelle said.

"Me," Jesse said. "You ever see any thirty-year-old people sitting on the wall here, smoking dope?"

Michelle gave a big sigh.

"Oh please," she said, drawing out the second word.

Again Jesse nodded.

"Yeah," he said. "I know. Lectures suck too."

She almost smiled for a moment, and then looked even more sullen to compensate. The boys by the shopping center had tired of watching them and drifted off. On the front porch of the town library, across the common, a young woman with a small child clinging to her skirt, and another on her hip, was sliding books into the library return slot. Jesse wondered briefly when she got time to read.

"You think I'm going to end up like her?" Michelle said, nodding at the woman.

"No," Jesse said.

"Well, I'm not," Michelle said.

Jesse was quiet.

"So what about right and wrong?" Michelle said after a time.

"Right and wrong?"

"Yeah. You said stuff was just legal or illegal. Well, what about it being right or wrong? Doesn't that matter?"

"Well, I'm not in the right or wrong business," Jesse said. "I'm in the legal and illegal business."

"Oh, that's a cop-out," she said. "You just don't want to answer."

"No, I don't mind answering," Jesse said. "That was

part of my answer. There's something to be said for trying to do what you're paid to do, well.''

He was aware that she was suddenly looking at him directly.

''And sometimes that's the best you can do. The other thing is that most people don't have much trouble seeing what's right or wrong. Doing it is sometimes complicated, but knowing the right thing is usually not so hard.''

''You think so,'' Michelle said in a tone that said she didn't.

''Sure. You and I both know, for instance, that sitting on the wall all day smoking grass isn't the right thing for you to do with your life.''

''Who the hell are you to say what's right for me?'' Michelle said.

''The guy you asked,'' Jesse said. ''And chasing you off the wall is obviously not the right way to help you do the right thing.''

''So why the hell are you sitting here blabbing at me?'' Michelle said.

Jesse smiled at her.

''Trying to do the right thing,'' he said.

Michelle stared at him for a long moment.

''Jesus Christ,'' she said. ''You're weird.''

Jesse took a business card out of the pocket of his white uniform shirt and gave it to Michelle.

''You need help sometime,'' Jesse said, ''you can call me.''

Michelle took the card, as if she didn't know what it was.

''I don't need any help,'' she said.

''You never know,'' Jesse said and stood up. ''It's what else we do,'' Jesse said, and turned and walked back to his car.

She stared at him as he walked and watched the car as it pulled away. She watched it up Main Street until it turned off onto Forest Hill Avenue and out of sight. Then she looked at the card for a moment and put it into the pocket of her jeans.

Chapter 41

The disk jockey at the 86 Club wore a ruffled white shirt and a tuxedo vest with silver musical notes embroidered on it. He played records and did some patter but the noise with or without the music was so loud in the low room that no one could hear what he said. A few people danced, but most of them were sitting and drinking at tiny tables, jammed into the space in front of the long bar.

Tammy Portugal was alone, crowded onto a barstool, drinking a Long Island iced tea and smoking Camel Lights. She was wearing tight tapered jeans and spike heels and no stockings and a short-sleeved top that exposed her stomach. She had put on her best black underwear, too, in case anything developed. She had cashed her alimony check. There was money in her purse. The kids were at her mother's until tomorrow afternoon. She had a night, and half a day, when she could do anything or nothing, however she pleased.

Across the room she knew he had been looking at her and finally she let her eyes meet his. He looked like Arnold

Schwarzenegger, but handsomer. Fabio, maybe. Big muscles, long hair. His pale eyes had a dangerous look, she thought, and it excited her. She had seen him before on her night out, and she had watched him as he moved through the bar. Watched how careful other men were around him. Watched how many of the women looked after him as he walked past. She had, she knew, been thinking of him when she put on the good black underwear. She wondered if he was gentle in bed, or rough. She felt the sudden jolt along her rib cage as she realized he was walking toward her.

"Hi," he said. "What are you drinking?"

She liked the way he came on to her. He didn't ask if she was alone. A man like him wouldn't have to worry about whether she was alone. If he wanted her, he'd take her.

She told him what she was drinking, trying to keep her voice down. She liked the throaty sound one of the actresses made on one of her soap operas, and she practiced it sometimes with a tape recorder when she was alone.

He wedged his body into the crowded bar, making room beside her where there had been none. "Seven and ginger," he said to the bartender, "and a Long Island iced tea."

He leaned one elbow on the bar and looked straight on into her eyes. She swiveled on her barstool, as if to talk with him better, and managed it so that her knee would press against his thigh.

"I've seen you before," he said to her.

They had to lean very close to each other to be heard over the clamor of the hot room.

"I'm out about once a week," she said, "looking for the right guy."

"Maybe you're in luck," he said.

"Maybe I am."

She tilted her head back a little and lowered her eyelids and gave him an appraising look.

"You must be single," he said. "I had something like you at home, I wouldn't let you out."

"Divorced," she said.

"Because?"

"Because my husband was a jerk."

"Was?"

"He's still a jerk," she said, "but he ain't my husband anymore."

"Kids?"

"Two. My mother's got them until tomorrow afternoon."

He nodded as if that answered the final question. He was wearing a dark blue polo shirt and white pants and boat shoes with no socks. Everything fitted tightly over his obvious musculature, and when he raised his glass to drink, his bicep swelled as if it would burst the short sleeve.

The disk jockey said something into the microphone which nobody could hear, and played a record. She couldn't hear it but she knew it was slow because the few people on the floor were touch-dancing.

"Dance?" he said.

She slid off the barstool.

"Sure," she said.

There were two big speakers at opposite corners of the small dance floor and when they got onto the floor they could hear the music. It was slow. Pressed against him, she felt the tension building in her. She could feel the thick slabs of his muscles. Muscles where she didn't know people had muscles. They danced two numbers, his huge hand low on her back, pressing her steadily in against him.

"You're free until tomorrow afternoon," he said as the

second record stopped playing, and the DJ began his chatter while he cued a new record.

"As a bird," she said.

"You wanna go someplace?" he said.

"And do what?" she said, looking upward at him as seductively as she knew how. She had practiced that in the mirror at home.

"We could get naked," he said.

She giggled and thought about seeing that body without clothes on. It was a little frightening and a little enticing and she was interested in a way she didn't understand but which was not merely sexual. She giggled again.

"Yes," she said. "Let's go someplace and get naked."

chapter 42

Anthony DeAngelo had never seen a murdered person before. He'd seen a couple of people killed in car accidents, and he'd even done mouth-to-mouth on a guy who was having a heart attack and died while DeAngelo was working on him. But the naked woman in the junior high school parking lot was his first murder victim. There were bruises on her face, and her head was turned at an awkward angle. Someone had written SLUT in what looked like lipstick across her stomach. DeAngelo tried to look at her calmly as he called in on his radio. He didn't want the kids being herded past the scene by teachers to think he was frightened by it. But he was. This wasn't accidental death. This stiffening corpse lying naked in the dull mist, on the damp asphalt in the early morning, had died violently during the night at the hands of a terrible person. He didn't know exactly what he should do, standing there talking into his radio. He wanted to cover the poor woman but he didn't think he ought to disturb the crime scene. Rain wasn't heavy. Probably didn't bother her anyway. He wished Jesse would hurry up and get there. In the school the kids were crowded at the windows despite the best efforts of the teachers. The school bus driver who had spotted the body first was standing beside DeAngelo's cruiser. She looked for people to talk to, to tell about what she had seen and how she was the first to see it, and oh God, the poor woman! But DeAngelo was still on the radio and the junior high school staff was fruitlessly busy trying to protect the kids from seeing the corpse. He felt better when Jesse pulled up in the unmarked black Ford with the buggy whip antenna on the back bumper swaying in decreasing arcs as the car stopped and Jesse got out.

"Anthony," Jesse said.

He walked over and looked down at the body.

" 'Slut,' " he said.

"Yeah. Like the car. Like the cat," DeAngelo said.

Jesse nodded, still looking at her.

"Clothes?" he said.

DeAngelo shook his head. "I haven't seen any."

The town ambulance pulled into the parking lot and behind it Peter Perkins in his own car, a Mazda pickup. Two young Paradise firemen who doubled as EMTs got out and walked almost gingerly toward the crime scene. Peter Perkins got out of his truck. He was in jeans and a tee shirt with his gun strapped on and his badge on his belt. A thirty-five-millimeter camera hung around his neck. He went to the bed of his pickup and got his evidence kit. One of the EMTs knelt beside the body and felt for a pulse.

After a moment he said, "She's dead, Jesse."

"Un huh."

"What do you want us to do, Jesse?"

The EMT was not quite twenty-five. His name was Duke Vincent. Jesse played softball with him in the Paradise town league. Like DeAngelo, Vincent had seen death. But never murder. Vincent's voice was calm but soft, and Jesse knew he was feeling shaky. Jesse remembered the first time he'd seen it. It was a lot worse than this, a shotgun, close up, he remembered.

"You think her neck's broken, Dukie?" Jesse said.

Vincent looked at the corpse again. Jesse knew he didn't like it.

"I guess so," Vincent said.

"Yeah, me too," Jesse said. "Probably what killed her. You and Steve stand by with the ambulance for a while. We'll have the county M.E. look at her, and there'll be some state investigators along."

"Why did he write 'slut' on her, Jesse?" DeAngelo said.

"Maybe the word means something special to him," Jesse said.

"So is it the same guy that did the car and Captain Cat?"

"Might be," Jesse said.

"But wouldn't he know that it would connect him to the other crimes?"

Jesse smiled to himself at the TV locution his own officer was speaking in the presence of a murdered person. There were so many cop shows. It was hard for real cops not to start talking like them.

"Might want us to see the connection," Jesse said. "Or it might be someone else who wants us to think there's a connection."

Most of the rest of the force had showed up, some in uniform, some dressed for off duty. For all of them it was their first murder and they stood by a little uneasily watching Jesse, except for Peter Perkins, who had stretched his crime-scene tape around the murder scene, and was now taking pictures. The other cops looked as if they envied him having something to do.

"John," Jesse said. "You and Arthur put up some horses and keep people behind them."

"There's nobody around, Jesse."

"There will be," Jesse said. "Suitcase, you talk to the bus driver. Get everything she saw, thinks, hopes, dreams, whatever. Let her talk, pay attention. Ed, go in, talk to the principal. We're going to have to talk with the kids, maybe we can do it class by class, find out if they saw anything. We also may have to search the school."

"For what?" Burke said.

"Her clothes," Jesse said. "I'd like to find her clothes."

"Maybe he killed her someplace else and brought her body here nude," Burke said.

"We find the clothes, it'll help us decide that," Jesse said. "The rest of you spread around and look for her clothes or anything else. Tire tracks, bloodstains. He whacked her around pretty good. But there's no blood on the pavement."

"Rain might have washed it," DeAngelo said.

"Watch where you walk, go in wider and wider circles around the body. Maybe he hit her with something. See if you see anything. Anthony, start knocking on doors, see if anybody lives around here heard anything, or saw a car come into the school parking lot during the night."

The cops did as they were told. They were happy to be given direction, happy to do something but stand and look at the battered body.

"Dukie," Jesse said. "You can cover her. And pull the ambulance up so it screens her from the school. Doesn't do the kids much good to look out at her all morning."

Behind him in the parking lot, parents had begun to arrive. Already they had heard of a murder at the junior high school. Already they were there to see about their children. Jesse knew he'd have to talk with them. He knew a number of them would want to take their children home. He would like to have kept all the kids here until they had been questioned, but he knew he couldn't and knew that trying to would accomplish nothing beyond his own aggravation. Other people were gathering too. Not parents. Just people from the town, who, as the word spread, began to gather silently as close to the scene as they could. He saw Hasty Hathaway moving importantly through the gathering crowd with a plastic rain guard over his snap-brimmed hat. Probably wearing rubbers too, Jesse thought. Jo Jo Genest was there, hatless, in a crinkle finish trench coat. Jesse's glance paused on Jo Jo. Jo Jo returned it and smiled. Jesse's glance lingered a thoughtful moment and then moved on. He looked for Abby, but didn't see her. Past the silent crowd Jesse saw the medical examiner's car arriving, and behind it an unmarked state car. That would be the homicide guy.

Hathaway cleared the crowd and spoke to John DeLong guarding the barriers, and came on past him toward Jesse. I was right, Jesse thought. He's wearing rubbers.

chapter 43

Jesse sat in his office at midnight with a state police captain named Healy, sipping single-malt scotch from a water glass. Healy had taken the bottle from his briefcase when he came in and set it on Jesse's desk. The green-shaded desk lamp was the only light in the room. Outside the rain continued to mist down, too light for a drizzle, too heavy for a fog. The day's dampness seemed to have incorporated the dampness of the shore and the scent of seawater was strong even though they were a half mile from the harbor. Except for the voices and the occasional creak of a chair when one of them shifted in it, the silence in the office and outside had the kind of weight that existed only in the middle of the night in a small town. Healy was about Jesse's size but older, and a little thinner. His short hair was gray. He had on a gray suit, and a blue oxford shirt, and a red and blue striped tie. His black shoes were still polished this late in the day.

"You're the homicide commander," Jesse said.

"Yeah."

Healy's eyes had the flat look that Jesse had seen before. The eyes had seen everything and believed nothing. There was neither compassion nor anger in Healy's eyes, just a kind of appraising patience that formed no prejudgments and came to conclusions slowly. Occasionally when Jesse had come unexpectedly upon his reflection in a mirror or a darkened window, he had seen that look in his own eyes.

"So how come we draw you?" Jesse said.

Healy shrugged, sipped a small taste of the scotch, held the glass up to the light for a moment, and looked at the color.

"I used to work up here, Essex County DA's office. I live in Swampscott. So when the squeal came in I thought I'd swing by myself."

"Chance to get out of the office for a while," Jesse said. Healy nodded.

"Don't like the office," he said. "But I like the Captain's pay. Somebody told me you used to work homicide."

"L.A.," Jesse said. "Downtown."

"You know Cronjager out there?"

"Yep."

"So how'd you end up here?"

"Cronjager fired me. I was drinking on the job. This was the only job I got offered."

"How you doing now? Tonight excluded."

"I'm not drinking on the job," Jesse said.

"It's a good start," Healy said. "Heard you used to play ball."

"People do talk. Yeah, I was a shortstop. Dodger organization. Tore up my shoulder playing at Pueblo." Jesse shrugged. "Sayonara."

"I was a pitcher," Healy said. "Phillies signed me."

"And?"

"And the war came and I went. When I came home there

was the wife, the kids. I went on the cops."

"Miss it?" Jesse said.

"Every day," Healy said.

Jesse nodded. They were both silent for a moment. Healy took another small sip of scotch.

"So what have we got," he said.

"Got her I.D.'d," Jesse said. "Name's Tammy Portugal. Twenty-eight years old, divorced, two kids. Lived on the pond, other end of town. Left the kids with her mother yesterday afternoon, her alimony check always arrived on this date and the mother always took the kids, give her daughter a break, let her spend some of the alimony. Tammy was supposed to pick the kids up at noon today." Jesse glanced at his watch without really seeing it. "Yesterday. When she didn't show, the mother called us."

"Where's the husband?" Healy said.

"Don't know. Mother says he took off two years ago, right after the divorce. Says he always sends his alimony on time. But she doesn't know where he is."

"And the alimony check came today?"

"Yesterday." Again Jesse did the automatic glance at his watch. "Day before, actually."

"So she must have cashed it before she went out," Healy said.

"Yeah, and we could trace it. We'll check on that in the morning. We didn't get all of this until the bank closed. Even if she cashed it someplace else," Jesse said, "it will probably clear through the Paradise Bank, and the president is one of our selectmen."

"So he'll be cooperative."

"Probably," Jesse said.

Healy looked at him and waited. Jesse didn't add to the "probably." Healy let it slide. Jesse saw him let it slide, and also saw him file it away. Stone has some reservations about the bank president.

"You got her movements established, prior to death?" Healy said.

"Not yet. Thought the M.E. might help us on that."

"He might," Healy said. "She had drunk a fair amount of alcohol."

"I figured. And, single kid, twenty-eight, night out, she probably went to a place where she could meet guys."

"Narrows it down," Healy said.

"Well, maybe it does," Jesse said. "I'm guessing she didn't go clubbing in Boston. Not many people from this town go into Boston."

"Christ no," Healy said. "Must be fifteen miles away."

"This is an insular town," Jesse said. "She went clubbing, I figure she went around here."

"Including Route One?"

"Yeah."

"So you only got about five hundred clubs to check."

"We're talking to people who knew her. She may have had some favorite places. Most women don't like to go to a strange place alone. She probably went to the same places or a few of the same places every time."

"I can give you some help along Route One," Healy said.

"I'll take it. What else the M.E. say."

"Not too much that you couldn't see looking at her. She'd been raped. She'd been beaten with a blunt instrument, possibly a human fist. Her neck was broken, which is almost certainly the cause of death. She wasn't killed here. There's no blood at all at the scene and there would have been. The word 'slut' was written on her with lipstick, probably hers, it matches traces found on her lips. You got any thoughts about 'slut'?"

"You know it was spray-painted on one of our squad cars, and later the station-house cat was killed and a sign was attached to it that said 'slut.'"

"Sometimes words have private meanings to the people who use them," Healy said, "especially if they're nuts."

Jesse nodded.

"You figure it's the same person?" Healy said.

"Be a logical guess, and if it is it may not be about the victims, it may be about us," Jesse said.

"Or it's a copycat who wants you to think that?"

"You believe that?" Jesse said.

"I don't believe anything, but it's possible."

"Yeah, but is it likely. This has got every mark of an unpremeditated act of rage or sadism or insanity or all of the above. It doesn't have any hint of some kind of calculating smart guy who pretends to be part of the other deal to confuse us."

"Unless the guy is even smarter than that and knows you'll think that way."

"How long you been a cop?" Jesse said.

"Forty-one years," Healy said.

"Got me by some, but in forty-one years how many criminal masterminds you run into on a murder case?"

Healy smiled.

"About the same number you have," he said.

"Which is the same number of big-league at-bats we got between us," Jesse said.

"Which is zip," Healy said.

They both sipped whiskey in the dim office.

"You got a suspect?" Healy said.

"Not based on evidence."

"But you got somebody in mind."

Jesse shrugged.

"Got a guy in town with maybe a grudge against the

department, or probably, more accurate, a grudge against me.''

''Not many towns don't have somebody like that,'' Healy said. ''Sort of goes with police work.''

''I know,'' Jesse said.

''And you don't care to tell me his name, anyway,'' Healy said.

Jesse shrugged.

''Doesn't seem right,'' he said. ''Even to you. I got absolutely nothing to back it up.''

Healy nodded. ''You know the former chief here?''

''No.''

''You know he was murdered out in Wyoming?''

''Boy, you don't miss much,'' Jesse said.

''I like to read the stuff that comes through,'' Healy said.

''Got blown up,'' Jesse said. ''On the road to Gillette.''

''Town like this doesn't have a murder a decade,'' Healy said. ''You get two in a month.''

''Hate coincidence,'' Jesse said. ''Don't you?''

''Yeah. You see any connection?''

''Not yet,'' Jesse said.

''But you're looking.''

''I'm going to.''

Healy nodded again.

''Course sometimes there are coincidences,'' he said.

''We're keeping it in mind,'' Jesse said.

Healy nodded, finished his drink, refilled Jesse's glass, and put the bottle in his briefcase.

''I'll be in touch,'' he said.

chapter **44**

Hasty Hathaway wandered into Jesse's office and closed the door behind him and came and sat with one leg on the corner of Jesse's desk.

"What did that state police captain want?" he said.

"And good morning to you too, Hasty."

Hathaway shook his head as if he had water in his ear.

"What did he want?"

"His name's Healy," Jesse said. "He's the state homicide commander. He wanted to talk about Tammy Portugal's murder."

Hathaway shook his head again, slowly this time.

"We don't want that, Jesse," he said. "We solve our own problems here."

"I haven't got the forensic resources for a full-fledged homicide investigation, Hasty. He does."

Hathaway reached over and gave Jesse a clap on the shoulder.

"We have every confidence in you and your men, Jesse,

we don't need the state government sticking its nose under the edge of our tent, so to speak.''

Jesse hated to be touched and he especially hated to be clapped on the shoulder.

"I'm a good cop," Jesse said. "But a good cop is mostly the product of a good support system. We're not geared for a homicide investigation.''

"We don't want that policeman nosing into our business," Hathaway said. His geniality was dissipating.

"Well, I'm not sure there's much to be done about that," Jesse said. "Even if I didn't want him, which I do, I got no way to keep him out.''

Hathaway was silent. One leg slung over the corner of Jesse's desk, he drummed quietly with the fingers of his right hand on the desktop. His face seemed to have tightened in on itself. The lines had deepened and the pale blue eyes seemed smaller. He looked feral.

"Jesse, you need to be clear about things," Hathaway said finally. "You are either with us, or you are not. We value loyalty above all things. It was ultimately Tom Carson's failure.''

"Whatever happened to him," Jesse said.

Hathaway glanced away from Jesse and stared out the window.

"We had to ask for Tom's resignation," Hathaway said.

"Because?''

"Because his loyalty was in question.''

"Loyalty to who?" Jesse said. His voice was gentle and there was nothing in it other than interest.

"To us," Hathaway said. "To the people of this town who matter.''

"Like you," Jesse said.

"Yes. And Lou Burke, and everyone in this town who cares about preserving democracy at the grass roots.'' Hathaway's voice seemed to scrape out of his throat.

"So where is Carson now?"

"I have no idea," Hathaway said.

"Me either."

Hathaway looked hard at Jesse, but there was nothing on his face, nothing in his voice, except the hint of something seething behind the bow tie and glasses.

"I don't want to hear that you are opening up to this state policeman in any way," Hathaway said finally.

"The surest way to bring them down here in droves," Jesse said, "is to try and keep them out."

"You don't have to keep them out. But you can stone-wall them."

"You haven't had much dealing with people like Healy," Jesse said. "I have. He's been in this business forty years. He's taken guns away from hopheads and chil-dren away from molesters. He's seen every mess, heard every lie. He's been there and seen it done. You can't stonewall him any more than you can scare him."

"So we throw the town secrets open to him?"

"No, but we let him help us catch the guy who killed that girl," Jesse said.

Hathaway sat silent as a stone on the corner of the desk, shaking his head slowly.

"A damned divorcee," he said finally, "out to get laid."

"Or the mother of two kids," Jesse said, "out for the evening. All depends on which truths you tell, I guess."

Hathaway continued to sit and shake his head. Then he rose abruptly and walked stiffly out of Jesse's office. Jesse watched the empty doorway that Hathaway had gone through for a while, his lips pursed slightly. He realized his jaw was clamped very tight and he opened it and worked it back and forth a little to relax it. He breathed in deeply and let it out slowly, listening to his own exhale, easing the tightness along his shoulders, relaxing his back.

"And Lou Burke," Jesse said aloud.

He got up and went to the file cabinet and got out Burke's personnel file and took it back to his desk and began to thumb through it.

Chapter 45

Finding Tammy Portugal's husband was easy. The alimony check had been cashed at the Paradise Bank and the address was printed on it. Jesse drove out to Springfield and talked with him at 10:30 a.m. in a coffee shop on Sumner Avenue at an intersection called the X. The restaurant was out of the 1930s. Glass brick, and a jukebox near the kitchen.

"I'm a loser," Bobby Portugal said to Jesse. "Tammy thought she was marrying a winner, but that was just my bullshit. I been a loser since I graduated high school."

Portugal was medium height and husky. His dark hair was longish and he had a neatly trimmed beard. He wore a Patriots warm-up jacket over a gray tee shirt and jeans.

"We went together in high school. I was a big jock in high school. Running back, point guard. She thought I was a big deal."

The waitress brought an order of English muffins for Jesse and a fried-egg sandwich for Portugal.

"Made All–North Shore League, junior and senior year,

football and basketball. Got a partial scholarship to B.C.''

Portugal paused while he peeled off the top layer of toast and poured ketchup on the fried egg.

''And when you got there,'' Jesse said, ''everybody had made all-league and a lot of the leagues were faster than yours.''

''You better believe it,'' Portugal said.

He took a bite of his sandwich and put it down while he pulled a paper napkin from the dispenser on the table and wiped ketchup from the corner of his mouth.

''I lasted six weeks,'' he said. ''And quit. Went to work for the highway department in town. Thought I was making a ton. Tammy and I were still going out, and she got pregnant, and . . .'' Portugal shrugged and shook his head. He picked up his sandwich and held it for a moment and put it down. His eyes filled and he turned his head away from Jesse.

''Take your time,'' Jesse said.

Portugal continued to sit with his head turned. Without looking he pushed his plate away from him. Jesse waited. Portugal took in a deep breath and let it out. He did it again. Then he straightened his head and looked at Jesse. His eyes were wet.

''We got married,'' he said. ''She still thought I was a big deal. Nineteen, money in my pocket, a star in the Paradise softball league. She was thrilled to be marrying Bobby Portugal.''

Portugal's voice was perfectly calm. Remote, Jesse thought, as if he were talking about people he knew casually, and found mildly interesting. Except that he was teary.

''And then we had the babies and two hundred and fifty bucks a week didn't look like so much. I tried selling Amway for a while. That was a joke. I tried insurance, got through the training program and got fired. I didn't earn much money, but I played a lotta ball with the guys and drank a lotta beer. Finally she dumped me. You blame her?''

''What are you doing out here?'' Jesse said.

''Security guard. Downtown at the big mall. When I get off work, I got a room with a sink in the corner and bathroom down the hall. You ever play ball?''

''Some,'' Jesse said. ''Why Springfield?''

''I had to get away from Paradise,'' Portugal said. ''This seemed far enough. Nobody ever heard of me here.''

''Tell me where you were Tuesday night.''

''Did my shift at the mall till ten. Had a date. Girl works at the mall. Got home around three-thirty, she spent the night. That when she was killed? Tammy? Tuesday night?''

''Can I talk with the woman you dated?''

''You gotta?''

''Be good to know what you were doing that period of time.''

''Yeah, if you gotta. But can you be sort of cool about it? Her old man is a long-distance trucker. When he's out of town we . . . we got a little arrangement.''

''I can talk to her at work,'' Jesse said.

''Okay. Her name's Rosa Rodriguez, she works in the little candy kiosk in the mall.''

''Can you give me the address of the mall?'' Jesse said.

Portugal told him and Jesse wrote it down.

''You own a car?''

''No. With my alimony? Mostly I ride the bus. Buses are pretty good here. I guess there's no more alimony, is there?''

''Child support,'' Jesse said.

He nodded.

''They okay?'' he said.

''Your children?''

"Yeah."

"They're with your mother-in-law."

Portugal nodded.

"You wanna give me the name of your supervisor, please," Jesse said.

Portugal told him.

"What time you get to work on Wednesday?"

"Ten a.m. About five hours' sleep. Man!" Portugal shook his head. "You think I done it?"

"Not if your story checks," Jesse said. "She was out clubbing, probably, Tuesday night, there was alcohol present. You know any of her favorite places?"

Portugal shook his head.

"No favorites," he said. "I know she used to go out once a week, but she'd never go the same place. Didn't want to get a reputation, you know. Bad for the kids, she said. So she wouldn't go to any place regular. She'd always go where nobody knew her. She was a good mother, man."

"Sorry to have to ask, but did she go to meet men, you think?"

"Yeah, sure, why wouldn't she? We was divorced. She was free. She liked sex, I know that. I mean that's pretty much what we had was sex, and after a while, when I wasn't working and didn't do much but play ball and drink with the guys, we didn't even have that."

"Because she didn't want to?"

"Because I wasn't much good," Portugal said.

"Too much defeat," Jesse said.

"And beer," Portugal said. "Way too much beer."

"You got an arrangement with the trucker's wife, though," Jesse said, and smiled. "Looks like you're making a comeback."

Portugal shrugged.

"Arrangement is just that, we both like to get laid, it don't mean much."

"You have any thoughts on who might have killed your ex-wife?"

Portugal's eyes teared again. He lowered his head.

"No," he said.

They talked in the anachronistic restaurant for nearly an hour. Jesse asked about male friends of the deceased, about female friends. Had she ever worked anyplace? Had she any enemies? Had he any enemies? Did she have debts? Did he? How often did he see her? When had he last seen her? When it was through, Jesse paid the small bill and they left the restaurant. The fried-egg sandwich remained uneaten on Portugal's plate.

"I wasn't such a loser," Portugal said, "she'd be all right. She figured she was marrying Mr. Big, guy that was going somewhere. And look where I took her."

"Maybe you're taking on more than you need to," Jesse said.

"And maybe I ain't," Portugal said.

Jesse had nothing else to say about that and he got in his car and drove away while Portugal stood on the corner looking down Sumner Avenue at Jesse's receding car.

chapter 46

There was a harvest fair on the common. It meant that tables were set up outdoors and people sold handicrafts and bakery products and pumpkins to benefit the Paradise Woman's Club. Inside the meeting Cissy Hathaway in a mop hat and apron was selling cider and donuts. Jesse stood with Abby against the far wall, near the door.

"The Paradise Woman's Club," Abby said. She shook her head. "Makes me blush."

"Maybe it has evolved into a powerful force for feminism," Jesse said.

"And maybe pigs fly," Abby said.

"And whistle while they do it," Jesse said.

They got in line for cider. In line ahead of them was Jo Jo Genest, massive and alien in the Saturday-morning suburban crowd. When it was his turn he lingered at the counter talking to Cissy. Jo Jo stayed too long. The line built up behind him with people looking toward the front to see what the holdup was. Jesse watched Cissy as she talked to Jo Jo. Her body seemed to lose some of its stiffness and her pale face seemed to gain color. She shifted behind the cider table in a way that made her hips move. Jo Jo finally moved on, the crowd parting carefully as he moved ponderously through it. He didn't look at Jesse and Cissy's eyes followed him before she turned back to the next customer.

When it was his turn Jesse ordered two ciders and two donuts, paid for them, and carried them away from the table to where Abby was standing.

"She's not as mousy as she looks," Jesse said.

"Cissy?"

"Un huh."

Abby looked at him as if he were crazy, as they walked across the common toward the wall across the street where the burnout kids usually sat.

"How could she be more mousy?" Abby said.

They sat together on the stone wall, where they could watch the people.

"I'm telling you, did you see her get almost wiggly when Jo Jo bought some cider?"

"Oh come on."

"I'm telling you, there's something there."

"You can tell by just looking."

"Absolutely," Jesse said. "I am wise in these matters."

"And why is that?"

"Because I am blessed with a penis," Jesse said.

"Yeah, and you think with it," Abby said. "Like every other man I know."

Jesse ate some donut and took a sip of cider. The leaves had begun to gather on the ground, yellow mostly, but with enough red and partial green to give it the New England effect. The smell of them mixed with the smell of the ocean. The ocean smell was so pervasive, Jesse thought, that unless it were offset by something else you didn't notice it.

"Any progress on the killing?" Abby said.

"Not in the sense that you mean," Jesse said.

"What other sense is there?"

"Well, like any investigation, each time you eliminate a suspect that's progress. You've narrowed the pool, so to speak. But progress in the sense of a solid lead to who did it, no."

"Who have you eliminated?"

"Her ex-husband. He's got a verifiable alibi for the time she was killed and several hours each side of it."

"And I suppose the ex-husband would always be the prime suspect in a case like this."

Jesse nodded.

"We like to start simple," he said.

"So has the pool now narrowed to everybody but her ex?"

"Well," Jesse said, "sort of. But there's odd-looking bits and pieces sort of floating up, nothing like a nice hard clue or anything, just odd things that don't look like they're part of the soup."

"Like what?"

Jesse shrugged and finished his first donut.

"You know the old instruction on how to sculpture a horse out of granite. You take a piece of granite and chip away everything that doesn't look like a horse."

"What the hell kind of answer is that?" Abby said.

Jesse drank some cider.

"I was trying to be folksy," he said.

Abby leaned away from him and stared at his face.

"Jesse, you don't want to tell me," she said.

"Talking about a case doesn't usually do the case much good," he said.

"Goddamn it," Abby said. "You don't trust me."

Jesse didn't say anything. The paper cup from which he'd drunk his cider was empty. He crumpled it and tossed it into a green trash barrel.

"Two," he said.

"Jesse, you can't not trust me."

He turned to look at her.

"Ab," he said. "I guess the ugly truth is, I don't trust anybody."

"For Christ's sake," she said.

"Nothing's quite what it seems to be around here," Jesse said. "Makes me careful."

"Including me?"

"Don't be hurt," he said. "It's just the way I have to be."

"I am hurt, but I'm also sad—for you. Not to trust me! You have to be able to trust somebody."

Jesse shrugged. He did trust someone. God help me, he thought, I guess I trust Jenn. He decided not to mention that. It wasn't an answer that would make Abby feel better.

"I didn't mean to hurt you," Jesse said.

Abby's eyes looked as if she might cry.

"I know," she said. "I know you've had a hard go and being a cop you've seen a lot of bad things."

Jesse put his hand out and patted her leg. He felt sorry that she was hurt, but it was an abstract sorry, more of an idea than a feeling. You need to be able to hear the truth, he thought. You can't hear the truth, you got nowhere to start.

Across the street, standing near a table where they were selling dolls made out of cornstalks and dressed in pink gingham, Jo Jo Genest stood and stared at Jesse. As if he felt the stare, Jesse looked up and met Jo Jo's gaze. Silently Jo Jo mouthed the word "slut." Jesse saw it and his eyes locked with Jo Jo's. He nodded slowly. Then Jo Jo spat and turned and walked slowly away. Jesse watched him go.

So I was right, Jesse thought. It's Jo Jo.

Abby was too involved in her own issues to see the interchange.

"I feel sort of foolish," she said softly, "being hurt and not being able to hide it. I really have a problem with being left out, and to have this relationship and to think you don't trust me . . ."

Jesse shifted his attention to her. He nodded gently.

"I know how you feel," he said. "I don't blame you. Maybe I'll be more and better later on. But right now, this is what you get."

"Yes," she said. "And this is a very nice man. But . . . oh hell," she said.

She stood up abruptly and began to cry. With her head down, trying to hide the fact that she was crying, she walked away briskly. Everybody's got baggage, Jesse thought. I just tripped over some of hers. He saw her get in her car and drive away. She had left her cider. He picked it up and drank some of it. The taste of her lipstick was on the cup. He drank the rest of her cider and crumpled the cup and shot it into the trash can. Outside shot is working. He nodded congratulations to himself.

"Okay, Jo Jo," he said softly. "No secrets between us."

Chapter 47

Jesse was in his office early when Suitcase Simpson, fresh off the three-to-seven shift, came to the doorway and stood.

"I, ah, got my report to make," Simpson said.

"Close the door," Jesse said.

Simpson closed it and came and sat in front of Jesse's desk. He took a small notebook from his shirt pocket and licked his thumb and opened it about five pages in. Jesse turned sideways and put one foot on the open desk drawer so that he could look out the window while he listened.

"I, ah, tried to be sort of cool about it," Simpson said. "You know, not like I was investigating or anything."

Jesse nodded.

"Best estimate is that about seventeen people applied for gun permits over the past five years that didn't get them," Simpson said. "Not all of this is firsthand, but that's what I heard from people who applied, or friends of people who applied, that kind of thing. So there's probably some I missed. But seventeen seems like a pretty solid low guess."

"Any of them Horsemen?" Jesse said.

"No."

"Surprise."

"Another thing," Simpson said. "Looking at the list, at least five people on it are Jews."

"Because the names sound Jewish?" Jesse said. "Or because you know it for a fact."

"That's why I said 'at least.' I know the five Jewish people."

"You got any idea how many Jewish-sounding names are on the membership list for Freedom's Horsemen?" Jesse said.

"Well, I never really thought about it," Simpson said.

"I have. I went through it a couple times. Want to guess?"

"None," Simpson said.

"Surprise."

Simpson sat back in his chair, holding his little blue notebook in his thick square hand, his forefinger keeping the place.

"Shit," he said.

"Yeah," Jesse said.

"I hate that," Simpson said. "I hate thinking stuff like this about my hometown."

"You don't have to think it about the town," Jesse said. "But you may have to think it about the Horsemen."

Simpson sat frowning. It looked odd. His big pink-cheeked baby face wasn't supposed to frown.

"What about us, Jesse? We don't have a Jewish cop."

"No blacks either," Jesse said.

"I know, but, hell, I don't think there's any black people in town."

"That would weed out a lot of applicants," Jesse said.

"But there's plenty of Jewish people in town. Christ,

there were tons of them in school with me."

"Who hired the force?" Jesse said.

"I don't know. Tom hired me. Selectmen approved."

"Which means Hathaway," Jesse said. "The other two go along with what Hasty decides."

"I guess so."

"I checked," Jesse said. "Tom hired everybody, with Selectmen approving, except Lou Burke. Lou was here before Carson came. Know any Jews who wanted to be cops?"

"Oh hell, Jesse, I don't know. I mean I never thought much about it. I never even noticed there were no Jews on the force until we started talking."

"So what do you think?" Jesse said.

"About what?"

"About all of this. No permits for people who aren't Horsemen. No permits for Jews. No Jews in the Horsemen. No blacks. No Jews."

"Oh hell, Jesse, I ain't a thinker. Jesus! I come on the cops because it was a nice job for a guy with no college. You know? Some prestige, some benefits. People pay attention to you. I can't figure out shit about Jews and gun permits and the damned Horsemen."

Jesse grinned.

"Don't kid me, Suit. You came on the cops because you were born to be a crime buster. Think about some things: Who runs the town?"

"Selectmen."

"All of them?"

"Well, no. Mr. Hathaway, really."

"Yes," Jesse said. "And who runs Freedom's Horsemen?"

"Hathaway."

"Right again. And, what is the connection between Freedom's Horsemen and the Paradise Police Department.''

Simpson sat back frowning, like a slow earnest kid trying to get the right answer. Then suddenly his face cleared and he sat up.

''Lou,'' he said.

Jesse nodded slowly.

''And does it appear the Freedom's Horsemen are influencing policy in the Paradise Police Department?''

''Not since you came, Jesse.''

''Before me?''

''Yes.''

They were quiet. Through the office window Jesse watched the yellow school buses pulling out of the town lot.

''What's this all mean, Jesse?''

Jesse kept looking at the school buses as they pulled out onto Main Street and peeled off in different directions. Then he swiveled his chair around so he could look at Simpson directly.

''Suit,'' he said. ''I don't know what it means exactly. But one thing I think it means is that we better not talk about this with anybody but you and me.''

''Not even the other cops?''

''No.''

''Jesse, I known some of these guys all my life.''

''Just you and me, Suit.''

Simpson nodded.

''Capeesh?'' Jesse said.

''Capeesh.''

Jesse nodded approvingly. Suitcase didn't know, and didn't need to know, yet, about Tom Carson's murder. He didn't need to know about Jo Jo's silent taunt at the Harvest Fair.

"I don't like all this," Simpson said. "All this stuff that isn't what it's supposed to be."

"I don't either, Suit, but I guess we're stuck with it. What do you know about Cissy Hathaway?"

The pink in Simpson's cheeks deepened and spread over his whole face.

"What do you mean?" he said.

"She fool around?"

Simpson was in full blush. He started to speak and stopped and shifted a little in his chair.

"Suit," Jesse said. "I watched her talk to Jo Jo at the Harvest Fair Saturday. I was asking about her and him."

Simpson settled into the chair. His face seemed to cool slightly.

"Gee, Jesse, I haven't heard a thing about that."

"But I'm missing something. What am I missing, Suit?"

Simpson shrugged.

"Come on, Suit. I asked you about Cissy Hathaway and you looked like you just swallowed a squirrel."

Simpson smiled. It was a complicated expression, Jesse thought. Uneasy, proud, confidential, evasive. He would not have thought Suitcase could feel that many things at the same time.

"Suit," Jesse said, "you been plonking Cissy Hathaway."

There was a long pause while Simpson looked around the room as if he were thinking about escape.

Then Simpson said, "Yes, sir. I have."

Chapter 48

Charlie Buck liked cowboy boots. He had never ridden a horse in his life, but he had seven pairs of cowboy boots. He liked the height they gave him. With his feet up on his desk he was admiring a new pair he was wearing for the first time, made from rattlesnake skin. He took a Kleenex from a box in the bottom left drawer of his desk, and rubbed a small stain off the toe of his right boot. It looked like a splash of coffee had dried on there. While he was doing this a uniformed deputy came in.

"Nice boots," the deputy said.

"Rattlesnake."

"I could see that. I got a guy downstairs, Charlie, wants to talk with somebody about the guy got blown up on Route Fifty-nine a while back."

"That'd be me," Charlie said.

He crumpled the Kleenex and put it in the wastebasket under his desk. Then he swung his boots down and stood up.

"Tell you anything else?" Charlie asked.

They started down the corridor to the elevator.

"Nope."

"What do you have him for?"

"Armed robbery. Him and another guy tried to knock over the bank at the shopping center down on South Douglas."

"You got him good?"

"Talk about a bad day," the deputy said. "Two of our guys walked in on him, going to cash their paychecks."

Charlie Buck smiled.

"So he hasn't got much room to bargain."

"He's a lot of priors. He's looking at twenty, easy," the deputy said.

They got in the elevator and started down.

"What's his name?" Charlie Buck asked.

"Matthew Ploughman. Says he's from Denver."

"He in the interrogation room?"

"Not yet. I didn't know if you'd want to talk with him."

"I'll go in," Charlie Buck said. "You bring him to me."

The interrogation room was small with gray cinder block walls and no windows, and only a one-way observation port in the door. There was a shabby maple table and two chairs. A sign on the wall read "Thank You For Not Smoking." Charlie went to the far end of the room and leaned on the wall. He waited silently while two deputies brought Ploughman in and left, closing the door behind them.

Ploughman was short and scrawny with a long beard and a lot of hair. His eyes were small and close together and his nose seemed insufficient compared to the rest of his face. He stood, not sure whether to sit, just inside the closed door.

"You got a smoke, man?" he said.

Buck nodded at the sign on the wall.

"Sit down," he said.

Ploughman pulled out one of the chairs and sat, his clasped hands resting on the table edge.

"What have you got for me?" Buck said.

"I can help you with that bomb killing on Route Fifty-nine," Ploughman said.

"Go ahead," Buck said.

"Do I get something back?"

Buck shrugged.

"Hey, I ain't trying for Eagle Scout, you know. I scratch your back, I want you to scratch mine."

"Matthew," Buck said. "You're looking at twenty years, maybe more. You and I are not negotiating as equals."

"Hey, don't I know it. I'm the one sitting in a holding cell with no cigarettes. But I can help you, and if I do, you could get me a break in court."

"Maybe."

"Lemme get my lawyer in here, we can work out some sort of deal."

Buck shook his head.

"You give me what you got, I like it, then we talk with your lawyer."

"I got a right to an attorney," Ploughman said.

"You been arrested, Matthew. You're not being questioned. You asked to talk with me. You want to talk, talk. Otherwise I go back upstairs and finish my coffee."

Ploughman was silent, the tip of his tongue ran back and forth across his lower lip. Buck waited a moment, then shrugged and started for the door. He knocked, and the door opened immediately.

"Wait," Ploughman said.

"For what," Buck said.

"I'll do it your way," Ploughman said.

Buck turned and walked slowly back to the end of the room and leaned on the wall. The door closed. Buck folded his arms on his chest.

"Go ahead," Buck said.

chapter 49

Jesse resisted the impulse to smile. "So," he said, "she fools around."

"She does with me, yes, sir."

Simpson was like a good boy in the principal's office.

"Stop calling me sir," Jesse said. "You think she fools around with anyone but you?"

"I don't know."

"How'd you and she get started?"

"Jeez, Jesse, I'm sorry, but I don't see where it's any of your business, you know?"

Jesse knew that Simpson was right. Unless it connected to something, Jesse had no business asking him personal questions. There wasn't any particular reason not to tell about Jo Jo. But Jesse didn't know his situation, didn't know quite what was going on, and when he found himself in circumstances like that his instinct was to close down, trust no one, and watch carefully. But he needed information, any information, and here was some and it might be helpful.

"I think Jo Jo killed the Portugal girl," Jesse said.

"You think he killed the girl?"

"Yeah, and he had to let me know it."

"He told you?"

"No, nothing I can arrest him for, but he told me."

"Why the hell would he do that?"

"Because it's about me and him," Jesse said. "He did the patrol car and he did Captain Cat, because I knocked him around in front of his wife."

"So why wouldn't he come straight after you?"

"Because he's afraid to. I'm a cop. I've got authority. I've got a gun. He assaults me and I can have him in jail."

"So he does stuff to embarrass you?"

"Yeah. Just like I embarrassed him. But it's no good if I don't know it's him, so he had to let me know."

"What'd he do?"

"He stood across the common from me and smiled and mouthed 'slut' at me."

"But that doesn't mean he did it. He could be ragging you about it even if he didn't."

"He did it," Jesse said. "I been at this too long to be wrong. He needed to tell me."

"So what's that got to do with Mrs. Hathaway?"

"Just before Jo Jo told me he did it, she was making goo-goo eyes at him over the cider table."

"That doesn't mean she's having an affair with him."

"It's not something you expect to see," Jesse said. "I see something I don't expect, I want to know about it. The fact that I opened the door and you were behind it is an accident."

Simpson sat and thought about this. Jesse waited. There's too much coming at him, Jesse thought. He doesn't know enough. He's not old enough yet. He wants to talk about it, hell, he's dying to, but he thinks it's dishonorable.

"I met Mrs. Hathaway at the Yacht Club," Simpson said. "Some kind of big wedding reception, I was doing a paid detail. She started talking to me, and at the end of the party she asked me to drive her home, because her husband was going out with a few of the men afterwards and she was tired. So I took her home and she asked me in and . . ."

"Okay," Jesse said. "I don't need the details. In effect she picked you up."

"Yes."

"And she was both affectionate and expert."

"You better believe it," Simpson said.

"Way to go, Cissy."

Simpson blushed more darkly.

"It's not like she was my first," he said. "But . . ."

"She was your first grown-up," Jesse said.

Simpson nodded.

"She's amazing," he said.

"I don't want to sound harsh here, Suit, but you might not be the only guy she ever picked up."

Simpson shrugged.

"She say anything about her husband?"

"She said they get along fine, but the fire's gone out."

"In his furnace only," Jesse said.

"I think she likes him though," Simpson said.

"You think he knows?"

Simpson shook his head.

"I don't know. She's not all that careful. I don't think he wants to know."

They were quiet, until Simpson said, "I still don't see what it's got to do with Tammy Portugal."

"I don't either, Suit. Maybe I will later. If she's connected to Jo Jo, and if Jo Jo did the Portugal girl . . . knowing is always better than not knowing."

"Always?" Simpson said.

"If you're a cop," Jesse said, "always."

Simpson sat for a time thinking. Jesse knew he didn't believe it was always better to know. But he was getting older every minute, and Jesse knew he would believe it, if he stayed with the cops.

Chapter 50

"You know about the militias," Ploughman said.

Buck nodded.

"Well, I know some guy from one of the militias, come to me, said he needed something done for a comrade in arms back east. That's what he called him, a comrade in arms."

Buck waited.

"They talk funny as a bastard, these guys, you ever notice? He says that there's a guy out here that threatens the comrade in arms back east and he has to be deactivated."

Ploughman waited for Buck's reaction. Buck had no reaction and Ploughman looked disappointed.

"Deactivated! They want him clipped, why don't they just say so, you know? So I tell this guy, No. I steal shit, but I don't kill people. I mean I'll carry a piece sometimes and make people think I would, you gotta make them think so, otherwise whaddya do, go in the bank and say gimme the money or I'll yell at you? But I never used it. I ain't a life taker. So I says no. And the militia guy kind of nods and looks at me like I'm a freaking enemy of the people and he says, well perhaps they will have to send someone.''

Ploughman stopped, looking pleased. Buck waited.

"And that's it," Ploughman said.

"That's what you got to buy off twenty years?"

"Hell, it's good. It tells you who ordered the hit and that they probably sent their own man. That's golden, for crissake.''

"Who did they send?" Buck asked.

"I don't know. They found out I wasn't the man, they didn't have anything else to say to me."

"You hear of them approaching anyone besides you?"

"No."

"How much were they going to pay you?"

"Five."

"Five thousand?"

"Yeah. They're all cheap bastards," Ploughman said. "I never saw a militia guy willing to go first class."

"Where in the east?"

"Didn't say. But I figure you guys know where he came from.''

Buck didn't answer. He stood with his arms folded, leaning on the wall, admiring his boots. Then he shifted his look to Ploughman.

"Tell your lawyer to see me," Buck said finally.

"Can you work something out?" Ploughman said.

"Have him call me," Buck said and went and knocked on the door.

chapter 51

Jesse was drinking scotch at the counter in his tiny kitchen when Jenn called.

"Is it later there or earlier," Jenn asked.

"It's eight o'clock where you are," Jesse said, "and eleven o'clock where I am."

"Are you drinking?"

"I'm having one scotch before bed," Jesse said.

"Just one?"

"Funny thing, Jenn. There's a lot of pressure here all of a sudden, and it seems like I don't need a drink. I haven't had more than one since the pressure began."

"Are you in trouble?"

"There is trouble," Jesse said. "I don't know yet if I'm in it."

"Can you tell me about it?"

"The trouble? Sure. The guy I replaced in this job got murdered in Wyoming. A woman got murdered and I think it's a way of getting at me."

"Was she close to you?"

"No, I didn't know her. But I know who did it, and I think he did it to challenge me."

"Are you scared?"

"Yes," Jesse said. "It's probably why I only have one drink."

"So you'll be ready?"

"Something like that."

"Can't you arrest the man?"

"I can't prove anything," Jesse said.

"Is the man in Wyoming part of this?"

"I don't know. It's crazy that a town like this, where there hasn't been a killing in fifty years, suddenly has two in a month. It makes you want to think they're connected."

"But you don't see a connection."

"No. There's some kind of militia group in town. Not like the National Guard, the other kind, and there's something funky about them."

"Do you like the men you work with?"

"I like them, but I don't know who I can trust."

"No one?"

"Well, I'm sort of forced to trust one of them. My guess is he's okay."

"What about that woman. Weren't you seeing a woman?"

"Abby. She's mad at me."

"Have you broken up?"

"I don't know. The last time I saw her she walked away in a huff."

"What is she mad at?"

"I wouldn't tell her about this."

" 'This' being the stuff you're telling me?"

"Yes. She said it meant I didn't trust her."

"Does that mean you trust me?"

"Yes."

"Even though . . . ?"

"Even though," Jesse said.

The phone line made phone line noise while both of them remained silent.

"You should come home," Jenn said after a time.

"I don't know where home is, Jenn."

"Maybe it's with me."

"I got too much going on, Jenn. I can't walk down that road right now."

"Even if you don't come home, why not get out of there? I've never heard you say you were scared before."

"I can't leave it, Jenn. You know when they hired me, I was drunk? Why would they hire a guy to be police chief who was drunk in the interview?"

"I don't know," Jenn said. "Maybe they didn't know you were drunk."

"They knew," Jesse said.

Again the cross-country silence broken by the low-voltage sound of the circuitry.

"I'm scared, Jesse."

Jesse didn't say anything.

"Will you call me soon," Jenn said.

"Yes."

"I mean tomorrow, every day, so I'll know you're okay?"

"Yes."

"I still love you, Jesse."

"Maybe," Jesse said.

"I do, Jesse. Do you still love me?"

"Maybe," Jesse said.

After they had hung up he sat looking at the half-empty glass with the ice cubes melting into the whiskey. He picked it up and took a sip, and let it slide down his throat, warm and cool at the same time. His eyes felt as if they would fill with tears. He didn't want them to, and he pushed the feeling back down.

Jenn, he thought. Jesus Christ!

chapter 52

Michelle sat and talked with Jesse on the wall. A couple of other burnout kids sat farther down the wall pretending that they weren't listening, and were too cool to pay any attention to the police chief if he chose to sit on the wall with them.

"You got a cigarette?" Michelle said.

"No."

"You don't smoke?"

"No."

"You ever?"

"No."

"How come?"

"I was a jock," Jesse said. "I thought it would cut my wind."

"That's weird," Michelle said.

Jesse stared at the leaves on the common, crimson now in places, and maroon, and yellow, the yellow tinged along the edges with green. It was something he'd never seen except on calendars, growing up in Arizona and California.

"I live next to your girlfriend," Michelle said. "Abby Taylor."

"That so?"

"Yes. Sometimes I see you come home real late with her and go in."

"Un huh."

"You have sex with her?"

"Why do you want to know?" Jesse said.

"I don't, I don't care. I just think if you're going to be telling people what to do you shouldn't be having sex with people."

"Why not," Jesse said.

"Why not?"

"Yeah, why shouldn't I be chief of police and have sex with people?"

"I don't care what you do, but it's gross to do that and then be telling other people not to."

"Have I ever told you not to?"

"You think I should?"

"There's no should to it," Jesse said.

"Well, that's not what most adults think."

"I'd be willing to bet," Jesse said, "that you don't know what most adults think. You know what a few of them think and you assume everyone thinks that."

"Well, do you think it's okay?"

"Sex? You bet."

"For me?"

"For anyone," Jesse said, "that knows what they're doing, and why they're doing it, and is smart enough not to get pregnant when they don't want to, or get AIDS, or get a reputation."

"I've had sex," Michelle said.

Jesse nodded soberly.

"I figured you had," Jesse said.

"I don't think it's such a big deal."

"Sometimes it is," Jesse said. "Depends, I guess, on who you have sex with and when and how you feel about them."

Jesse paused and smiled.

"Though I gotta tell you," he said. "I've never not liked it."

Michelle glanced down at the two ratty-looking boys at the end of the wall and lowered her voice.

"If a guy, you know, shoots off, and you get some on you, can you get pregnant?"

"He needs to shoot off in you," Jesse said.

"In . . . down there?"

"In your vagina," Jesse said. "There may be someone who's gotten pregnant by getting it on her thigh, but it's not something I'd worry about."

Michelle was silent, her feet dangling, looking at the ground between her feet.

Jesse looked across the common some more at the fall foliage. What made the leaves of the hardwoods so bright, he realized, was the undertone of evergreens behind and between them. The turning trees were made more brilliant by the trees that didn't turn. Must be a philosophic point in there somewhere, Jesse thought. But none occurred.

"So are you?" Michelle asked.

She was still looking at the ground, and as she talked she pointed her toes in and then back out.

"None of your business," Jesse said.

"Embarrassed to say?"

"No," Jesse said. "But you don't go out with someone and then tell everybody what you did."

"I'll bet you talk about it with the other cops."

"No," Jesse said.

"That's weird. You ever been married?"

"Yes."

"You divorced now?"

"Yes."

"Is it because you didn't love each other?"

"No. I think we love each other."

"So what is it?"

"None of your business," Jesse said.

"Jeez, another thing you won't talk about."

"I don't talk about you and me, either," Jesse said.

Michelle was startled.

"We're not doing nothing," she said.

Jesse grinned at her.

"That makes it easier," he said.

Michelle tried not to, but she couldn't help herself. She giggled.

"Jesse, you are really crazy," she said. "You are really fucking-A crazy."

"Thank you for noticing," Jesse said.

And Michelle giggled some more and looked at the harlequin leaf bed beneath her dangling feet.

chapter 53

Madeline St. Claire, M.D., had her office in a building on Bedford Drive in Beverly Hills a block north of Wilshire, on the corner of Brighton Way. Jenn liked the location. It made her feel important to go there twice a week. Jenn loved Dr. St. Claire and hated her. She was so implacable.

"What we are after in here," Dr. St. Claire had said to her in one of her early visits, "is the truth."

"So how come you are an authority on truth? Maybe your truth isn't my truth."

"We want your truth," Dr. St. Claire said. "We want you to know why you do what you do."

"Who's to decide my truth?"

"You will."

"So why do I need you?"

"Why do you?" Dr. St. Claire had said and Jenn had felt the stab of panic that she often felt when she realized that something was up to her.

She had gotten past that and now she understood why

she needed help with the truth. But the rebellious child angry at the stern teacher never entirely disappeared, and many of the therapy sessions were combative. Sometimes Jenn cried. Dr. St. Claire remained unmoved. She was kind, but she was firm, and nothing Jenn did, no trick from Jenn's considerable repertoire, could divert her. Under Dr. St. Claire's steady gaze the strictures of pretense with which Jenn had defended herself for so long began to loosen.

They were talking about Jesse.

"The thing is," Jenn said, "that I feel so much more than I used to feel when I talk to him. I feel stronger. It's like, sometimes I imagine the skin of a valley girl laying shriveled on the floor, and a kind of new pink me standing up, a little damp, kind of scared, but genuine. Is that too fanciful?"

Dr. St. Claire made one of her little head movements which managed to encourage Jenn while remaining non-committal.

"I know I haven't been here long enough to be what I'm going to be. But when I talk to Jesse I know he's in trouble, and I know he's a little scared. Jesse is never scared."

"Or never shows it," Dr. St. Claire said.

"He's really very brave," Jenn said.

Dr. St. Claire nodded.

"And the funny thing is, when he sounds a little scared, I feel a lot braver. You know. I feel like I could help him."

"Why do you suppose that is?"

"I don't know. Maybe I'm glad he's not so damned perfect, you know? That he can be scared?"

"Perhaps you don't need to be quite so much less than he," Dr. St. Claire said.

"What do you mean?"

"You have learned to get what you want by submitting to men. They had power. You, as I believe you said once, knew how to 'bat your eyes' when you needed something."

"And now I don't?"

"Now you may need to less," Dr. St. Claire said. "I don't think you are all the way yet."

The room was very plain. The walls were beige. The rug was gray with a pink undertone. The only thing to look at other than Dr. St. Claire was her framed diplomas. Her medical degree was from UCLA. There was some kind of psychoanalytic certificate too, and other things behind her that Jenn had never turned around to look at.

"But I am taking care of myself."

"Yes," Dr. St. Claire said.

"You mean more than earning my own money."

"Yes."

"You mean this too, don't you."

"Yes."

"So I'm starting to take better care of myself, and that means I can take better care of Jesse."

"Or whoever," Dr. St. Claire said.

Jenn sat back a little in her chair and thought about that.

"Often," Dr. St. Claire said, "circumstances of heightened intensity can accelerate things."

"Like rising to the occasion," Jenn said.

"Yes," Dr. St. Claire said. "Very much like that."

chapter 54

After work on a Tuesday evening, Jesse bought a large sandwich with everything on it at a shop called the Italian Submarine near the town wharf, and brought it home for supper. He would have two drinks. One before the sandwich and one with it. He was on his first drink when Abby called him.

"I'm ready to forgive you," Abby said.

"That's good."

"I wish you trusted me, but you don't. Maybe you can't. But I find that I'm missing you and decided that not seeing you was punishing me as much as you and so I want to see you."

"Okay."

"Control yourself," Abby said. "I hate it when you get giddy with excitement."

"You want to go with me to the Halloween dance at the Yacht Club?" Jesse said.

"Well, yes," Abby said. "I mean I want to go with you, but I wish it didn't have to be to the Yacht Club dance."

"Sort of part of my job," Jesse said.

"I know. Chief of police and all that," Abby said. "Actually I guess I'm supposed to go too, being town counsel."

"Want to come here first for a drink?" Jesse said.

"Yes. What time?"

"Say seven, we don't want to get to the ball too early."

"I guess," Abby said.

They were quiet for a moment. Jesse sipped his drink. He suspected that Abby was sipping hers.

"How have you been?" Abby said.

"Good."

"Any progress on who killed that young woman?"

"Some," Jesse said. "I know who did it, but I need evidence."

"You know who did it?"

"Yeah."

"Well who . . . I guess you can't say, can you? Have you heard from your ex lately?"

"Yeah."

"She hasn't let you go, has she," Abby said.

"I hear from Jenn pretty regularly."

"Have you let her go, Jesse?"

"No, I don't suppose I have, altogether."

"So where does that leave me?"

"Where you've always been, Ab. You're a really wonderful woman. But I am not really finished with my first marriage yet."

"I know."

"You shouldn't put all your eggs in this basket, Ab."

"I know."

"I'm sorry it's that way," Jesse said.

"Hell," Abby said, "let's play it as it lays. The worst we can do is have a hell of a good time for a while."

"I don't know how it will turn out, Ab."

"Me either, but let's start with the Halloween dance, and a drink beforehand."

"And maybe we won't have to stay long," Jesse said.

"And have the rest of the night to kill," Abby said.

"We'll think of something," Jesse said.

"I already have," Abby said.

Chapter 55

The morning of the Halloween dance Jesse got a Federal Express envelope from Charlie Buck in the Campbell County, Wyoming, Sheriff's Department. Inside was a letter and a list of names.

"We have a cooperative witness in custody," Buck wrote, "who says that Tom Carson was killed by a man sent by a militia group back east. Since Carson was from Massachusetts, we got a list of everybody who flew from Boston to Denver a week on either side of the crime. See if you recognize any names. The witness may be selling us a plea. Or the killer may have flown from New York, or drove out in a 1958 Rambler. But it makes sense to start with Boston–Denver."

There followed a list of names, three columns, eighteen pages. On the twelfth page was Lou Burke's name. Jesse stared at it for a long time, then he reorganized the list and put it in a manila folder along with Buck's letter and locked the folder in the file cabinet in his office. He took Lou Burke's personnel file out and brought it back to his desk and looked at it. Lou had been a twenty-year man in the Navy, before he retired and joined the police. Jesse ran his eyes down the list of Lou's military occupation specialties until he found the one he remembered.

1970–1972 Underwater demolition specialist

Jesse's fingers tapped softly on the desk as he read the personnel sheet.

1970–1972 Underwater demolition specialist

Holding the file in his lap, he swiveled his chair so he could stare out the window, past the driveway where the fire trucks parked, and look at the full strut of the Massachusetts fall. Jesse was never one for nature's grandeur, and he wouldn't get in a bus and ride very far to look at the leaves either. But since it was there it was nice to look at. Nothing like it in L.A. He watched the bright leaves for quite a while holding Lou Burke's personnel file facedown in his lap.

He was still sitting when Molly Crane came in from the dispatch desk, and stood in the doorway, leaning on the jamb. She often did that, didn't really come in, didn't really stay out, just lingered in the doorway to talk.

"You thinking?" she said. "Or daydreaming."

"Looking at the leaves," Jesse said.

"I'm on break," Molly said.

Jesse nodded.

"You going to that dance at the Yacht Club?" Molly said.

"Yeah. You?"

Molly laughed.

"Are you kidding? The police department dispatcher?"

"You're a full-time police officer too," Jesse said.

"Yeah, that'll make a difference. See how many other guys from the force are there."

"You ever been?"

"I never even been inside the Yacht Club, except once when some lady got drunk and started to strip right in front of all the guests, and I had to go over there and drag her out."

"Drunk and disorderly?"

"Yeah, that was the charge. Pretty good-looking babe, too," Molly said. "By the time I got her in the cell she had taken off every stitch. I gave her my coat but she wouldn't wear it. Kept saying she was free and was going to live free, or something like that. She was pretty drunk. Anyway all of my fellow officers were really worried about her and kept checking on her regularly to make sure she didn't hurt herself or escape or anything."

Jesse smiled.

"She still in town," he said.

"Oh sure. President of the little theater group, parent-teachers group, art association, you name it."

"She ever talk to you?"

"Pretends she doesn't know me," Molly said.

"Maybe she doesn't," Jesse said. "Drunks don't always, you know."

"I'm Irish," Molly said. "I know about drunks."

"She still drink a lot?"

"I guess so. I don't move in her circles, but she hasn't required the cops again."

"Kind of a status-conscious town, you think?" Jesse said.

"Oh yeah. Funny thing is that's where all the prejudice is. The WASPs and the rich Jews get along fine. Neither one of them wants anything to do socially with working types.''

"Maybe you're generalizing a little," Jesse said.

"Oh yeah, whatever that means, I'm probably doing it. Don't get me wrong. I don't wish I was going to the Yacht Club. I'm just looking forward to your reaction.''

"Maybe I won't have one," Jesse said.

Molly smiled, still leaning on the doorjamb.

"I know what you're like, Jesse," she said and pushed herself erect. "You'll have one. But you won't show it.''

With that Molly walked away, letting the door swing shut behind her. That was also something she did. Molly was a great one for exit lines.

Jesse looked back out the window and sat for a while longer. Then he stood and carried Lou Burke's personnel folder back to his upright file and put it away. Then he went back to his desk and dialed up Charlie Buck in Wyoming.

chapter 56

Paradise Neck was a narrow jut of land that angled out to form the eastern shore of Paradise Harbor on its inner shoreline, while it kept the open ocean at bay with its outer. There were two roads on the Neck. One along the outer shoreline and one along the inner. They joined at Plumtree Point, where the lighthouse stood. The Yacht Club was off the inner coast road on the Neck, down a narrow drive thickly arched with trees and into a broad parking area beside some outdoor tennis courts behind a huge, haphazard, white clapboard two-story building. Jesse was amused that when you approached this tabernacle of Paradise high culture, you came at it from the rear. The Yacht Club faced the ocean, cantilevered out over the rust-colored boulders and bedrock that the sea had unearthed over time, its vast picture windows beaded with sea spray. Jesse was amused also at the understated arrogance of the membership, naming it simply The Yacht Club, as if there were no other. At night, coming from the leaf-thick tunnel into the brightly lit lot was rather like coming on stage. He parked nose in to one of the green composition tennis courts and got out and opened the door for Abby. She looked very elegant in black tuxedo trousers and a white blouse that looked somewhat like a boiled shirt. At her throat was a string of pearls. Jesse wore a dark suit.

In the ballroom, walled with windows, apparently floating over the harbor, the guests were generally in formal dress accented by Halloween-themed accessories. Several women sported satin half masks trimmed with rhinestones. Hasty Hathaway was wearing a black-and-orange bow tie with his tux. The bow tie had orange lights in it that flashed on and off. A four-piece orchestra in one corner was playing music by Andrew Lloyd Webber. At the far end of the room a bar was open, and along the wall opposite the water view a buffet table was laid with orange and black paper, covered with food, and anchored at each end by a large carved jack-o'-lantern.

"Hasty is drawing a crowd with his bow tie," Abby said in Jesse's ear as they pushed toward the bar. "It's his party trademark. At Christmas he has one with red and green lights."

"He's a sporty guy," Jesse said.

He got Abby a martini and himself a scotch and soda at the bar. They came in the same-sized clear plastic glasses. Abby sipped hers and made a face. Jesse needed to be careful with the scotch. This was not a good place for the chief of police to get drunk. Abby drank again.

"Got to get some of this in quick so that the rest of it won't taste so awful."

Jesse smiled. He started to drink his scotch and thought better of it. Take your time, he said to himself. Sip now and then. Nurse a couple of drinks. You don't have to stay here forever. They edged over to the buffet table: potato chips; a boiled ham; salted peanuts; cream cheese and bologna roll-ups; pretzel sticks; potato salad; a large molded salad made of lime Jell-O and cabbage; pigs in a blanket; goldfish crackers; small meatballs in a sauce made from red currant jelly; a salad made with green beans, wax beans, and red kidney beans in oil-and-vinegar dressing; a platter of sliced American processed cheese food, two colors, yellow and white; some Ritz crackers; some salami chunks; a bowl of caramel corn; and a large bowl of something Jesse didn't recognize. He asked Abby.

"That's called nuts and bolts," Abby said.

"Yeah, but what is it?"

"Cereal."

"Cereal?"

"Yeah, Cheerios, Wheat Chex, bite-sized shredded wheat, stuff like that, sprayed with oil and salted and baked in the oven. Then you add pretzel sticks, maybe some peanuts if you're at the cutting edge. Some people sprinkle on garlic salt, some people put on some Kraft grated Parmesan cheese. Toss lightly and serve."

"Oh," Jesse said.

"One year they had a Crock-Pot of blushing bunny," Abby said.

"Which is?"

"Kind of a Welsh rabbit. Campbell's cheese soup and Campbell's tomato soup mixed equally and served over toast."

"It's gotta be Campbell's?"

"Yes. WASPs are very brand-name loyal."

Abby's glass was empty. He stood near the end of the buffet table trying not to hear the music while she went for a refill. He looked at the buffet table and smiled. I hope I don't get hungry, he thought. He took another drink. Carefully.

"You're all alone, you poor dear," Cissy Hathaway said.

Her speech was slow and careful, the way people speak when they're drunk and trying not to show it. She had on more makeup than usual and behind the makeup Jesse could see that her cheeks were very red. She wore a long-sleeved formal gown, cream-colored with a red-and-green floral pattern and a high neck. The dress was very tight. Her high-heeled shoes were the same green as the leaves in the floral pattern.

"Abby's getting a drink," Jesse said.

"Well pooh on her," Cissy said. "Come dance with me."

If he said no, she'd insist. Jesse could see it in her face. Jesse put his glass down and let Cissy take him to the floor. The band played "We've Only Just Begun." Jesse was a good dancer. He had good coordination and he could hear the music. But dancing wasn't really what Cissy had in mind. She pressed against him as they moved among the dancers, pushing her pelvis against his and moving her hips slightly without regard to "We've Only Just Begun."

"Do you like my dress?" she said. Her face was turned up to his and her lips almost brushed his face as she talked.

"Yes, ma'am," Jesse said.

"You don't think it's too tight?"

"No such thing," Jesse said.

"Men are all alike," Cissy said. "They judge clothes by how much of a woman they show."

"You're probably right," Jesse said.

"When a man is with a woman," Cissy said, "clothes are just in the way."

Jesse said, "Un huh," emphasizing the second syllable, trying to sound both interested and noncommittal. Not easy, he thought, while being dry-humped on the dance floor.

"It's why when I'm with a man," Cissy said, her lips

now actually brushing Jesse's as she spoke, "I wear as little as possible."

The band segued into "I Left My Heart in San Francisco."

"Hasty's a lucky man," Jesse said. He was looking past Cissy's shoulder for Abby.

"Oh, Hasty," she said. "I can't wait around all year for Hasty."

Jesse smiled without speaking. He couldn't think of anything to say to that. He was thinking of Suitcase.

"Can you tell," she whispered against his mouth, "that I'm not wearing anything under this dress?"

"I wasn't sure," Jesse said.

Cissy had a good body under her ridiculous dress. It was becoming difficult for Jesse to remain detached.

"Is it something you might want to see?" she whispered.

Christ! Jesse thought. Where's Suit when you need him.

"Is it?" Her mouth was against his.

"Not right here," Jesse said.

"But somewhere you would, wouldn't you. I can tell."

Jesse was still struggling for gallantry.

"Anyone would," he said.

Cissy clamped her mouth against his and began to kiss him aggressively. Jesse felt a tap on his shoulder. It was Hasty, his bow tie blinking steadily.

"Mind if I cut in?" Hasty said.

Cissy continued to kiss him.

Jesse pulled away and said, "No, not at all," and turned Cissy, her eyes still half closed, into Hasty's arms.

The band began to play an old Beatles tune. He found Abby near the bar, with a martini. The bar had cleared somewhat as people danced.

"Last Tango in Paris?" Abby said.

"Help," Jesse said.

He ordered a fresh scotch from the bar.

"How's she stack up as a kisser?" Abby said.

"There's better," Jesse said.

"Good to know."

Abby's eyes were bright and Jesse realized that she might be a little drunk too. He knew their relationship wasn't helping her drinking. He picked up his scotch. Careful. He sipped a small sip and put the drink back down on the bar. Morris Comden, one of the other selectmen, came across the room and asked Jesse if he could have the next dance with Abby. It was the boldest thing Comden had done since Jesse had been in Paradise. At selectmen's meetings, he sat quite still and watched Hasty so he'd know how to vote.

"Ask her," Jesse said.

Abby smiled and said, "Of course," and went to the dance floor with him. Over Comden's shoulder on the floor, she stuck her tongue out at Jesse. Jesse smiled at her and sipped his scotch. Hasty Hathaway came to the bar.

"Wild Turkey," he said to the bartender. "Straight, one ice cube."

He got his drink and turned and put an arm around Jesse's shoulder.

"Wife gets a little giddy," he said, "when she drinks."

"Sure," Jesse said.

Hasty took a drink.

"Mother's milk," he said.

Jesse nodded. The dancers labored about the floor. Most people were terrible dancers, Jesse thought. He wondered if Comden had been dispatched to dance with Abby, so that Hasty and he could talk man to man. He didn't see Cissy anywhere.

"Women are hard to figure, aren't they, Jesse?"

"Yes," Jesse said, "they are."

"I guess you've had your share of trying to figure them out."

"Un huh."

"Being divorced and all."

"Still trying to figure that out," Jesse said.

"Well," Hasty said, "that's just how women are, I guess. When you want faster, they want slower. And when you want slower, they want fast."

Hasty shook his head.

"You and Cissy seem happy," Jesse said.

"Ciss? Oh hell, sure we are. But even a happy marriage isn't easy, is it. There are adjustments."

Hasty drank the rest of his Wild Turkey and ordered another.

"Sexual problems?" Hasty said.

"Who?" Jesse said.

"In your first marriage. It's usually sexual stuff that makes a marriage hit the reef."

"No," Jesse said. "We didn't have sexual problems."

Unless, Jesse thought, your wife boffing a producer could be considered a sexual problem.

"What was your deal," Hasty said.

Jesse shrugged.

"I'm not sure I know," he said. "We didn't seem to want the same things."

"Let's get some air," Hasty said.

With his arm still on Jesse's shoulder Hasty steered him toward the sliders and out onto the deck over the water. The strong salt smell reminded Jesse again of how far he was from home. The Pacific never smelled like this that he could remember. Maybe it was the cold weather made the ocean smell different. The light from the ballroom spilled out for a little way onto the black water. There was a small chop. Across the harbor the lights of the town were strung along the coastline and rose up from the water to Indian Hill, where the park was.

They leaned on the deck rail. Below them, Jesse could hear the water moving over the rocks.

"Man to man," Hasty said.

Jesse nodded to himself. Comden had been dispatched. He was not a good choice. He was too dull to carry on a conversation. Poor Abby.

"Your ex ever fool around?" Hasty said.

He wasn't looking at Jesse. Arms resting on the railing, he stared out across the water.

"Yes."

"How'd it make you feel?"

"Bad."

Hasty nodded.

"You fool around?" he said.

"Not till we separated," Jesse said.

"You ever wonder why you weren't enough?"

"Yes."

Hasty nodded again. He was silent for a time. Through the glass doors behind them the band had finished its set and the sound of conversation and glassware replaced the sound of music.

"When we were dating," Hasty said, "she was hotter than a cheap pistol. Part of the reason I married her, I suppose. I never had many girlfriends, and when I started dating her . . ." He shook his head at the memory. "But as soon as we got married she wasn't interested anymore. The funny thing is when we dated we did everything but it, you know. Heavy petting, I guess you'd say. But never the dastardly deed itself. Didn't want to cheapen the relationship."

Hasty laughed at himself derisively.

"Talked a lot about saving it for marriage," he said. "Then we got married and she wasn't interested. You know? She'd lie back and close her eyes and think of England. But it was pretty much of a duty.''

"I guess marriage is different from dating," Jesse said.

"I guess it is," Hasty said.

Across the harbor a small tender plugged in toward the town wharf from one of the yachts moored in deeper water. Its running lights looked like slow shooting stars in the dark. Hasty finished his drink. Jesse had already finished his.

"I finally just decided that she was frigid and that the hot stuff before marriage was a way to get me. But you know how it is in a marriage. You figure you're supposed to stick it out. After a while the way it is gets to seem like the way it's supposed to be.''

"Yes," Jesse said. "I know."

"She seem frigid to you?" Hasty said.

"Hard to say."

"Come on, Jesse. She embarrassed us both on the dance floor ten minutes ago. She seem frigid to you then?"

"No."

"So how come she's frigid at home, and hot with other men?"

"I'm a cop, Hasty. That's a shrink question."

"Aw, they're all crazy themselves," Hasty said.

Jesse didn't say anything.

"Well, anyway, I've come to terms with it. We have our life together. Except for the sex, I like her. We get along good. What she does when I'm not home, I know she sees other men. I'm sure she's hotter than Cleopatra with them. I . . . I . . .'' Hasty made an aimless hand gesture. "We get along," he said.

"Whatever works," Jesse said. "You have anyone?"

"On the side, you mean? No."

Jesse nodded.

"Anyway," Hasty said, as if finishing a difficult chore, "I wanted you to know that I don't blame you. I apologize for my wife."

"Sure," Jesse said. "No problem."

Again they were quiet, the two men looking at the black harbor, forearms resting on the railing, each holding an empty plastic cup in his hand. The tender had reached the wharf and disappeared. Its running lights were out. The darkness between the men and the town across the water was unbroken and palpable. Hasty clapped Jesse on the back.

"Well, look at all that food," Hasty said. "Better go in and get some before they eat it all up."

"That's right," Jesse said. "That's what we better do."

chapter 57

Jesse was at his desk when Molly brought Bobby Portugal in.

"Remember me?" Portugal said.

"Sure," Jesse said. "Have a seat."

"They're cleaning out the house," Portugal said.

"Where you and Tammy lived?"

"Yeah, and I had to come in from Springfield to get some stuff I left there. Probably hoping it would give me an excuse to come back. So I thought I'd stop by, see how the case was coming."

"Not much hard evidence," Jesse said.

"You got her diary?"

Jesse was silent for a moment. Then he got up and walked around Portugal and closed the office door.

When he was back behind his desk again he said, "Diary."

"Yeah. You didn't mention it when you was in Springfield, but I figure, cops. You know? I'm not bad-mouthing the police, I'm just figuring you got it and don't see no reason to talk about it with me.''

''She kept a diary.''

''Long as I knew her, every night, last thing. Even if we had sex, when we was done, she'd write in the freaking diary.''

''You ever read it?'' Jesse said.

''No. It was one of those leather ones with a lock on it. She wore the key on a chain around her neck. Little gold key. She had a lotta ambition. I think she thought she could write down everything she did and someday she could get someone to help her and they'd write a book about all her exciting adventures.''

Portugal shook his head and smiled grimly.

''Like getting knocked up by me.''

Jesse was quiet.

''So if you had the diary I figured it might tell you something, who she was seeing, who she went out with that night. Something. She wasn't somebody to stay home and watch TV.''

Jesse shook his head slowly.

''You don't have it, do you?'' Portugal said, slowly surprised.

''No. Did you see the drawer where she kept it?''

''Yeah, sure. It's what made me think of it. It wasn't in there. You find the key on her when you . . . found her.''

Jesse shook his head.

''You might have missed it.''

''No.''

''She always had it on her.''

''She was stark naked,'' Jesse said as gently as he could. ''We'd have seen it.''

Portugal sat still a minute, looking at nothing.

"Yeah, sure," he said after a moment, "you'd have seen it. You find her clothes?"

"No."

Portugal nodded as if that were meaningful.

"If you keep a diary for a long time," Jesse said, "you fill up the pages. Did she keep the old ones?"

"Yeah. I think so. She bought a new one when we got married and that's the only one I know. She probably left the other ones home, at her mother's house, when she got married."

"You think her mother took it?"

Portugal shrugged.

"She could have. They were in there cleaning out the place. It's going on the market Monday. I don't get any. They get it all. Her old lady didn't even want me in there to get my things. She never got over me knocking up her baby girl. But the old man's not a bad guy. He called me, told me to come get my stuff. The old lady woulda chucked it in the Dumpster."

Jesse tapped gently on the desktop with his fingers.

Finally he said, "I have your phone number. I know anything, I'll let you know."

"I'd appreciate it."

"You can count on it," Jesse said. "And I'd appreciate it if the diary was something you didn't talk about with anybody else."

"Sure," Portugal said. "No sweat."

"Thanks," Jesse said.

"I already told my girlfriend how Tammy used to keep a diary," Portugal said.

"Well, ask her not to discuss it as well," Jesse said.

"Well, since her husband don't know about me," Portugal said, "I guess she can keep a secret."

"You better hope so," Jesse said.

And they were both laughing as Portugal left.

Chapter 58

Lou Burke was getting into his car when Jesse opened the passenger door and got in beside him.

"Patrol supervising?" Jesse said.

"Yeah."

"Mind if I ride along?" Jesse said. "I spend too much time in the office."

"Come ahead," Burke said.

Burke backed the car out of the parking lot and turned up Main Street. Between them was a shotgun, locked barrel up on the transmission hump.

"See if there's any gum wrappers in the barrel," Burke said. "Peter Perkins had the car before me."

Jesse looked into the shotgun barrel. He blew some dust out.

"No gum wrappers," he said.

"Boys don't seem to have the proper respect for a weapon," Burke said, "do they?"

"Never make it in the Corps," Jesse said.

"You in the Marines?"

"Semper Fi," Jesse said. "You?"

"Navy."

"What was your job?"

Burke smiled.

"Lot of stuff. I was a lifer."

"Twenty years?"

"Yeah. This is my retirement."

Jesse smiled. Burke drove the car up Indian Hill Road. The startling leaves had finished turning, Jesse noticed. Many of the trees were leafless, or nearly so. And, puzzlingly, some of them still had leaves and the leaves were still green.

"Ever do any demolition work?" Jesse said.

Burke's eyes shifted almost imperceptibly as he glanced involuntarily at Jesse and then looked back at the road.

"Yeah, some."

Jesse nodded. At the top of Indian Hill, Burke drove the patrol car slowly into the park. It was during school hours, and it was chilly. There was no one in the park except a white-haired man in a black-and-red wool jacket walking an aging yellow Lab.

"Funny how quiet a town is during school hours," Jesse said.

Burke didn't say anything.

"Ever been to Denver?" Jesse said.

"Denver?"

"Yeah."

"Why you asking?"

Jesse smiled at him.

"Why not?" Jesse said.

"Jesse, you got something on your mind, I think you just better say it right out."

"I am saying it right out," Jesse said, still smiling. "You ever been to Denver?"

"Yeah."

Jesse's smile was gone.

"When's the last time you were in Denver?" Jesse said.

From Indian Hill, you could see the whole harbor, uneventful in the late fall, and the old town, weathered shingle, red brick, and church steeples beside the dark water. You could see across the harbor to Paradise Neck, the big glass facade of the Yacht Club teetering over the water. And you could see across the Neck, mostly evergreen trees, with white and gray houses among them, and look at the Atlantic Ocean.

Burke didn't answer. He turned the car back down the hill toward the center of town.

"When's the last time you were in Denver, Lou?"

Burke shook his head.

"Drive us back to the station, Lou."

Burke was silent. Jesse let the silence stand. There was no reason to let Burke in on what Jesse knew. Jesse had never gotten in trouble saying too little. The patrol car pulled into its slot outside the station.

"I'm going to ask you to take a leave of absence, Lou."

Burke turned toward him and started to speak, and stopped.

"Leave the handgun and the badge with Molly," Jesse said.

As they got out of the car Burke turned and looked across the roof at Jesse.

"You sonova bitch," he said.

Burke's voice was thick, as if forced out through a closing throat. And there was something in Burke's face that Jesse felt with a force he wasn't used to. You didn't work South Central without seeing hatred. But the passion in Burke's face was beyond hatred. Jesse felt something like revulsion, as if he'd seen something grotesque for a moment. He felt as if he needed to hold steady against it, the way you lean into a strong wind.

"Gun and badge to Molly, Lou," Jesse said.

chapter 59

Tammy Portugal's maiden name was Gennaro. Her mother and father lived in a small ugly house that had once been a summer cottage, facing a swampy saltwater estuary which the local kids called the eel pond. The process of converting the cottage to a full-time home had been apparently a slow one. The rear wall of the kitchen above the sink was still unfinished, the area between the studs filled with the silvery foil backing of the fiberglass insulation.

The kitchen table where Jesse sat was made of metal covered with white enamel. There was a small fold-up leaf at either end. The mug from which Mr. Gennaro was drinking instant coffee was formed in the shape of a gnomish-looking man with a beard. Mrs. Gennaro, in a flowered housedress and white sneakers, was at the stove boiling water, in case there was a call for more instant coffee. The sneaker on her right foot had a hole cut to relieve pressure on her small toe. She was a sturdy woman, not fat, but wide in the hips and shoulders. She had white hair which she wore in a tight perm, and rimless glasses.

"You sure you won't have coffee?" Mrs. Gennaro said.

"No, thank you, ma'am," Jesse said.

Jesse hated instant coffee. Across the table from him, Mr. Gennaro put a spoonful of Cremora in his coffee and stirred. He was a wiry little man, no taller than his wife. He worked sometimes as a fisherman, and sometimes as a landscaper, and in snowstorms he drove a plow for the town.

"How are you both doing?" Jesse asked.

Mr. Gennaro shrugged.

Mrs. Gennaro said, "We get through the day."

"It'll get better," Jesse said. "I know it doesn't feel like that now, but in time, it'll get better."

Neither one said anything. Probably didn't want it to get better right now, Jesse thought, probably were so into the grief that it was their life, and without it they wouldn't have anything at all.

"I see you have your daughter's house on the market," Jesse said.

"Yeah," Mr. Gennaro said. "No sense paying for an empty house."

"You selling it furnished?" Jesse said.

"No," Mrs. Gennaro said. "We got a man to come in and take everything out. He paid us for the furniture."

"That's good," Jesse said. "It would be painful doing that yourself."

Mrs. Gennaro nodded. The steam began to spout from the kettle. She turned the heat down beneath it and came to the table.

"I hope you were able to keep some memories," Jesse said.

Mr. Gennaro shifted a little in his seat.

"What do you mean," Mrs. Gennaro said.

"You know," Jesse said, "pictures, letters, diaries, stuff like that."

They were silent.

"She keep a diary?" Jesse said.

Simultaneously, Mr. Gennaro said "Yes" and Mrs. Gennaro said "No."

Jesse smiled politely and didn't say anything. The Gennaros looked at each other. Jesse waited. No one said anything. Jesse could hear the hot water in the teakettle stir restlessly on the stove over the low heat.

"If she kept a diary it might help us find who killed her," Jesse said.

The Gennaros looked at each other and back at Jesse. Still they didn't speak. Jesse knew they were silent because they didn't know what to say. He needed to get them started.

"I want to punish the man who killed your daughter," Jesse said.

Silence. Mr. Gennaro shifted again in his chair. Mrs. Gennaro's face was clenched like a fist. Her cheeks were red.

"I know there are diaries," Jesse said.

Mrs. Gennaro shook her head.

"I need to see them."

Still she shook her head. Jesse looked at her husband.

"You want the man that killed your daughter?" Jesse said.

His voice was still quiet, but the pleasantness was gone.

"You embarrassed by what's in there?" Jesse said. "What would she say? Would she say, 'Cover up for me and let the man who killed me get away'? Would she say that?"

"No," Mr. Gennaro said.

"Eddie," Mrs. Gennaro said sharply.

Gennaro stared at the tabletop, shaking his head slowly. "No," he said again.

Then he stood and walked into the next room.

"Eddie," Mrs. Gennaro said again, louder, and sharper.

Gennaro came back into the kitchen with a cardboard beer case filled with small books covered in red imitation leather, each little book with a brass lock. Gennaro put the diaries on the table in front of Jesse and went back to the other side of the table and sat down.

"This is them," he said. He nodded at his wife. "She got the keys."

"I won't give them to you," Mrs. Gennaro said.

"You don't have to, ma'am," Jesse said.

"I raised a decent girl," Mrs. Gennaro said. "She was a decent girl until that Portugal . . ."

"She was decent anyway," Gennaro muttered.

"I don't want him prying into those books, Eddie," Mrs. Gennaro said.

"He's going to," Gennaro said and kept his eyes on the table. "I want him to."

"Don't you care what I want?" Mrs. Gennaro said.

"I want the guy caught," Gennaro said.

Jesse picked up the beer case with the diaries carefully stacked in it.

"How you going to open them without the keys?" Mrs. Gennaro said.

"Probably pry them open," Jesse said, "with a screwdriver."

Mrs. Gennaro looked at the diaries without speaking for a moment, then she said, "Wait a minute."

She left the kitchen. Jesse waited. Gennaro sat silently staring at the kitchen tabletop. After a moment Mrs. Gennaro returned and gave Jesse a collection of little brass keys tied together with a red ribbon.

"I want them books back," she said, "with no damage."

"I'll get them back to you, ma'am," Jesse said.

Neither of Tammy Portugal's parents said anything else as Jesse carried the diaries from the house.

chapter 60

They sat in Hasty's car in the parking lot of the Northshore Shopping Center. The nose of the car pointed north so that the afternoon sun streamed in over Hasty's shoulder and made him a dark silhouette as Burke turned in the seat to look at him.

"Something will have to be done about Stone," Burke said, squinting, trying to look at Hasty. But the sun was too fierce. Burke gave up and looked away.

Hasty was silent.

"He knows," Burke said. "He knows I was in Denver. He knows more than that. Sonova bitch doesn't say much, but he knows."

"Maybe he doesn't say much because he doesn't know," Hasty said.

"He knows," Burke said. "We made a bad mistake with him."

"Mistakes are part of life," Hasty said. "The important thing is to overcome them."

To Burke, Hasty's voice seemed disembodied, coming

as it did out of an unseeable place in the hard middle of the sun glare.

"Well, we better overcome this one pretty quick," Burke said. "Or he's going to overcome us."

"What do you recommend?"

"We have to kill him."

"The death of a second police chief from this town in less than a year?"

"Better than having him take us all down," Burke said. "We can find a way to cover it, an accident or something."

"All of us?" Hasty said.

"Well, you know what I mean, he gets me, sooner or later he'll get you, and . . . everybody."

"You are required in these circumstances to give only your name, rank, and serial number."

"For crissake, Hasty, I'm not a fucking prisoner of war."

"Of course you are. If our movement is about anything, it is about war with the forces of international mongrelization."

"I know," Burke said. "I understand that. But they're going to arrest me for murder, Hasty."

"What they do has no effect on what we know to be true," Hasty said.

"Hasty, I can't afford theory right now. My ass is on the stove, you know? We need to get Stone out of the way."

In black silhouette Hasty nodded slowly.

"To save us all," Hasty said.

"Absolutely," Burke said.

"What have 'us all' to do with your trip to Denver, Lou?"

"Christ, Hasty. You sent me."

"To do what?"

"To blow Tom Carson up."

"Because?"

"Because he knew too much and you didn't trust him to be quiet about it."

"Un huh."

There was silence in the car. Across the parking lot, people in bright fall clothing surged in and out of the vast mall. Shop early for Christmas. Take advantage of pre-holiday sales. No payments until January. Many of the people in the late-afternoon surge were teenaged mall rats. For them the mall had replaced playground, Boys Club, street corner, home. The new marketplace.

"I wouldn't tell them, of course," Burke said. "But once they start they're bound to find out."

"How?"

"Well, I mean they investigate."

"What?"

"Well, you know, they backtrack my story . . ."

"And?"

"And who the hell knows what physical evidence they have. Who knows what the Wyoming militia might tell them. They get somebody in jail they can squeeze them, make a deal, go easy on you if you give us the others, you know . . . I would never do that, but we don't really know the Wyoming people."

"Yes," Hasty said. "Of course. Who's to do the killing?"

"I figured you could get Jo Jo to do it. He's got a mad on about Stone anyway."

"Well," Hasty said. "I don't know, Lou. I can promise at least to give it serious theoretical consideration."

"What the hell does that mean?"

"I'll think about it, Lou. Meanwhile you sit still, and keep your mouth shut. Until you hear from me."

"We need to move fast," Burke said.

"I'm aware of that, Lou. And we will, but we will move

with deliberate speed. I agree with you that we've underestimated Stone, and we don't want to underestimate him further.''

"Yeah, sure, Hasty. Just as long as we get him before he gets us.''

"He won't get us, Lou,'' Hasty said. "You're on suspension. Go home, sit in your house, stay there, and say nothing.''

"I'm counting on you, Hasty,'' Burke said.

"Of course,'' Hasty said.

Chapter 61

Jesse began reading Tammy's diaries from the most recent entry back. It took him a day to reach the parts that seemed interesting, and yet another day to cut and paste them together into a narrative that he could study.

May 11—Talked to Hasty Hathaway at the post office. He is the most important man in Paradise, kind of old.

Memorial Day—Hasty Hathaway was talking to me today at the Parade. He acts kind of interested. Its hard to tell with a guy as geeky as he is, but a girl can listen.

June 28—Had a drink at the 86 last night. Looking good if I do say so. New white sweater, the black jeans I got that make my butt look really good. Hasty Hathaway bought me a drink, took me home. We stopped at Indian Hill on the way, and I thought he was going to come on to me, but we just talked. He's really kind of nice, sort of a sad person. Who'd think so, all that money and everything. But he says him and his wife haven't got much going in the sex department. Says he's pretty lonely. Said he needs somebody like me to talk with. I told him he could take me out to dinner sometime if he wanted. He said he had to be careful in town, him being a married man and all, but we could go into Boston maybe. I said sure. He said did I mind him being married, and I said no. His wife's married I said, not him. He thought that was pretty cute. Then he took me home and never even touched me. Strange guy. Fun, maybe.

July 9—ate at the Ritz—Wow!!!—fancy as hell, lotta food I didn't know what it was. We had caviar. I didn't like it much. Hasty was asking me a lot of questions about Bobby and me and how come we got divorced and did I have a boyfriend. Mostly I think he was trying to find out about our sex life, sort of weird, but he can show you a pretty nice time.

July 13—We had lunch at a place in town called Loc Ober's. Really fancy. Had French Champagne too. After, he said he had a room at the Parker House and would I want to go there with him. Just like that, he said it. Like he was inviting me to go fishing or something. I didn't answer him at first, cause I was thinking about how he'd be kind of funny looking with his clothes off, but I've done worse than Hasty, and I was feeling no pain and a girl needs to think about her future. So I say, sure, I'd love to, and we did. I figured a guy his age and all I'd have to work pretty hard to get his motor going, but Hasty was so excited when we got into bed that I thought he was going to come on the bedspread. No work at all. In fact it was over so quick I never really got going myself. After, Hasty gave me a nice ring. Solid gold with a little diamond in it. A real one.

July 29—Hasty's getting better. He lasts long enough now so I get something out of it. I mean it's not like Bobby and me, but he's getting the idea about touching me a little bit, first. I'm teaching him different positions. It's like he thought there was only one. No wonder his old lady isn't interested. I hope what I teach him doesn't get her interested. He's a good thing for me. I don't want to lose him.

August 13—Hasty says he loves me. He gave me a real pearl necklace for our one month anniversary (since we first did it).

August 24—We had our first fight. Hasty doesn't want me dating any other guys and I say to him "what about you. You got a wife. Maybe you should stop fucking her, you want me to stop." Hasty says they only do it twice a month, but he can't stop because she'd be suspicious. And I tell him he stops fucking her, I'll stop dating other guys. I told him everybody knew his wife was fucking other people. And he said he didn't like that kind of talk, like if he didn't talk about it it wasn't happening. At the end he cried and said he loved me and we did it twice and he gave me a nice gold ankle bracelet.

August 31—Hasty heard about me dating Joe Hudson. He wanted to know what we did, and I told him none of your business and he got real mad and said he was going to break up with me if I kept going out with Joe. I told him you do what you want Mister nosy. I go out with anybody I want, unless you want to divorce the old lady and marry me. Well you should have seen his face. But then we did it and he cried while we were doing it and said he could never lose me and after he gave me a really nice set of pearl earrings to match the necklace.

September 7—I told Hasty I thought it was sick, him asking all that stuff about Joe Hudson and if we had sex and what we did. He said he loved me so much he needed to know everything, and nothing would be as bad as what he imagined. Divorce your wife I told him and marry me, and then we can talk about whatever you want.

September 8—Poor Hasty is so agitated about me and

Joe Hudson, and me wanting him to get divorced. I didn't really mean I'd tell him about me and Joe. That would be tooo weird!!!!!! But if it gets him, it's just a little white lie. I don't really get it anyway. I do the same thing with Joe as Hasty. What's so different about it???

September 11—I told Hasty I was going to go public about me and him. I got all his letters. I said it was time for him to either go or get off the pot.

September 15—Hasty says give him a week. He said he would make it right. I said okay, but I wouldn't see him until he decided.

September 17—Got some new jeans at Marshall's and one of those great midriff sweaters. Going to take myself out for a few drinks tonight at the 86.

September 17 was the last entry. Jesse read his cut-and-paste narrative sitting alone on the little balcony overlooking the harbor. It was too cold to sit out there, even with his jacket on. But somehow it made the reading less painful to be out there, as if the openness of the setting compensated for the hermetic quality of the small life lived so briefly in the excerpted pages. When he was finished he sat for a long time looking across the harbor at the lights from the Yacht Club.

"I want you to know," Hasty said, "that I fully support you in whatever decision you make about Lou Burke."

Jesse nodded without comment. They were sitting at the counter in the Village Room. Jesse had coffee. Hasty had coffee and a large cinnamon roll with white icing on it.

"We both know it's not a popular decision," Hasty said. "But you're the professional. You run the department your way."

Jesse nodded again. He poured some half-and-half into his coffee.

"When I hire a man I back him until he proves I shouldn't," Hasty said.

He took a bite out of his cinnamon bun. Jesse stirred two sugars into his coffee.

"I just hope to God you know what you're doing."

"Me too," Jesse said.

"You do, don't you?" Hasty said.

He was talking around his mouthful of cinnamon bun. There were crumbs on his tie.

"Yes," Jesse said.

"I mean you better have some solid evidence, everybody likes Lou in town."

Jesse nodded and drank some of his coffee.

"You do, don't you?"

"Yes."

"It would help me support you if I knew what you know," Hasty said.

Jesse shook his head.

"Why not," Hasty said. "For God's sake, Jesse, I'm the chairman of the Board of Selectmen."

"I've never gotten in trouble," Jesse said, "being quiet."

"Jesse, damn it, I'm your boss."

Jesse smiled at him and said nothing. Hasty started to speak again, and caught himself. He took a deep breath and exhaled slowly.

"You are going to need me on your side," Hasty said finally. "And don't forget it."

"I'm counting on you, Hasty."

"You could count on me more," Hasty said, "if I had a better idea of what you're doing."

Jesse finished his coffee and put the cup down carefully in the saucer.

"You'll be among the first to know," Jesse said and got off the stool. "Coffee on you?" he said.

Hasty nodded. Jesse stopped at the end of the counter to say hello to a couple of postal clerks having pie and coffee on break. Then he left the Village Room and walked back across the common toward the police station.

Chapter 63

"Stone has to go," Hasty said to Jo Jo.

They were in Hasty's car cruising Route 128, north toward Gloucester.

"Mistake," Jo Jo said.

"No, he has to go. He'll ruin everything if he doesn't."

"You can't kill the chief of police," Jo Jo said, "and think it'll keep things quiet. You seen that state cop, whatsisname."

"Healy."

"Yeah. You think that he's going to kiss it off when the second police chief in less than a year dies in this fucking town?"

"It's a risk we'll have to take," Hasty said. "We're too close to the arms deal. The arms deal is crucial."

"What's this 'we' shit, paleface? I'm the guy has to do the clip."

"We're in this together, Jo Jo."

Jo Jo looked almost amused.

"Sure," he said. "Why don't we ace Lou Burke?"

"Lou?"

"Yeah. He's the only thing connects you to Tom Carson. Deep-six Burke and the connection's gonzolla."

"Lou Burke?" Hasty said. "I've known Lou Burke for thirty years."

"I dump him," Jo Jo said, "hide the body, make it look like he took off after Stone suspended him."

"Lou's one of us," Hasty said. "He's a Horseman."

"And you think they ain't going to find somebody out in the wild west to finger him, say, yeah, he's the guy blew Tom Carson up? And you think when they get that they won't squeeze him, and when they squeeze him you think he won't spill his freaking guts?"

"Lou wouldn't talk."

"You think so, huh? I don't know how they do it in freaking Montana . . ."

"Wyoming," Hasty said.

"Whatever," Jo Jo said. "I don't know if they electro-cute you or hang you or do it with an injection or a fucking firing squad, but just say you're Lou Burke and you're sit-ting in jail and they tell you they are going to hang you or, if you don't like that idea, you can give us something and maybe we won't. You think Lou's gonna say gimme that noose, baby?"

"Are you afraid to kill Jesse Stone?" Hasty asked.

"I ain't afraid," Jo Jo said. "And I ain't stupid either. It's a lot smarter to take out Lou Burke than it is to clip Stone."

"I can't betray the movement."

"You hit Stone and it'll turn into a bowel movement," Jo Jo said.

As they talked about the crime Jo Jo's vocabulary be-came more and more like a movie tough guy. Hasty hated him at that moment, more than he thought was possible. Jo

Jo was a sneering, posturing bully. He cared for no cause, no person. No question of honor had ever penetrated that thick Neanderthal skull. He cared only about his muscles and the fear he could instill in people. Except Stone. Stone wasn't afraid of him, and Hasty was pretty sure that Jo Jo was afraid of Stone. What made the hatred worse, though, so that it trembled in his solar plexus, was the fact that Jo Jo was probably right this time.

"How would you hide the body?" Hasty said.

"Let me figure that out," Jo Jo said. "What you don't know you can't tell the cops later."

"You think I'd tell the police anything?"

Jo Jo looked at him without answering.

"You don't understand, do you," Hasty said. "You don't understand commitment, or honor, or loyalty. And you certainly do not understand responsibility. You don't even know what these things mean. All you understand is fear."

Jo Jo snorted.

"What I understand, Hasty, is you want some guy iced, but you haven't got the balls to do it. We both understand that, don't we."

Hasty was silent for a time. They reached the Gloucester circle, and went around it, and started back, southbound, on Route 128.

"All right," Hasty said. "Kill Lou Burke, and hide the body. Make it look like he took off."

"There's a little matter of price," Jo Jo said.

"Thirty pieces of silver."

"What the hell is that?" Jo Jo said.

Hasty shook his head.

"Same as Tammy," Hasty said.

"No, Lou's a cop, and I got to hide the body. I want double Tammy."

Hasty felt very tired.

"Okay," he said. "It's a deal."

"Up front," Jo Jo said.

"Of course," Hasty said. "Just do it quickly."

"What would you do without me, Hasty?" Jo Jo said.

The weariness Hasty felt was nearly overwhelming. He had trouble concentrating on the road. He didn't respond to Jo Jo and they drove in silence the rest of the way.

Chapter 64

When Jesse answered the phone there was a pause and then he heard Jenn's voice.

"Jesse?"

He felt a small tug in the center of himself. He had always felt it when he heard her voice or saw her. Goddamn it.

"Hello, Jenn."

"I was in the middle of a swallow," Jenn said, "when you answered. How are you?"

"I'm fine."

"Are you having a drink?"

"Yes."

"How many?"

"First one."

"It's later there, right?"

"Yes."

"Are you really all right, Jesse?"

"So far."

"Are you still scared?"

"Sort of."

"Say more about that, Jesse. Can you get any help?"

"I don't know."

"Well, have you caught the one who killed the girl?"

"I know who he is. I can't prove it yet."

"Is he what scares you?"

"No, it's more . . . well. The guy I replaced, guy named Carson, got blown up by a bomb out in Wyoming. Wyoming cops have evidence of a militia movement involvement back east. One of my cops, guy that was acting chief before me, that interviewed me for this job, guy named Lou Burke, flew to Denver just before Carson got blown up. Burke was a demolition specialist in the Navy. He's a member of the local militia movement which calls itself Freedom's Horsemen."

"You think he did it?"

"I'll bet," Jesse said.

"Have you arrested him?"

"Not yet. I suspended him."

"Why not arrest him, turn it over to the Wyoming police?"

"I'm not sure they can make the case yet, but even if they can, I want more," Jesse said. "The chief selectman in town, the guy that hired me, is also the commander of Freedom's Horsemen."

"You think he's involved?"

"He's a married man. He's having trouble with his wife. And he was having an affair with the girl that was murdered."

Again there was silence while Jenn drank some wine. Jesse's drink sat untouched on the kitchen counter.

"But you know who killed her," Jenn said.

"Yeah, but now I'm not so sure I know why."

"You said last time it was about you."

"Yeah, and maybe it is, but now maybe it was about more than me."

"So why don't you confront, or arrest, or call in the FBI or whatever."

"I don't know exactly if any of what I suspect is true. I don't know who I can trust. Maybe I can't trust anybody."

"Even your own policemen?"

"Even. I'm alone here, Jenn."

"I could come."

Jesse was silent. He felt suddenly overwhelmed by the desire for her to be there.

"Jenn . . . I can't . . ."

"I know, Jesse. I know."

Jesse was silent, struggling not to fail. "I can't have that, Jenn. At least not yet."

"I know."

"I want it more than I can tell you, but I can't let that happen to me again. First I have to do this. Then we can see about us."

"It's awful to be alone, Jesse."

"If you can't be alone," Jesse said, "you can't be with someone. I can't have you here because I'm scared. You can't come here because you're scared for me. You understand?"

"Yes."

They were quiet. Jesse picked up his drink and took a sip. He had switched his scotch from on-the-rocks to with-soda.

"You seeing anybody?" Jesse said.

"No. You?"

"I'm still dating that woman, but it's not going anywhere."

"Because you don't trust her?"

"I guess."

"Can't have a relationship with someone you don't trust," Jenn said.

"I know."

"It must be very hard, Jesse, to be alone in trouble where there's no one to trust."

Jesse drank more scotch and soda.

"Yes," he said.

"Stranger in a strange land," she said.

"I want to get them all," Jesse said slowly. "Everybody. I want the town cleaned up. I want to know when I see somebody that they're not a murderer or an anarchist, or whatever, you know? I want the pleasant little town I thought I was getting when I came here."

"Maybe that's more than you can have," Jenn said.

"I want to find out."

"Get some help, Jesse."

"I can't," Jesse said. "I need to do this alone."

"Are you proving something to me, Jesse?"

"No."

"To yourself, then."

"I guess so."

"I know you, Jesse," Jenn said across the continent, "I know how tough you are. I know how smart you are. If you need to do this, you'll do it. You won't lose this, Jesse."

"I don't know, Jenn, I mean thank you for what you said, but it's like wrestling with smoke in the dark."

They were quiet again at each end of the wire.

"You seem a little different, Jenn," Jesse said after a time.

"You think so?"

"Yeah. You getting any help?"

"Yes."

"Shrink?"

"Yes."

"A real one, not some guy does full body rolfing?"

"No. It's a woman. She might be tougher than you, Jesse."

"Nobody's that tough," Jesse said and heard her laugh and felt excited as he always had when he made her laugh.

"Yes," Jenn said, "that's the Jesse I know."

"It helps to talk with you, Jenn."

"Good."

Again they were quiet.

"I guess I better hang up," Jesse said.

"Okay," Jenn said. "Be very careful."

"Yes."

"I'm here, Jesse."

"I know. It helps, Jenn."

They hung up and Jesse stared a long time at his half-empty glass with the excitement pulsating in the pit of his stomach. He stood finally and picked it up and emptied it into the sink. Then he went into the bedroom and opened his bureau drawer and took out a picture of Jenn and set it upright on the top of the bureau.

chapter 65

There were two Paradise cruisers and the fire department rescue van parked in a semicircle on Indian Hill. Lou Burke's car, a six-year-old Buick sedan, was parked, doors open, against the safety barrier at the verge of the rust-colored granite cliffs which dropped two hundred feet straight down to the surf. The car's ignition was on, the gas tank was empty, and the battery was dead. Jesse popped the hood and put his hand on the engine block. It was cold. He walked to the barrier and looked down to where the dark shape tossed and wallowed in surf, caught among the rocks.

"Do we know if it's Lou?" Jesse said.

"Not yet," Peter Perkins said. "No way down the cliffs from here. Suitcase is coming around with the police boat and a couple of divers, but it'll take him a while."

Jesse nodded and walked back to the Buick. On the steering wheel, attached with a piece of gray duct tape, was a typewritten note:

Jesse,

I can't stand it any more, suspected of murder, suspended.
It's on you, Jesse.

                                                    Lou Burke

"Bag the note," Jesse said.

Peter Perkins picked up the note by one corner and put it carefully into a transparent plastic envelope.

"You think Lou killed himself, Jesse?" Perkins said.

"Don't know," Jesse said.

"There's Suitcase," Perkins said.

The police boat from the town wharf nosed around the ragged jut which marked the end of the harbor, and pushed through the hard morning chop toward the base of the cliff. Jesse could see Suitcase Simpson and two men in wet suits. The light was pale in the early morning and the late-fall sun gave a weak yellow light, and no warmth. The wind off the ocean was strong and cold.

The boat steered in as close as it could to the surf line below the cliffs, and the two men in wet suits went over and into the black water. It took them almost ten minutes to work their way to the dead man, bumping against the boulders, facedown in the seafoam. One of the divers attached a line, and with the two divers steering the body, Suitcase reeled it in toward the boat. The body bumped against the side of the police boat and flopped inhumanly as Suitcase and the two divers got it in over the gunwales and laid it faceup on board.

"Is it Lou?" Jesse yelled, but his voice was lost in the wind and surf sound. He could see Simpson looking up at him. Simpson yelled, but Jesse could not hear him. Jesse cupped his hands as if making a megaphone, and Simpson went into the cabin and came out with the bullhorn.

"I think it's Lou," Simpson yelled, his voice amplified and dehumanized by the bullhorn. "He's been banging around down here for a while and it's hard to tell."

Jesse nodded and gave Simpson a thumbs-up and the police boat swung in an arc away from the foot of the cliffs, opened the engines, and roared, with the east wind behind it now back around the point toward the town wharf.

"See what you can do here," Jesse said to Peter Perkins.

He got into his cruiser, set the blue light flashing, and headed for the town wharf. There was barely anyone on the road at 6:10 in the morning and he had no need of the siren. I really can pick 'em, he thought as he drove through the old town with its narrow streets and narrower sidewalks and narrow old houses built right up against them. Three homicides in a year. Towns like this you're supposed to get about one a career. He thought about Jenn for a moment, and then he was there. He could see the police boat slow now as it passed through the boats winter-moored in the harbor. He got out of the car with the wind pushing at him. Seagulls were roosting on the tops of pilings and along the edge of the big town float. He went into the wharf office and poured himself some coffee and drank it with Cremora and sugar while he waited for Simpson and the body. He still had some left when the boat docked against the float, and he was still sipping it when he stepped over the gunwales of the police boat and squatted on his heels next to the sodden corpse.

"You're right," Jesse said to Simpson. "It's kind of hard to say who it is. You find any I.D. on him?"

Simpson looked like he might be a little seasick. "Once we got him in the boat," he said, "I didn't touch him."

Jesse nodded. He rolled the body over and found the

pants pockets and with some trouble got a soaked wallet out. He opened it.

"It's Lou's wallet," Jesse said.

"Jesus," Simpson said.

The two divers and the boat captain looked elaborately elsewhere.

"Yeah," Jesse said. "We'll get a positive I.D. from the M.E., I guess. But it sure seems to be Lou."

"Why'd you suspend him, Jesse?"

"I'll tell you about it later," Jesse said.

"Did you really suspect him of murder?"

"Later, Suit."

"Yeah, sure, Jesse. Lou didn't seem the type, you think?"

"I don't know if there is a type," Jesse said. "But if there is, no, Lou didn't seem to be it."

"I guess there's a lot we don't know yet," Simpson said.

"Yes," Jesse said, "there sure as hell is."

chapter 66

Jo Jo recognized the voice on the phone. It belonged to the pretty young man who worked for Gino Fish.

"Mr. Fish asked me to tell you that the product you asked for is now available."

"How do we pick it up?" Jo Jo asked.

"Go to the information booth at the South Shore Plaza with the correct amount of money, in cash, as specified. Someone will meet you and tell you the rest. You'll be expected at two o'clock today."

"I gotta talk to my guy," Jo Jo said.

"You can talk to anyone you want," the pretty boy said. "But you're there at two or the deal is canceled."

"For crissake," Jo Jo said.

But the pretty boy had hung up.

"Faggot bastard," Jo Jo said aloud.

Then he called Hasty Hathaway and at 12:30 they were in Hasty's Mercedes, with a suitcase full of small bills, heading for the South Shore.

"It's right there where Route Three splits off from the expressway for the Cape," Jo Jo said.

"Well, how are we to transport the arms?" Hasty said. "Didn't they say anything?"

"Just what I told you," Jo Jo said.

They parked near the entrance to Macy's and walked through the mall, it was busy in the early afternoon. The stores were already pushing Christmas. There were Christmas trees and pictures of Santa Claus, and miniature village scenes and railroad trains that circled endlessly through the fake snow. There were Salvation Army troopers with their bells and buckets, and tinsel and shiny ornaments and a lot of people, mostly women, often with small bored children dressed too warmly. Jo Jo and Hasty stopped beside the information booth. Jo Jo was carrying the money in a green sports equipment bag that said Adidas on it in white letters. The women behind the information desk were wearing Santa Claus hats. There was a big clock on the booth. It read ten minutes of two.

At 2:15 a smallish man in a longshoreman's cap and a Patriots warm-up jacket walked up to Hasty and said, "I'm from Gino."

"Money's in the bag," Jo Jo said.

With the bag still on Jo Jo's shoulder, the smallish man zipped it open enough to peer in. He nodded.

"Okay," he said. "You give me the bag. I give you the keys to the truck and tell you where it's parked."

"You don't get the dough until we see the product," Jo Jo said.

"Nope, deal goes down like I said, or it don't go down at all."

"And maybe I grab your scrawny little fucking neck and squeeze it until you tell me where the truck is," Jo Jo said.

The smallish man shrugged, and glanced over toward a

bookstore fifty yards down the mall. Vinnie Morris was leaning against the wall outside the bookstore with his arms folded across his chest.

"Maybe not," the smallish man said.

"You know if you double-cross us," Hasty said, "I can bring an army down on you."

"Sure," the smallish man said. "You want the deal or not?"

"Give him the money, Jo Jo."

Jo Jo shrugged. The sight of Vinnie Morris had taken a lot of the ferocity out of him. He took the bag off his shoulder and handed it to the smallish man. The smallish man handed him a set of two keys on a small orange plastic key tag.

"It's a Penske rental truck," the smallish man said, "Mass plates 354-6AV. It's parked outside the entrance next to Charlie's Saloon."

Then the smallish man turned and walked away down the mall. Jo Jo and Hasty looked after him for a time and then looked back at Vinnie Morris, but Morris wasn't anywhere in sight. They turned then and headed back down the mall toward the parking lot outside of Charlie's. Hasty could feel the excitement in his stomach. Things had gone badly for a while. This was a good thing. They'd be armed properly. They could hold off anyone. State police, ATF, FBI, Marshals, anybody. At 2:35 in the afternoon, the parking lot was full. By 2:45 they hadn't found the truck. By three o'clock they realized they weren't going to.

There was no truck.

chapter 67

Jesse stood with Abby Taylor on Indian Hill, looking over the railing down at the rocks where they had found Lou Burke.

"Right here?" Abby said.

"Yes."

"How could he do it?" Abby said. "I mean, maybe I could put a bullet through my brain, or take too many sleeping pills, or whatever if I were really depressed. But to climb over this fence and jump off the cliff . . ." She shuddered.

"Maybe he didn't," Jesse said.

"Didn't jump?"

"Maybe."

Abby stepped back from him and stood with her hands pushed into the pockets of her long blue coat.

"Jesse," she said and stopped.

He waited.

"Jesse, a lot of people think you've gone off the deep end here. You see conspiracy everywhere. Yet you don't talk to anyone about it. People are wondering about you.''

"And you?" Jesse said.

She took another step away from him. Jesse knew she was unaware of it.

"I don't know. I mean, we've been so intimate, and yet, you don't trust me. You don't trust anyone. That's not healthy, Jesse.''

Jesse leaned his forearms on the railing and looked at the gray water. It was like the last night in L.A., except he wasn't drunk. L.A. seemed much longer than six months ago.

"I'm not going to explain myself, Abby. I've done this kind of work most of my adult life. I'm doing it the best way I know how.''

"A lot of people blame you for Lou's death.''

"Because I suspended him?''

"Yes. The thinking is that if you had anything on him, arrest him for it, otherwise leave him alone. People in town liked Lou. He grew up here. He's part of the militia.''

"And that's a good thing?''

"The militia, oh for God's sake, Jesse. They're like the Ancient and Honorable Artillery Company. They march in the Fourth of July parade, for God's sake. Sure I think they're silly, and so do you. But they aren't some criminal enterprise.''

"I hadn't heard you defend them so strongly," Jesse said.

He was still staring at the choppy gray water below him. Above them a splatter of herring gulls soared and stooped. The sound of them was as constant as the movement of the sea. Abby seemed cold, she thrust her hands deeper into her pockets, hunched her shoulders so that the high collar of her coat was a little higher.

"Jesse, I live here and I work here. I am with a good law firm, I have a chance to be a partner."

Jesse nodded silently.

"What are you nodding about?" she said.

"I'm agreeing that it is not going to be good for your career if you stick by me."

"I didn't say that."

"Yes," Jesse said. "You did. You just didn't use those words."

It was an overcast day, and raw. There was a spatter of rain with snow mixed. The snow didn't last on the blacktop of the parking lot, or the rocks. But it had a short life on the grassy parts of Indian Hill, and a small residue had collected around the base of the windshield of Jesse's car. Abby stood drawn in upon herself. She shook her head slowly.

"This isn't happening right," Abby said.

"No," Jesse said.

"I . . . have had a very nice time with you, Jesse."

"Yes," Jesse said. "It's been nice."

"People think you should resign."

Jesse nodded.

"Want a ride back to your office?" Jesse said.

"No," Abby said. "I'll walk back. I need the time alone." She smiled without pleasure. "Clear my head."

"Sure thing," Jesse said.

He was still leaning on the rail.

"Jesse," she said. "Turn around."

He did. She stepped to him and put her arms around him and pressed her face against his chest.

"I'm sorry, Jesse."

He patted her gently on the back.

"It's okay, Abby," he said.

Then he let her go and she walked away down the hill

toward town, the spit of snow glistening momentarily in her hair. Then she was out of sight and he turned back and looked at the gray water and listened to the gray gulls and thought about the other ocean and the night he left it. He smiled after a while.

"Here's looking at you, Jenn," he said out loud.

His voice was small and nearly soundless mixed with the wind and the ocean sound and the noise of the gulls.

chapter 68

Hasty didn't like driving in city traffic. But he had to see Gino Fish, so the big Mercedes was wedged into the northbound commuter traffic on the Southeast Expressway. Hasty was nearly in tears.

"You dumb bastard," he said to Jo Jo.

"What the hell are you yelling at me for?"

"Because this was your deal. You were the one vouched for Fish."

"Bullshit," Jo Jo said. "You come to me, I was trying to do you a favor. Don't whine to me it didn't work out."

"You bastard," Hasty said.

He turned off at Mass. Avenue and drove past Boston City Hospital. He didn't like the city, and didn't spend much time there. It took him two or three false turns to find Tremont Street and another ten minutes to find the block where Gino Fish had his storefront.

"You needa be careful about this," Jo Jo said. "That Vinnie Morris is a quick sonova bitch."

"I thought you were a tough guy," Hasty said. "Are you scared of these people?"

"No, but it don't make no sense," Jo Jo said, "go charging fucking in there? Yelling and waving your arms, you know?"

"The goddamned fairy took my money," Hasty said. "The Horsemen's money. If I have to I'll bring the whole militia company in here. And I'm going to tell him that."

Hasty parked beside a hydrant near the Cyclorama, and got out.

"You going to back me?" he said to Jo Jo.

"I didn't cut in for that," Jo Jo said. "I set up the deal. They welshed on it. It's between you and them."

"You yellow belly," Hasty said.

He slammed the door, and turned and went down Tremont Street to the storefront. It was empty. The door was locked. Hasty groaned in anger and disappointment and turned and went back to his car. He got in and started up without a word.

"Nobody there?" Jo Jo said.

Hasty nodded as he yanked the Mercedes out into the traffic and drove out of the South End on Tremont Street.

"I knew there wouldn't be," Jo Jo said. "Why I didn't waste time walking down there."

"You're a yellow belly," Hasty said.

"You want to go one on one with me?" Jo Jo said.

"These are your people, Jo Jo. I want my weapons, or I want my money."

"You been stiffed, asshole. Don't you get it? There aren't any fucking weapons." Jo Jo said "weapons" in exaggerated scorn. "There never were any weapons. They saw you coming."

"You brought me to them. You get the money back."

Jo Jo shook his head.

"I mean it, Jo Jo. You are in this far too deeply to just walk away."

Jo Jo felt a little tingle of fear race up the backs of his thighs. His glance shifted onto Hasty's face, and held. He pulled his chin down into his neck almost like a turtle retracting, and his neck thickened.

"I may be in it, Hasty, but I sure as shit ain't in it alone."

Hasty didn't answer right away. He had driven out of the South End and onto Charles Street where it ran between the Common and the Public Garden. The city rose up all around them. A cold rain had begun to spit and Hasty turned the windshield wipers on to low intermittent.

"I do not believe what I am hearing," Hasty said finally.

He was choosing his words carefully, talking as if to an adolescent, trying to speak with the icy assurance of command.

"We have paid you well for work you were willing to do. Now you speak as if, somehow, that gave you knowledge which you would use against us."

"Hey, you're the one talking about getting in deep," Jo Jo said.

"And you are in deep. There is no information you have which you could use against us that would not also incriminate you."

"You want people to know about Tammy Portugal? Or how you had me throw Lou Burke off the rocks? You think that might not get you in just a little fucking trouble?"

Hasty shook his head as if saddened. He turned left onto Beacon Street, past the Hampshire House with its line of tourists outside the Cheers bar.

"Jo Jo, you haven't the intestinal fortitude. You inform on me and you go to the electric chair. It's as simple as that, and you know it. You have great big muscles, and you are mean as hell, but you are as yellow as they come. You have nothing on me that won't get you in trouble too.''

Jo Jo stared at Hasty with eyes that seemed without pupils, opaque eyes too small for his crude face. As Hasty watched him, between glances at the road, Jo Jo's color deepened, and a small muscle twitched in his cheek.

''I oughta just throw you off the fucking rocks,'' Jo Jo said.

''My men would tear you apart if that happened,'' Hasty said. ''Don't threaten me, Jo Jo. I'm not afraid of you.''

''You think I'm bluffing?''

''I think you better think about how to get the money back that you allowed us to be cheated out of,'' Hasty said.

At Berkeley Street he turned the car onto Storrow Drive and they headed back to Paradise in utter silence.

Jesse stood alone in Lou Burke's small garden apartment. What struck him most was the anonymity of it. No
pictures of family. No books. No old baseball gloves with
the infield dust ground into the seams. Jesse walked slowly
through the three small rooms. No newspapers stacked up.
No magazines. A television set with a twenty-six-inch
screen glowered at the living/dining area off the kitchenette.
A small desk near the entry. Some bills due the end of the
month. Two canisters of coffee on the kitchen counter, a
Mr. Coffee machine. Some milk and some orange juice in
the refrigerator. A couple of pairs of slacks in the closet, a
blue suit, a starched fatigue outfit with Freedom's
Horsemen markings. Clean police uniform shirts in the bureau drawer. An alarm clock on the bedside table. No fishing equipment. No hunting gear. No cameras. No
binoculars. No rugs on the floor. No curtains on the windows. The shades were all drawn to precisely the middle
of the lower window. The bed was tightly made. There was
no dust. No plants. No bowling trophies. The floors were

polished. In the front hall closet was an upright vacuum cleaner.

Not much of a life, Lou.

Jesse stood in the middle of the living room and listened to the silence. He turned slowly. There was nothing he was forgetting. Nothing he'd overlooked. He wondered if his apartment would look like this to a stranger, empty and lifeless and temporary. He was glad Jenn's picture was on his bureau. He looked once more around the small empty space. There was nothing more to see. So Jesse went out the front door and locked it behind him.

Back at the station Jesse stopped to talk with Molly.

"We got a typewriter around here anywhere?" Jesse said.

"Nope. Got rid of them five years ago when we got the computers."

"Don't have one left over in the cellar or the storage closet in the squad room, or anyplace?"

"No. Tom made a deal with a used-typewriter guy, from Lynn. When we went computer the typewriter guy came in, took all three typewriters. You want me to see if I can get you one?"

Jesse shook his head.

"No, just curious. Lou Burke have any family?"

"None that I know, Jesse. Parents died a while back. Far as I know he never married."

"Brothers? Sisters?"

"Not that he ever talked about. Pretty much the department and the town was what he had."

Jesse didn't miss the cutting edge in the remark. The department was Lou Burke's life, and Jesse had taken it from him.

"There was no typewriter in his apartment," Jesse said.

"I'm sure there wasn't," Molly said. "Lou was a wonderful cop but he hated to write anything. I used to do half his reports for him.''

"So where did he type out his suicide note?" Jesse said.

Molly looked up at Jesse and started to speak and stopped and frowned.

"There's no typewriter at his house," she said.

"That's correct," Jesse said.

"The note wasn't printed out of a computer."

"No," Jesse said.

"Maybe he went to somebody's house that had a typewriter," Molly said.

Jesse picked up a pad of blue-lined yellow paper from Molly's desk. There were fifty pads just like it in the office supply cabinet in the squad room.

"Wouldn't it have been easier to have handwritten the note?" Jesse said.

"That is odd," Molly said. "Though suicidal people are, you know"—Molly tossed her hands—"crazy."

Jesse put the notepad back down on Molly's desk. He didn't say anything.

"Unless he didn't write the note," Molly said. "And whoever did it just assumed that there'd be typewriters in the station. But even if there were, we'd find out pretty quick that they weren't used for the note."

"Which means whoever wrote it was stupid," Jesse said.

"That's not all it means," Molly said.

"No," Jesse said, "it's not."

He walked back toward his office. Molly watched him as he went.

"Jesus," she said softly.

chapter 70

Jesse parked his car in the curving cobblestone driveway of the Episcopal church rectory. It was a big brick building with a green center entrance door and green shutters. It was a bright morning, and the grass of the rectory lawn was wet with the early morning frost that had melted in the sun. A woman wearing an apron over a flowered dress answered Jesse's ring.

She said, "Reverend is expecting you, Chief Stone."

Jesse followed her into the study, where the reverend was at his desk. The room was lined with books, and there was a fire burning in the fireplace. Reverend Cotter was gray-haired and pink-cheeked. He was wearing a brown tweed jacket over his black minister's front-and-backwards collar. He stood and shook Jesse's hand and gestured him to a chair beside the desk. He waited until the housekeeper had left before he spoke.

"Thank you very much for coming so promptly," he said.

He had a deep voice, and he was pleased with it.

"Glad to," Jesse said.

Cotter unlocked the middle drawer of his desk with a small key on his key chain, and tucked the key chain back into his pants pocket. He opened the drawer and took out a five-by-seven manila envelope and placed it on his desk, taking time to center it and to adjust it so that it was neatly square in the middle of his clean desk blotter.

"This is very embarrassing," he said.

"Whatever it is," Jesse said, "it won't be as embarrassing as other stuff I've been told."

Cotter nodded.

"Yes, I'm sure. Indeed I often reassure my own parishioners in the same way when they come for help."

Jesse nodded and smiled politely. Cotter took in a big breath of air and let it out. Then he handed the envelope to Jesse. It was postmarked the previous day from Paradise. It was addressed to Reverend Cotter, probably with a ballpoint pen, in block printing, no return address. Inside was a Polaroid picture. Jesse took it out, handling it by the edges, and looked at it. It was a picture of Cissy Hathaway, naked and provocative on a bed. There was nothing else in the envelope except a piece of shirt cardboard used to protect the picture. There was nothing in the picture to identify the room.

"Just this?" Jesse said.

"Yes," Cotter said.

"Any idea why this would be sent to you?"

"No."

"It came this morning?"

"Yes."

Jesse sat quietly looking at the picture. He could see no real expression in Cissy's face, though the harsh light of the Polaroid flashbulb would wash out subtlety.

"Mind if I keep this?" Jesse said.

"Please," Cotter said. "I certainly don't want it."

"Anything else arrives let me know," Jesse said. "Or if anything occurs to you."

"Of course," Cotter said.

Jesse put the picture back in the envelope, and slid the envelope in the side pocket of his jacket.

"What are you going to do?"

"We'll check it for fingerprints," Jesse said.

"Are you going to speak to Cissy?"

"Yes," Jesse said.

"I . . . I am her minister," Cotter said. "If I can help . . ."

"Sure," Jesse said. "I'll let you know if we need you."

Chapter 71

Jesse sat with Cissy Hathaway in her kitchen, looking out at the backyard now flowerless, the grass yellow in the weak sunlight. He handed her the Polaroid.

"This came today in the mail addressed to Reverend Cotter," Jesse said.

Cissy took the picture and stared at it. As she looked at the picture she began to blush. Jesse was still. Cissy kept her eyes fixed on the picture, her face expressionless except for the bright flush that made her look feverish. She didn't say anything, and Jesse didn't say anything, and the silence grew stifling the longer it went on.

Finally Jesse said, "As far as I can see, there's no crime here. You can tell me to buzz off, if you want to. But I thought you should know."

Cissy put the picture facedown on the kitchen table and stared at the blank back of it. Jesse waited. Cissy got up from the table suddenly and walked to the counter. She got a pack of cigarettes, lit one, and stood with her back to him looking out the window over the sink at her driveway and the neighbor's yard beyond it. She took a deep inhale and let the smoke dribble out. Jesse was silent.

"Jo Jo," she said with her back still to him. "Jo Jo Genest took that picture. He has others."

"Did he coerce you?" Jesse said.

"No."

"Do you know why he sent the picture to your minister?"

Cissy took another big inhale and let the smoke out, still with her back to Jesse. She seemed to be memorizing every detail of the neighbor's lawn. Jesse was quiet. It was going to come, he knew that. All he needed to do was wait.

"Yes," Cissy said. "I know."

"Can you tell me?" Jesse said.

Cissy took a last drag on her cigarette and dropped it into the sink, turned on the water, flicked the disposal switch, and watched the butt disappear. Then she shut off the disposal, turned off the water, and turned from the sink. The high color had left her face. Her eyes seemed larger than Jesse remembered.

"I am going to have to tell you things that mortify me," she said. "I will. But you have to promise not to be judgmental."

"I won't be judgmental, Cissy."

"No, I think you won't. It's why I think I can tell you."

Jesse nodded gently and waited. Cissy stood at the sink and folded her arms.

"You have to help me, Jesse," she said. "You have to help me say these things."

Jesse stood and walked over to the sink and put one arm around Cissy's shoulders. She stiffened but she didn't move.

"I was a cop," Jesse said, "in the second-largest city in the country. I have heard stuff you can't even imagine. I have seen stuff you don't even know exists.''

She nodded slowly, her arms still folded, his arm still around her shoulder.

''You're human, Cissy. Humans do things that they're ashamed of. They get in trouble. They need help. I don't want to get too dramatic here, but that's what I'm supposed to do. I'm supposed to help you when you get in trouble.''

Cissy nodded again. Then they were both quiet, Cissy hugging herself, Jesse's arm around her shoulder.

''I have been married to Hasty for twenty-seven years,'' Cissy said softly. ''I don't know if I love him, sometimes I don't even know if I like him, but we've been together so long.''

She fumbled another cigarette out of the package and lit it.

''I think Hasty likes sex. I know I do. But somehow we don't seem to like it with each other. When we have sex it's . . . technically correct, I guess. But it is not much else and we don't have it very often. I feel very stiff and cold and awkward having sex with Hasty.''

She smoked for a time, watching the exhaled smoke drift toward the ceiling.

''The longer we have been together, the odder Hasty has become. He was an important young man from a good family when I first met him. All this business with Freedom's Horsemen . . .''

She shook her head.

''It occupies him more and more every year. I needed sex. And, I guess there is something very wrong with me, some of the kind of sex I needed.''

''No reason, right now, to decide if there's something wrong with what you needed,'' Jesse said.

''I know. I tell myself that. I took a series of lovers.

Some of them were nice normal men who were happy to do nice normal things with me.''

She took in some smoke and blew it out.

"I actually met Jo Jo through Hasty. He came to the house one day. He and Hasty talked business in the den and I brought them some beer. The way Jo Jo looked at me. It was like he knew. I could feel his look go right through my clothes. Right through everything I pretended to be. I knew he saw me. And I let him know I knew.''

She was still standing stiffly, but she had allowed her head to rest lightly against Jesse's shoulder.

"He wasn't the first man, but he was the worst one,'' Cissy said. "And the worse he was, the worse I was.''

She stopped talking and seemed to be thinking about her badness.

"The pictures?'' Jesse said.

"They were my idea. I . . . liked being that way and I liked to see myself that way.''

"There are more pictures?''

"Many.''

"And he has them?''

"Yes.''

"Probably been better,'' Jesse said, "if you kept them.''

"Maybe I half wanted him to tell,'' she said.

"Maybe.''

She half turned and dropped her cigarette in the sink and repeated the process of washing it down the disposal. Then she settled back against Jesse's shoulder.

"So why did he go public now?'' Jesse said.

"I think he's mad at Hasty,'' she said.

"About what?''

"They had some kind of a business deal that went badly. Hasty blamed Jo Jo.''

"What kind of business deal?''

"I don't know."

Cissy turned in against Jesse and put her face into his chest. It was hard to hear her voice, muffled as it was against him. He could feel her trembling and he patted her shoulder a little. Over her shoulder he looked at his watch. Whatever was coming was coming slow. Finally she spoke again, her voice muffled against his chest.

"Jo Jo killed Tammy Portugal."

There, Jesse thought. Cissy kept her face buried in his jacket. She was hanging on to him as if she might blow away if she let go.

"He used to tell me how he did it."

"How he killed Tammy?"

"Yes."

She began to sob against him. Big paroxysmal sobs, her body heaving. She said something he couldn't understand.

"What did you say?"

She shook her head.

"No, you've come this far," Jesse said, "and we're still okay. You can say it. I can hear it."

"I liked hearing about it," she said, gasping the words out between sobs. "And he knew I wouldn't tell anyone because then I'd have to tell how I knew."

Jesse was silent for a moment, patting her shoulder gently. He had hold, finally, of the grotesque animal he'd been hunting. And he would have to pull it, snarling and vicious, slowly out of its hole. He didn't know yet how big an animal it was going to be.

"I'm going to have to ask you to testify," Jesse said.

She nodded her head against him, her body shaking. He held her. The sobbing went on for a long time. He patted her gently. He could hear the occasional car go ordinarily by on Main Street. Somewhere he could hear a dog bark.

"You were brave to tell me," Jesse said.

She nodded against him.

"I had to tell you," she said. "I couldn't have those pictures all over town."

"The next brave thing you are going to have to do is get psychiatric help. Good help. An honest-to-God shrink."

"I'm sick," she said into his chest, "I know I am."

"You can get well," Jesse said. "You know a shrink?"

She shook her head.

"Your family doctor can refer you," Jesse said. "This is too hard to do alone. You need to save yourself."

"My God," she said. "Jo Jo will kill me."

"Jo Jo will be in jail," Jesse said.

Chapter 72

Jesse took Peter Perkins and Anthony DeAngelo with him to arrest Jo Jo. Both men carried shotguns. He didn't know if he could trust them either, but it was time to find out. He didn't want to have to kill Jo Jo; a show of force usually made an arrest go smoother. They waited in the parking lot in the back of the gym where Jo Jo trained and took him, shotguns leveled, without incident when he came out to his car. They brought him handcuffed to the station. Molly at the front desk watched in silence as they led him past her and locked him up in one of the holding cells in the back. DeAngelo and Perkins left. Jesse went back out front.

"I'll cover the desk," Jesse said to Molly. "You can go home."

"You sure you don't mind being alone with him?" Molly said.

"Be fine," Jesse said and smiled at Molly. "Give us a chance to really get to know each other."

"Won't that be swell," Molly said and got her things

together and left. Jesse watched her go down the front steps of the station, then he went to his office, got a tape recorder, and walked slowly back to the cell area. He pulled up a folding chair, plugged in the tape recorder, and talked with Jo Jo through the bars.

"That thing on?" Jo Jo said.

"Not yet," Jesse said.

He held the recorder so that Jo Jo could see that it wasn't.

"Get used to the cell, Jo Jo," Jesse said. "You're going to be in one the rest of your life."

"You can't prove shit," Jo Jo said.

"Jo Jo, you know you did her, and I know it, and we got a witness who'll swear you bragged about it. We're going over you and everything you own—your car, your house. We're going to find forensic evidence, Jo Jo."

"You been out to get me since you come to town," Jo Jo said.

"When's the last time you had sex with a woman?" Jesse said.

Jo Jo stared at him. "Why you want to know?"

"Because it's the last time," Jesse said.

Jo Jo continued to stare at him.

"Give you a chance to find out how tough you really are, though. Cons always like to test the bodybuilders, you know? See if they can back it up. Some guys at Cedar Junction be real proud to have Mr. Universe punking for them."

Jo Jo had been sitting on his cot. He stood now and walked to the bars.

"What do you want, Stone?"

"I want to help you, Jo Jo. I want to find some sort of deal for you."

"Like what?"

"Like maybe you shouldn't have to go down alone for

this. Maybe if we talked about what kind of business you are doing with Hasty Hathaway. Maybe you might be able to tell me something about Tom Carson's death, or Lou Burke's.''

''I don't know nothing about that.''

''Too bad,'' Jesse said.

Jo Jo walked to the back wall of the cell and turned and walked to the barred door again.

''What kind of deal?''

''Depends what I hear, and how good it is.''

Jo Jo walked to the back wall and turned and leaned on it, looking at Jesse.

''So I spill my guts to you and you don't promise me nothing.''

Jesse smiled.

''Works for me,'' he said.

''No deal,'' Jo Jo said.

Jesse waited.

''You can't even get me for Tammy, no way you can prove it.''

Jesse waited.

''If I did know something, I'm not going to fink out without something better than you're offering.''

''You need a little time,'' Jesse said, ''run this thing over in your mind, think about how your life is going to go from now on. I'll come back in a while and see you.''

''I got to know what the deal is,'' Jo Jo said.

Jesse turned and left him there standing alone in the dim light at the back of his tiny cell, the tape recorder silently waiting on the floor by the folding chair outside the bars.

chapter 73

When her husband came into the house Cissy Hathaway had already mixed the first of their two evening Manhattans. Hasty went as he always did to the living room and she brought the drinks in, as she always did, on a small silver tray someone had given them at their wedding. She put the tray down on the coffee table. She felt weak, as if she'd been ill, but steady enough, quiet inside now that the thing had got out. Hasty took his drink and sipped some without waiting for her. Then he took a Polaroid picture from his inside pocket and dropped it faceup on the coffee table.

"Oh God," she said.

"I got this in the mail this morning."

She nodded.

"Explain it to me, please."

Her husband's voice was thin and very tight. His face was white, and there were vertical grooves in his cheeks. The hand holding the Manhattan was trembling slightly. She felt the weakness open beneath her and it was as if she would slump into it and disappear. She didn't want her drink. It stood on the tray in front of her with the short thick glass beaded slightly and the amber light showing through it. She shook her head gently. She couldn't go through it all again.

"Explain." Her husband finished his drink. "I need you to explain."

She stared at her hands folded in her lap. They looked foreign to her. Her knees looked remote and unconnected to her. Her living room, in the house where she had lived for most of her adult life, looked like a museum room. Not hers, not anyone's. Why would someone make a chair like that? Why would someone sit in it?

Her husband's voice was so tight it seemed half strangled.

"Now, I want to know now."

"Jo Jo," she whispered.

It was so soft he couldn't hear her. He leaned forward. "What?"

"Jo Jo. He sent the pictures. I told the police."

"What police?"

"Jesse."

She was still whispering. He was still leaning forward. His face was bloodless and there was sweat on his upper lip.

"Did he force you?" Hasty said.

"No."

Her voice was barely audible.

"Goddamn you," Hasty said.

"Jo Jo killed that girl, too," she whispered. "I told Jesse."

Her husband didn't say anything. He leaned farther forward until he was doubled over and clutched at himself and began to moan. Then he stood and walked to the wall and pounded on it with both fists and began to scream. Then he stopped pounding and stopped screaming and turned back toward her.

"You . . . you don't know . . ."

He shook his head. He couldn't find words. She was still, staring at the hands folded in her lap.

"I'm sick," she whispered. "You have to understand, Hasty. I'm sick."

"Goddamn you," he said. "Goddamn you."

With the back of his hand her husband knocked a floor lamp over and when it was on the floor he kicked it. Then he turned and ran from the room. After a moment she heard the back door open and after another moment she heard the car start. She sat for a long time in the empty house before she got up finally and walked slowly to the kitchen and closed the back door that her husband had left open. Then she sat and rested her arms on the kitchen table and put her head down onto them, and cried.

Chapter 74

He had them assembled in Bob Merchant's carriage house, where they had their weekly meetings; all the Horsemen, in fatigues, with weapons, sitting on folding chairs among the children's bicycles, and the family garden tools: the wheelbarrow, power mower, snowblower, the rakes and hoes, the shovel, and the long-handled three-toothed cultivator, and coiled hoses hanging on the wall. That had been easy, there was a system in place to assemble the Horsemen. Now it was all on him. He stood in a near trance at the side of the room waiting for the men to settle. Now everything was in what he would say. He felt simultaneously frenetic and still. He remembered a phrase he read once in college—furious immobility. That's what he felt like. Furious immobility. Every moment since Cissy told him had been frenzied. If Jesse knew that Jo Jo killed Tammy Portugal, then soon he would know why, and once Jo Jo began to talk—and Hasty had no doubt that under pressure, Jo Jo would talk—he would tell everything. Tammy, Lou Burke, Tom Carson, the arms deal, everything, and all that Hasty had built for, all the plans, the mobilization, the slow expansion, all that Hasty was, the Horsemen, the bank, the prominent man in town. He didn't know how Jo Jo had gotten those pictures, but he knew why he had gone public with them. He should never have fought with him about the aborted weapons deal. He should not have blamed him. The blame goes to the commander. It had been a moment of weakness and frustration and it had betrayed him as such moments always would betray a man who had the burden of command. Later he could learn from that mistake. Now he must silence it. Stone knew. He didn't know how much, but Stone knew something about Lou Burke when he suspended him. He knew something about Jo Jo. Stone was another mistake. Hasty had wanted a pliable drunk. He had been deceived. That mistake had to be silenced too. Once he would simply have used Jo Jo. But now he could not. Now he had only one instrument, the Horsemen. However he was to save the situation, the Horsemen were what he had available. He had not told them yet of the aborted arms deal. If he could pull this off, the arms deal would fade. They wouldn't need the arms. Perhaps he could control the town without them. Enough good men, banded in the right cause . . . The room was quiet. Hasty walked out in front of the men. His insides felt jagged and unstable. My God, he thought, I hope I don't foul myself. He tried to tighten his stomach. He took in a deep breath through his nose so as not to let it show and tried to focus on what he wanted.

"Men," he said, and paused, and cleared his throat. "Men, we have been preparing—I think it is fair to say, that many of us have been preparing all our lives—for the moment that has come."

He could hear the nervous vibrato in his voice. Was he

to fail himself in the moment of crisis? Command, he said to himself. Command.

"You all know Jo Jo. He has his ways, but he has been one of us. Now they have him in jail on a manufactured charge and they will force him to incriminate us. He may resist them, but no one can resist long. They use science to pervert us. Injections, hypnosis, sleep deprivation. It will not be long before Jesse Stone knows our every plan."

They were listening. His voice was stabilized, though his insides were still turbulent.

"I know that many of us have come to like Jesse Stone, but that is part of his way. He is, at the very bottom line, a stooge for the state police."

From the inside pocket of his field jacket, he took a Polaroid picture of Cissy and held it up.

"He has even circulated this disgusting piece of trash. I don't know if any of you have received one; it is an obviously doctored picture purporting to be my wife. A man capable of that kind of deceit is capable of anything."

Several of the men leaned forward trying to make out the picture. Hasty paused, letting his eyes rove slowly over the room, meeting the look of as many of the men as he could. He let the pause build. After a long moment he put the picture back in his jacket pocket. His insides were settling. He was heartened by his rhetoric. He had felt the satisfaction of revenge as he had held up his wife's naked picture in front of the men. Bitch. He felt powerful. His voice was strong.

"He has to be stopped," Hasty said softly.

Hasty paused again, looking slowly around the room. Some of the men were nodding their heads.

"We will implement our plan to take the town hall," Hasty said. "We will take Jo Jo out of there . . . and we will eliminate Jesse Stone."

"You mean kill him?" one of the men said from the back.

"In a war of liberation," Hasty said, "we do what we must. Our forefathers eliminated the British agents of repression at Lexington and Concord. We've done this exercise often enough. We know how. Each of you should report to his squad leader now. First squad will disable telephone service from the town hall. Second squad will see to the electricity. Third and fourth squad will deploy to the town hall and establish a perimeter."

The silence in the room was jagged with excitement. What had been a kind of war game had suddenly become real and the men felt frightened and heroic.

"It is our moment," Hasty said softly. "Paradise will be ours. Quietly, without fanfare, and without opposition, we can establish a free white Christian community. And bit by bit, community by community, with ever-growing force as our communities proliferate and begin to connect, we will return this nation to its place of freedom and individual rights which our ancestors dreamed of when they threw off the British yoke."

Lying on her stomach behind a folded canvas pool cover in the loft of the carriage house, Michelle Merchant listened intently. Her father and her brother were both Horsemen. She thought that all the rah-rah crap that Mr. Hathaway was spouting was really bogus, but she kind of liked the movement because it was antiestablishment the way she was. And when her father got on her case she could say that she was just rebelling the way he did. Her father didn't like her knowing anything about the Horsemen, which was why she liked to hide in the loft during meetings and listen in. It gave her ammunition when he would yell at her. Her mother didn't care. Michelle suspected that her mother liked it when Michelle got her father back, like her mother wanted to, but was too wussy.

Below her the men had broken up into four groups. They checked their watches. Then two of the groups went out first. The other men waited. The tension was so strong that it even reached the loft and filtered through Michelle's nearly impenetrable scorn. She could feel her heartbeat quicken. The men kept checking their watches and after what seemed to Michelle a long time, the last two groups went out and the room was empty.

Michelle could feel her breath coming a little faster. Were they actually going to attack the town hall and kill Jesse? Did they actually believe that crap about starting a free town, whatever that meant? That was total crap. Even if they killed Jesse and got Jo Jo Genest out of jail, pretty soon other cops would know and they'd come and put all the dumb Horsemen in jail. Anybody knew that, for crissake. She smiled for a moment at seeing her father and jerkface brother hauled off to jail. She could go visit them, like in the movies, and talk to them through the bars. Cool. She was dying for a cigarette. The barn was empty. She sat up and lit a cigarette and took in a big lungful of smoke. Her old lady would poop her pants, Michelle thought. She smiled in the dark loft and smoked some more. The only thing that bothered her was Jesse Stone. He was the only adult she'd ever met who hadn't given her a load of bullshit when he talked to her. She kind of didn't like him getting killed. She didn't want to spoil this thing. It was kind of exciting. And she wanted to see what her old lady would do when Dad got arrested. What kind of lecture would they give Michelle then, she wondered. She kind of liked Jesse, though. She finished her cigarette and lit another one.

With the tiny red glow of the freshly lit Camel Light bobbing from the corner of her mouth, she slid out the hay loft door and climbed down the back ladder and set off across her backyard.

chapter 75

"I don't know exactly what it was Tom Carson did," Jo Jo said. "Maybe found out about Hasty laundering cash for Gino."

"You were the go-between?" Jesse said.

"Yeah. I set it up."

It was late, and Jesse was tired. He and Jo Jo were on their respective sides of the barred door to Jo Jo's cell. Jesse had a tape recorder. There was a single overhead light in the cell corridor with no shade.

"Hasty'd get a couple percent of what he laundered, and I guess he was using that money to finance the Horsemen."

"How did he launder it?"

"Just didn't fill out the cash deposit forms, I guess," Jo Jo said. "It was his freakin' bank, you know? Then he'd deduct his two percent, put it in the Horsemen's account, and wire-transfer the rest to checking accounts in other banks. Now it's in the banking system nice and legitimate. Gino would write checks on the new accounts. No nasty

CTRs pile up on some treasury agent's desk in Washington."

"And you think Chief Carson got wind of this?"

"My guess, yeah. And he wouldn't go with it. Everybody knows it's drug money. And I heard that Tom said he couldn't let that slide."

"And?"

"So they got him to resign, and set him up in a town out in Wyoming. Some Posse group out there fixed it. And after he was out there a while, they sent Lou out to blow him up. They wanted the local Posse guys to do it, but that didn't work out."

"Why didn't they just kill him right away?"

"We talked about it. Decided it would draw too much attention to kill a police chief. Figured an ex-police chief out in the freakin' boondocks someplace would go down easier. I think they thought the bomb would pulverize him and they'd never be able to get an I.D."

"Wyoming cops I.D.'d him," Jesse said. "How about Tammy?"

"Hasty was tapping her," Jo Jo said. "She wanted him to leave his wife and marry her. You know Hasty. He thinks he's a leading freakin' citizen. Can't have that. So he told me to dump her."

"Did he tell you to make it part of the pattern of the painted police car and the dead cat?"

"No, my idea. I had it in for you ever since you suckered me, in front of my ex."

"I know. I knew you were pulling the 'slut' stuff and I knew why."

"But you couldn't prove it. I thought it would be cool to do her in a way made you look bad."

"How about Lou Burke?" Jesse said.

Jo Jo smiled.

"Hasty wrote the damn suicide note. Didn't trust me to."

"Why'd you kill him?"

"Hasty said to. Said you were getting too close. Said Lou would talk eventually. So I got him to meet me up on Indian Hill. Told him it was Horsemen business. And I threw him over."

Jesse was silent for a moment. Jo Jo was finally getting a chance to brag. He was telling the stories almost eagerly, as if they were interesting things that he'd done on vacation.

"I knew about Hasty and Tammy," Jesse said. "It was in her diary."

Jo Jo shrugged.

"And Lou's suicide note was typewritten."

"Couldn't handwrite it," Jo Jo said. "Be too easy to see it wasn't Burke's writing."

"Except Lou didn't have a typewriter," Jesse said.

"Coulda typed it here."

"Nope. We're all computerized."

Jo Jo made a disgusted sound.

"Freakin' Hasty is so stupid, you know. He thinks he's Napoleon or something with his freakin' Horsemen."

"So how come you sent the picture of Cissy to her minister?" Jesse said.

Jo Jo smiled broadly. "Sent it to a lot of people," he said. "Sent one to Hasty too."

"I'll bet he was pleased," Jesse said. "You take it?"

"Yeah. Her idea. She liked being tied up. Spanked. Weird broad—big time. Had a lot of poon tang with that broad, and you know how most broads are—all the time moaning about love—she wasn't like that, she liked the sex, but she was always like mad while we was doing it. She liked to pretend I was forcing her, you know? Grim."

Jesse nodded.

"She was banging one of your cops too, you know."

"Probably pretended he was rescuing her," Jesse said. "How come you decided to go public."

"With the pictures? I was, ah, brokering an arms deal for Hasty. Gino was supposed to get him some heavy weapons—you know Gino?"

Jesse shook his head.

"Major dude in Boston," Jo Jo said. "Queer as a square donut, but really wired."

"And you know him through the money laundering," Jesse said. He was stroking Jo Jo's ego.

"Yeah, I know Gino. Hasty's a big deal in town here maybe, but on the street, he's nowhere. He had problems, he always had to come to me."

"So he asked you to get him heavy weapons?"

"Yeah. Machine guns, mortars, some kind of anti-aircraft missiles. I'm telling you, he thinks he's going to take over the town and, you know, defy the freaking government."

Jo Jo laughed. Jesse laughed along with him. Couple of good old boys, Jesse thought, chewing the fat in the back room.

"So I set him up with Gino and Hasty gets high and mighty with him when they have a meeting and when the time comes for the guns, they take his money and stiff him."

"No guns," Jesse said.

"None, and he blames me. Freaking twerp. Says it's my fault. Says I better get the money back or else. He's actually threatening me. Well, first I thought maybe I'd just break his scrawny neck for him, wring it like he was a chicken, you know? But then I think no, be smart, Jo Jo. Don't get mad. Get even. So I got some of the pictures of his old lady and I sent them out. I sent one to his minister and one to him and one to the president of the Paradise Garden Club that Cissy belonged to. Ought to freak them out. I was going to send a few out every day. Drive Hasty crazy.''

Jo Jo laughed again. Jesse felt like he'd bathed in dirty water. He shut off the tape recorder.

''Think about something, Jo Jo,'' Jesse said. ''When I suspended Lou Burke Hasty was so worried about what Burke might say that he had you kill him.''

''Yeah.''

''I've actually arrested you, and you know more than Burke.''

''You think he'll try for me?''

''He'll have to,'' Jesse said. ''Or he's a goner.''

''How's he gonna get me in here?'' Jo Jo said.

''My guess is he'll try to get you out of here, one way or another.''

''And?''

''And kill you,'' Jesse said. ''You know the Horsemen. Do they believe in him?''

''Yeah. Assholes. They think he's freakin' George Washington.''

Jesse nodded.

''You think he'll try to kill me?''

''I think he'll try to kill us both,'' Jesse said.

chapter 76

When Suitcase Simpson pulled up in his own car behind the men in battle dress fatigues gathered around the station, he could see Jesse on the front steps with a shotgun. There were no lights showing at the station, but several men in the crowd had flashlights focused on Jesse. Simpson parked quietly on the street and got out. He was in uniform, wearing a bulletproof vest. He carried a shotgun and his service pistol. He stood silently in the shadows behind the Horsemen.

Two steps forward of the other Horsemen, Hasty Hathaway stood very straight in front of Jesse.

"We're relieving you of your duties," he said to Jesse. "And we are coming to take your prisoner."

Simpson felt someone move up beside him. It was Abby Taylor. She had on something that looked like a navy pea coat and the collar was high up around her head so that Simpson could barely see her face. Her hands were deep in her pockets. She looked briefly at Simpson and then looked at Jesse on the station steps. Neither of them spoke.

On the steps Jesse worked the pump on his shotgun and jacked a shell up into the chamber. The sound of the action was very sharp in the quiet night. Jesse was wearing a vest too, Simpson noted.

"Couple of things, Hasty," Jesse said.

His voice wasn't loud but it carried and the men were very still, nearly trancelike, confronting the stunning thing they were about to do.

"First," Jesse said. "Anything happens here and I'll kill you."

As he spoke Jesse raised the shotgun slowly and aimed it directly at Hasty. Before he could stop himself, Hasty took a step back.

"Second," Jesse said. "I'm arresting you for the murders of Tom Carson, Tammy Portugal, and Lou Burke."

Peter Perkins's Mazda pickup pulled in beside Simpson's car, and Perkins and Anthony DeAngelo got out, with shotguns and vests. They looked at Simpson. Silently Simpson gestured that they should spread out behind the Horsemen. Molly Crane arrived on foot. She was wearing sweats and sneakers and her service pistol. Her badge was pinned to the sweatshirt. Simpson pointed her to the left and she nodded and went.

"You can't bluff us, Stone," Hasty said. He felt dreadful about stepping back. His face felt hot. He tried to make his voice cut like Jesse's had. "We have relieved you of duty. Step aside or . . . step aside . . . or be killed."

"I hear one round go up into one chamber," Jesse said, "and I will shoot you dead, Hasty."

Hasty didn't step back this time, but he glanced automatically around at his troops to see that no one put a round up.

"You are a murderer and a goddamned fraud. What you really want is to kill me, and to kill Jo Jo. What were you

going to do, rush the jail and shoot him? Claim it was a
stray bullet? Poor Jo Jo. You gotta kill him because he
knows. You tell your men how you got conned on the arms
deal? Jo Jo knows. You tell them how you were sleeping
with Tammy Portugal until she wanted to get serious, then
you had Jo Jo kill her? You tell them how you had Tom
Carson killed? Jo Jo could tell them.''

As Jesse talked the other cops drifted in: John Maguire,
Arthur Angstrom, Eddie Cox, Billy Pope, Pat Sears.

''You tell them that when I had some evidence on Lou
Burke you had Jo Jo throw him off the top of Indian Hill?''

Something like an inaudible sigh moved through the
Horsemen as Jesse talked. Hasty felt it. He looked at the
small dark eye of Jesse's shotgun only five feet away, and
he backed away.

In the darkness behind the Horsemen Suitcase Simpson
spoke softly to Abby, still standing beside him.

''Go to Peter Perkins's truck. When you see the lights
go on in my car turn them on in the truck.''

Sheltered among his troops, shielded by other Horsemen
from the gaze of Jesse's shotgun, Hasty said in as much
voice as he could command, ''Third squad marksmen, pre-
pare to fire.''

A set of headlights behind them went on, and then a
second set and the Horsemen were bathed in light. Then
Simpson's voice, amplified by a bullhorn, came from the
darkness behind the light.

''This is the Paradise Police,'' the voice said. ''We have
you surrounded. Put down your weapons.''

There was a long frozen silence. The Horsemen nearest
Hasty turned and looked at him, waiting. Hasty didn't know
what to do. He had not thought of this. He didn't know
what to do. With the shotgun held in his right hand and
pointing straight toward the sky, Jesse walked down the

steps of the station and shoved past three Horsemen to stand in front of Hasty. His face was right next to Hasty's.

"You have the right to remain silent," Jesse said. "You have the right to an attorney."

Hasty started to back away and Jesse stayed close to him, walking him backward through the Horsemen as he recited the Miranda rights. The battle-dressed Horsemen parted silently as Hasty backed out of the group and into the police perimeter in the darkness beyond the headlights. Behind the headlights Suitcase Simpson stopped him with a hand in his back. Molly came out of the darkness and handed Jesse a pair of handcuffs and Jesse snapped them onto Hasty's wrists. In the distance, sounding very clearly through the quiet night, came the sound of sirens.

"That'll be the state cops," Simpson said.

"You call them?" Jesse said.

"Yes."

"Good thought."

The sound of the sirens broke the last resistance among the Horsemen. They began to drop their weapons and move away from the station. As the sirens got louder the Horsemen began to move faster and soon they were running, out of the bright headlights, past the silent policemen who made no attempt to stop them, heading home in the darkness, leaving their rifles and shotguns on the ground where they had stood.

Chapter 77

The sky over the harbor was beginning to get light. Jesse felt gray and empty, his mouth dry and bitter, with the flat joyless contumescence of dissipated tension. He was at his desk in his office with Healy, the state police captain.

"How'd it go down?" Healy said.

Jesse's voice was soft and Healy had to lean forward to hear him.

"Kid named Michelle Merchant. Her father's a Horseman. She heard the plan and told a woman I know, Abby Taylor."

"The town attorney," Healy said.

"Sometimes. Abby called the station, but the phones were dead, so she called Suit—Simpson—one of my cops."

"Well, now you know whose side your department is on."

Jesse nodded.

"Good to know," Healy said.

Jesse nodded again, a movement so small that Healy wasn't sure he'd made it.

"You talk to Wyoming?" Healy said.

"Yeah. They want Hathaway for blowing up Tom Carson."

"The prosecutors will work it out," Healy said. "Genest going to stand up when it's time to testify?"

Jesse nodded again. "He knows Hathaway was trying to kill him last night," Jesse said. "He'll talk until you don't want to listen."

"What do you want to do about the rest of the mob?" Healy said.

Jesse didn't answer for so long that Healy thought maybe Jesse hadn't heard him. Finally Jesse shrugged slightly.

"I think most of them are harmless," he said.

"You know who most of them are?"

"I can put together a list of Horsemen. Be harder to prove that any particular one was here last night," Jesse said.

"Might be some federal charges," Healy said. "Armed insurrection?"

"I'll let the Feds worry about that," Jesse said. "Most of these guys are just guilty of being jerks."

"Lot of that going around," Healy said.

"A lot," Jesse said. "I'll settle for lifting their gun permits."

"Probably a way to do that," Healy said. "You know the kid blew the whistle on them?"

"Yes," Jesse said.

"Good kid?"

"Kind of a burnout," Jesse said.

"Well, she saved your ass."

"I plan to mention that to her," Jesse said. "Abby Taylor too."

The light from the east was whiter now, making the electric lights in Jesse's office look weak.

"You should get out of here," Healy said. "There's going to be a lot to do later."

Jesse nodded and swiveled in his chair and looked out his window. There was a television van with its odd-looking antenna parked next to the police cruisers. Channel Three/Action News was stenciled on the side.

"And the media is always with us," he said.

"I'm getting too old for this all-night shit," Healy said. "You got a bottle of whiskey somewhere?"

Jesse took it out of his bottom drawer and put it on the desk in front of Healy.

"Glass on the windowsill," Jesse said.

"Join me?"

Jesse shook his head. Healy poured about an inch and drank it down. Then he capped the bottle and pushed it back across the desk toward Jesse. Jesse didn't stir. He was too tired to put it away.

"How long you been on this job?" Healy said.

"About six months."

"Nice start," Healy said.

After Healy left, Jesse sat for a while until he got the strength to get up. He walked past the television crew without speaking, and got in his car and went home. He was so tired it was hard to focus on the road. The sun was up by the time he got home and there was a different tone to the black winter water in the harbor. He parked in his slot and walked heavily up the steps to his condominium. When he opened the door he heard the television. He closed the door quietly behind him and took out his gun and walked softly to the living room. Sitting on the sofa with her feet up on the coffee table watching the early-morning news was his ex-wife.

"Jesus Christ, Jenn," Jesse said.

She stood and smiled at him.

"You're okay," she said.

Jesse nodded.

"The janitor let me in," Jenn said. "I told him I was your wife."

"You're not," Jesse said. "We're divorced."

"I saw on the news about last night," Jenn said.

"It's over," Jesse said. "What the hell are you doing here?"

"I was worried about you. I missed you."

"Jenn, I don't know," Jesse said.

"You still seeing that other woman?"

"No."

Jenn smiled.

"I don't know either, Jesse. But here I am. At least you could hug me."

Jesse realized suddenly that he was still holding his gun. He put it back on his hip, and walked very slowly around the coffee table.

"Yes," he said. "I could do that."